Broken

Dawn Michele

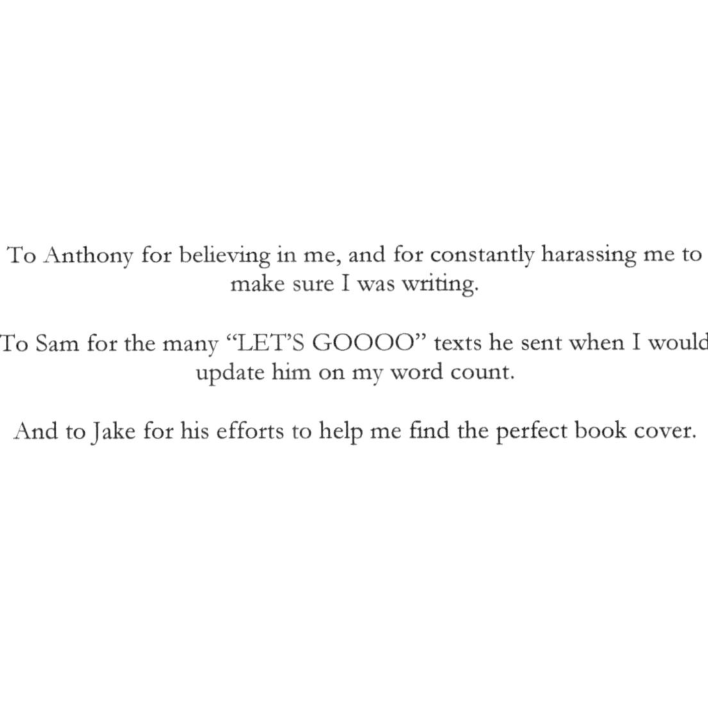

To Anthony for believing in me, and for constantly harassing me to make sure I was writing.

To Sam for the many "LET'S GOOOO" texts he sent when I would update him on my word count.

And to Jake for his efforts to help me find the perfect book cover.

Broken

CHAPTER ONE

"Allison?" Startled, I look up from my thumb, which I have been slowly working a sliver of rough skin off of, drawing a bead of blood. I had been lost in thought, wondering if it were possible to pinpoint the exact moment that the life I was living had become unrecognizable. Was it the impact of the crash, or the dozens of tiny choices I made throughout that day? What if I had fed my daughter frozen waffles for breakfast instead of cereal, which used up the last of the milk? What if I had stopped at the store on the way home from the park, instead of going home because she was cranky and needed a nap. What if I had decided to make rice for dinner instead of mashed potatoes, necessitating the need for someone to run to the store for milk? What if I had been the one to go instead of asking my husband to take our daughter and go to the store because I just wanted thirty minutes to myself where someone didn't need something from me? If I had gone alone there wouldn't have been extra time spent placing Tabby in her car seat, taking her out of her car seat, walking slowly in the store because she loved to walk rather than ride in the carriage. Would that difference in timing have changed the outcome? How far back can I go with all the different choices I could have made that would have prevented what happened? It's the "what if's" that torture me. What if, what if, what if. And milk. Milk is the reason I no longer have a family. Well, milk and Justin.

I stand, gathering my purse in my left hand and pressing the index finger of my right against my thumb to hide the blood. I slowly walk towards the woman with the friendly, open face, waiting for me in the doorway to her office. Dr. Marion Whitman motions me inside and gestures towards two chairs facing one another. I move towards the one closest to the door and settle myself on the edge. I'm strung as tight as a bow, desperate to be anywhere but here. It's only been 6 months since I lost my two reasons for living, and I have yet to fully allow myself to feel that loss. It feels too big; like if I allow myself to really and truly feel all of it at once it will destroy me, and I'm barely holding on as it is. It wasn't even my choice to come here. Not really. The idea of therapy has never appealed to me. Honestly the idea of tearing my emotional wounds open for someone else to poke around in is terrifying and a little nauseating. I don't want to share my grief with this stranger. I don't want to share my memories of my husband and my daughter. And I definitely do not want to talk about Justin. My mother pressured me into this. She is the only person who tolerates me, and her tears and pleading over her fear for my mental health and wellbeing were too much to bear up against in my current state. So I'm here, but I'm not happy about it.

Dr. Whitman is in her late 60s, with fluffy white hair and dozens of wrinkles. She immediately reminds me of Betty White. She's dressed in a short sleeve navy blue cotton dress printed with colorful peacocks and brown comfortable looking flats. She looks far too cheerful and upbeat for me. My tolerance for happy people is fairly low these days. I pretty much want everyone to be as miserable as I am. It's insane, I know this, but I also don't give a shit. My husband and child are gone, and I have trouble understanding how the world around me continues on without them, and I resent every happy, smiling person I see, which is why I stopped leaving the house months ago. One of the many reasons my mother guilted me into being here in the first place. Dr. Whitman sits in the chair opposite me and offers me a warm smile, but her eyes are sharp and assessing, and I know she isn't missing much.

"It's lovely out today, isn't it?" she begins, catching me off guard. It's such a benign question and certainly not what I expected. I assumed she would ask about my family, or their deaths, or how I'm coping, not about something as inconsequential as the weather.

"What? Oh! Yes, um, I guess it is," giving away too much information in that bumbling sentence. My eyes move to the window, and I see that it is, in fact, lovely out, which I also resent. It's sunny and the sky is a brilliant blue, and I remember wondering when it got so warm when I left the house this morning. "I hadn't really noticed," I say, stating the obvious.

Dr. Whitman chuckles softly and says "I gathered that."

I shift uncomfortably in my chair, unsure of what to do with my hands and feet. My limbs feel awkward and unmanageable, as if they belong elsewhere, I just don't know where that might be.

"I'm sorry," I mumble, looking down at my lap, although I'm unsure what it is that I am really apologizing for. My discomfort, maybe, or maybe my clear lack of desire to be here. It's not her fault my mother forced this on me, and while I may not want to be around happy people because the desire to slap the smiles off their faces is almost overwhelming, it feels so wrong to direct those feelings towards Betty White's doppelganger. I sigh deeply and shift in my chair.

She spends the next 30 minutes taking me through basic background information. Things like where I grew up, my parents' marital status, where I went to college. Questions that lull me into a false sense of safety that maybe this session will be easy. She hasn't touched on anything that would indicate she was leading up to asking about Will or Tabitha or Justin or *that day*. I should have known better.

"Allison," she says softly, looking at me with a gentle expression on her face, "tell me why you're here."

I stare at her, suddenly tense and angry. "I'm sure my mother told you what happened."

"That's not what I mean. I mean why are *you* here? Your mother is the one who called and provided the initial intake information. I know why she thinks you need to be here. What I want to know is why you are here."

Because I got my family killed? Because I stopped leaving the house because I was having homicidal fantasies when I saw people going about their lives when my life is gone? Because I dream of all the ways I wish I could torture Justin in the hopes of making him hurt just a fraction of the way I hurt?

"My mother is worried about me," I state banally.

Dr. Whitman smiles and says "Yes. She made that clear. Do you think she has reason to be worried?"

I cross my arms across my chest and sigh like a petulant child. I feel angry and defensive as I cross one leg over the other and bounce my foot against my calf. "My mother has her own ideas of how I should be handling my grief. Since I am not grieving the way she thinks I should be, she decided I needed therapy, and she can be," I pause, throwing out an arm and finish with a forceful "persistent." I know this is not a fair assessment. I know that the truth is so much more complex than what I just said, but I can't bring myself to explain how desperate and worried my mother has been – how my anger has changed me into someone vile and ugly that even I don't recognize, and how much that scared her.

Dr. Whitman writes something in the notebook on her lap and looks at me expectantly. The silence lingers so long that my discomfort grows exponentially. I know her game; stay silent until I'm so uncomfortable that I talk just to fill the void. I hate the person I've become since I lost Will and Tabitha. I am a screaming bitch now, and I know it. Before – before this wretched, disgusting life I am now living – I was nice. People liked me, and I liked people. No one would have ever described me as bitchy; they would have said I was sweet, or friendly, or outgoing. When Will and Tabby first died – God even thinking those words send shockwaves of pain coursing through me – friends and family tried so hard to be supportive, to visit, to "be there", but I eventually drove them all away with how hideously I treated everyone. I have no idea how to let go of all the anger inside of me, and I can't seem to stop myself from lashing out at everyone who tries to connect with me.

Giving in, because clearly Dr. Whitman is the queen of the silent game, I tell her the truth. "I hate everyone," I say. "I hate that the world still spins, I hate that people around me are happy. I hate when I hear someone laugh or speak, or, fuck, even breath. I am so fucking angry all the time," I spit, "and I don't know that I even care anymore."

Dr. Whitman nods, "You lost a great deal, and anger is completely normal - healthy even. Tell me this…how do you express your anger?"

"I'm a hateful, screaming bitch any and every chance I get," I say, honestly.

"Does it feel good? When you lash out and are, in your words, a screaming bitch, does it feel good?"

"Yes. It feels," I pause, searching for the right word, "freeing. Like, when you open the valve on a pressure cooker and the steam streams out? It feels like that; like a release of all the pressure building inside of me. And the thing is, no one will say anything. I'm the widow and the childless mother, I can say whatever I want, and no one is going to say a damn thing."

She nods and writes something down, then looks at me and asks, "Besides your mother, who do you have for support?"

I make a self-deprecating noise and state flatly, "No one. Not anymore." When she says nothing, I continue,

"I used to have a lot of friends. Friends from college, from playgroup, couples' friends that Will and I went out with often. Now? Now I have no one. I have systematically run every single person out of my life, and truthfully? I don't care."

I slump in the chair and stare out the window. I'm lying to her and myself, and I know she knows it. I do care, on a very deep level, that I am the loneliest person I know. I lost my whole world in an instant, and then proceeded to push away every single person who tried to support me and comfort me. I didn't want their comfort, or their kindness or their soft smiles of pity. Mostly though, I didn't want the, what? Reminders? No, because not one second goes by where I didn't *remember;* I didn't want the memories I associated with them and my loss. I didn't want to see Sarah, one of my closest friends from playgroup, because she got to leave me and my grief, and go home and cuddle her beautiful daughter, and I did not. I didn't want to see Jeff and Ann, a couple Will and I routinely had dinner with, because they have each other, and I would never have Will again. I couldn't bear to have tangible evidence of my "never agains" constantly in my face.

I turn from the window and regard Dr. Whitman. She's watching me with a thoughtful expression on her face, almost like she knows what I was just thinking. "I can't be around people. Seeing them have what I have lost, it's too much. It hurts too much. Why do they get to have their children when my baby is gone? Why are they still complaining about their husbands' leaving socks on the bedroom floor, when I would literally give my life to have to pick up Will's socks one more time?

The unfairness of it all just adds to how insanely angry I am all the time."

She nods and touches the pen to her mouth, thinking. "Your mother expressed concern that you don't leave the house and haven't in several months. How are you meeting your needs? How are you working or making sure you have food? How are you taking care of you?"

"I work from home. I edit books, so I can do that anywhere. I get my groceries and household supplies delivered. I do all my banking online. I literally have no reason to leave the house."

"What about self-care? Are you showering? Cleaning your house? Exercising?"

This question makes me uncomfortable, but I don't know why. When everything first happened, I was in such a fog that the first several days are just blank. I just remember going through the motions, robotically selecting a casket, burial plot, flowers, shutting out every feeling and emotion. I remember going to shower the morning of the funeral and just standing under the water, unsure what I was supposed to do. I was in there so long that the hot water turned so cold that I was shivering, and yet, I still just stood there. Eventually my mother must have become worried about me because I remember her coming in, helping me out of the shower and wrapping me in a towel, stroking my wet, but still unwashed hair, and murmuring soft words at me. I wore a hat to the funeral to cover my hair, since there wasn't time for the water to recover and wash it. In the weeks after the funeral I would go days without showering or eating.

"I'm better at it now," I answer honestly. "The first several weeks things like bathing and eating seemed so pointless, but now I try to remember to eat at least once a day, and I shower every day, or every other day at least. I really only use the family room, kitchen and downstairs bathroom, so it's not hard to keep those areas picked up. As for exercising, no, not really."

I noticed Dr. Whitman's eyebrows go up when I mentioned only using a few rooms in my house, so when her next question comes, it's not a surprise.

"You are only using 2 rooms and a bathroom?"

Even though her question was expected, it doesn't mean it isn't hard to answer. Coming here today I expected questions about Will and Tabby, questions about Justin, questions about how I'm grieving and what I am doing to "move on". God, I hate that expression…"move on". Like somehow I'm going to wake up one day and no longer feel like half of my soul, both of my reasons for living, are missing and just skip merrily into the next phase of my life, leaving my grief and sadness behind. I didn't expect that questions about my hygiene or which rooms in my house I'm occupying would be so difficult to answer. But they are. I feel ashamed and uneasy, which only adds to the intense anger I carry around with me.

I narrow my eyes at her and practically snarl "Yes", almost daring her to judge me for it. Except all she does is nod, like she understands, which makes me even more irrationally angry, so I glare at her.

God I am *such* a bitch.

"Do you have a fenced in backyard?" She asks, apropos of absolutely nothing.

"What?" I ask, stupidly, feeling unbalanced.

"A fenced in yard? Do you have a fence?"

"Uh…wha…a" I blink at her, "yes?" I answer, although it sounds more like a question.

"Can you go in a store?"

"A store?"

She crosses her legs and leans slightly forward, "You said you don't leave the house, and haven't in months. I'm asking, can you go into a store?"

I think about this and answer with a confused "Yes…"

She nods and then only furthers my confusion when she says "On your way home from here, I'd like you to stop at a second hand shop, Goodwill or the like."

I stare at her, trying to keep up with this sudden change of topic and wondering if it really is a sudden change. The first few months after losing Will and Tabitha, I would find myself zoning out and losing time or missing big chunks of conversation, but I thought I had at least gotten that under control. "What?" I ask, again stupidly.

Dr. Whitman smiles at me and says "I want you to go to a second hand shop. I want you to buy as many ceramic dishes and mugs as you can. Nothing glass though. Grab a sheet as well. I want you to go home and lay the sheet out on the ground in front of the fence. Then I want you to throw those dishes and mugs at the fence. Throw them really hard. Smash them. Shatter them. Scream at the top of your lungs while you do it. Embrace all that anger in you and send it flying with each plate you throw."

I look at her like she's lost her mind. She wanted me to….smash dishes?

I can tell she knows how confused I am. "Trust me," she says. "Trust me. Smash all those dishes and mugs.

Then gather up the corners of the sheet and place it, with all the pieces, in a box. Next week, when you come, bring the box with you."

"I…what? Why?" I ask, so confused by this request.

Dr. Whitman gives a soft chuckle and says "Next week Allison. Ok? Just bring the box next week. Just like grief is a process, therapy is a process too, and I need you to try and trust me to lead you through both of them. Eventually I will be asking you to trust me with much bigger truths, and feelings, and actions, but while we build up to that part of our relationship, I'm just asking you to trust me with broken dishes. Can you do that?"

I think about it, and decide that yes, I can do that. "Okay," I say. "I can do that."

She smiles at me, and for the first time in six months I don't want to slap the smile off of someone's face. Instead, I feel like I just passed a test I hadn't studied for, and I feel a little shimmer of pride light somewhere so deep inside of me it takes me a moment to recognize it. "Okay," she says, moving to stand and walking to her desk. She makes me an appointment for next week and hands me a little business card with the date and time, and then leads me to a side door and out into a small hallway that leads to an exit door. I had noticed when I came in that she had two separate exterior doors, and clearly this was why. So patients leaving their sessions didn't have to go into the waiting room and see or be seen by whoever was waiting for their appointment. For some reason I took comfort in this. I mumble goodbye and exit the building, get in my car and head to Goodwill before going home.

CHAPTER TWO

I drive to the house from Dr. Whitman and Goodwill feeling conflicted. For the first time in months I'm excited about something and there is an intense feeling of guilt associated with it. What right do I have to be excited about anything? Will and Tabby will never experience excitement again. They will never laugh or smile or feel joy. Am I diminishing their loss by looking forward to something? Objectively, I know that is crazy. While we do not grieve the same way, not by a long shot, hence her manipulating me into therapy, I know my mother grieves the loss of my husband and my daughter. She adored Will, and she loved Tabby to distraction, and she was devastated when they died. It's less obvious now, but that doesn't mean it isn't still there. What it isn't is her entire existence. She goes to book club and bridge club, she gardens and shops and goes out with her friends for lunch. She has a life that isn't just about the loss of her son-in-law and only grandchild. I resent her for this, just like I resent everyone.

In six months I haven't laughed once. I don't watch television. I don't listen to music. Even the books I edit no longer bring me joy. I used to love reading and thought I was the luckiest person in the world that I got paid to read books for a living. I would devour my authors' books. Romance and mysteries, dramas and psychological thrillers, page after page of new worlds and new friends and crazy enemies. Now? Now I edit dry, dull nonfiction books on financial planning, cabinet building, and engine repair. I have systematically removed anything from my daily life that might bring me even the slightest hint of joy. Feeling this spark of excitement is uncomfortable, like trying on shoes that don't fit correctly. It pinches and pulls in weird and painful ways, but it's there all the same, pushing its way towards the surface, making itself known.

I pull into my driveway and see my mother sitting in one of the Adirondack chairs on the front porch. I should have expected that. She knew my first therapy appointment was today, after all, she is the one who scheduled it. I should have anticipated she would be here waiting when I got back to see how it went. And seeing as her own house is only a block and half away, it's even less surprising to find her sitting here waiting for me.

I take in my house that is now just a house and no longer a *home*. I remember the day five years ago when Will and I pulled up to this house, having already seen close to a dozen that for one reason or another, were not right for us. There was the house wallpapered with giant yellow flowers in every room, and by every room, I mean *every* room including the bathrooms and weirdly, even the garage. There was the house with a slide-out toilet under the sink in the kitchen, which Will and I laughed ourselves sick over. Then there was the house with a basement that easily could have been the setting for a slasher film; I noped out of that one pretty quick. The day we pulled up to this house though, we knew. This one would be our home.

It's a beautiful two-story Craftsman, painted a deep dark blue, with gleaming bright white trim. The wood floor of the covered front porch is stained a gorgeous dark brown, and the wooden ceiling is a soft white. We installed a fan with wide wicker paddles and a beautiful chandelier on the ceiling. To the left of the front door we placed two white Adirondack chairs and a squat table and to the right of the door we hung a sturdy wooden porch swing we stained just a shade lighter than the floors. The front door is a bright sunny yellow, a color I was so in love with when this was a home, but now just mocks me with its cheerfulness. Maybe I should paint the front door black. It seems more fitting now.

I get out of the car and open the back door, reaching in for one of the three boxes across my back seat. This one is full of coffee mugs, a riot of mismatched colors and patterns. I have another box filled with dinner plates and one just of salad plates and bowls. A large serving platter with a jolly Santa in the center lays across the box of dinner plates. I'm particularly looking forward to smashing that stupid smile off of Santa's face. The expression the checkout lady had when I began unloading the dozens of plates, bowls and mugs from my cart was almost comical. I mean, I get it. Who buys 46 dinner plates with 8 different patterns and colors that clash violently? And who really needs 31 coffee mugs, including one that I'm pretty sure was a giant boob with a strawberry pink nipple on it? Not to mention the salad plates and the cereal bowls with everything from paisley print to Elvis Presley. She didn't ask, but I could tell she wanted to. The me *before* would have made a joke and let her in on why I was buying so many hideous dishes. Except, the me *before* wouldn't have needed to do this exercise to begin with, so there's that. Instead I just crossed my arms over my chest, pasted my bitchiest "don't talk to me" expression on my face, and waited while she rang me up.

My mom pushes to standing as I approach the steps to the porch and asks, "What *is* all this?"

I push the first box in her arms and say "I have two more boxes in the car," not answering her question.

"Okay, but Allison, what is this," she asks, peeking in the box. "Coffee mugs? I don't understand. Why do you need all these mugs? And oh my God, is that a boob?" she asks, sounding horrified.

"Homework," I call over my shoulder as I head back to the car for the next box.

"Homework? Allison, what? What in the world is going on? I thought you had your first therapy appointment today. Did you go?"

I reach into the car and drag the second box across the seat. Hefting it into my arms, it's far heavier than the first box, I turn and start back to the porch.

"Yes mom, I went. And this is homework." I walk up the stairs and tilt my head towards the front door, "Is it locked?"

"No, I went in when I got here to use the bathroom," my mother says, sounding confused but unsure if she should push me for more information.

I wrap my left arm around my box and balance it on my left thigh while pressing down the door latch with my other hand. I juggle the box back into both arms as the door swings wide, and step into the foyer and head to the kitchen, my mom following behind with her own box. I place my box on the island and turn, "I have one more in the car. You can just put that one on the island next to the other one."

I carry the last box into the house and set it beside the other two. I stare at them, unsure of what to do next. I want to start smashing them right now, but I also don't want my mother here when I do it. In the beginning I would just turn up the *bitch* and try and run my mother off like I did with everyone else. My anger is like a living, breathing thing that I wear like people wear clothing, wrapping it around me and using it as a shield from all the people in my life who wanted to comfort me. I didn't want their comfort or their support or their company or the constant reminders that they had what I would never have again.

My mother, though, didn't let me push her away. Growing up it was just the two of us. My dad left when I was an infant, preferring a life with no responsibilities to having a wife and child. I don't remember him, I've never seen him again, and I honestly have no idea how or if my mother grieved his absence. When I was growing up she never indicated she missed him. I know she dated occasionally, and she always seemed happy with life. My grandfather made some really smart investments and was extremely wealthy. My mother had a trust fund and never needed to work, so she was able to stay home with me for years. When I started elementary school she got a part time job in a bakery, just to have something to do with her day. Once a year she would leave me with my grandparents and go on a cruise with her girlfriends to some tropical destination. Our home was always filled with friends and family, cousins for me to play with, and so much laughter. I never really considered if she was lonely or not.

After the funeral, when I was at my absolute most wretched, I tried really hard to make her abandon me. To get her to give up on me like everyone else had. I treated her to the very worst of my anger, letting it burn as bright as possible, spewing so much hate and venom that even now I'm ashamed of some of the things I said. She still didn't give up on me. She kept coming back, week after week, month after month, letting me heap verbal abuse on her over and over until one day two weeks ago when she had had enough and she slapped me. Hard. Across the face. It stunned me silent. I lost my husband and my child and my mother had slapped me. I was a thirty-four-year-old woman and my mother had slapped me. I stood, breathing heavy, holding my cheek, anger blazing through me when she whispered "Enough."

I stared at her, drawing in ragged breaths.

"I love you," she said, tears running down her face. "I love you more than my own life. The thought of losing you is unbearable, so I cannot imagine how much pain you are in right now, losing Tabby…"

"Don't," I hiss.

She reaches out to take one of my hands but I snatch it close to my chest and curl it into a fist so she can't. "It's time," she says. "You can't go on like this. You are stuck, so stuck in your anger that I'm not even sure you have allowed yourself to actually grieve your loss."

My spine snaps straight and I practically growl at her "Stop talking."

"No. No, I will not stop talking. Allison, you experienced the absolute worst..."

"STOP," I scream, leaning forward into her face.

"NO," she shouts. "NO! Listen to me. Allison, please, listen to me. I don't know, I can't know, what you are going through. What I do know is you will never, never be able to move forward, have any kind of life at all, if you don't get some help."

"Move forward?" I ask, sarcastically. "Just, what? Forget they ever existed? Is that what you want Mom? For me to *move forward*?"

"Yes," she says, nodding her head and wiping at the tears on her cheeks. "Yes, I want you to move forward. Not move on. Not forget. Not *get over it*. How can you even think that? I loved them too. I miss them too. It in no way compares to what you lost, but baby, I lost them too. I feel their absence and my heart breaks, for me, but mostly for you. But Allison, you can't keep going like this. You can't. And honey, I know you don't want to hear this, but beautiful girl, Will would not want this life for you."

"You don't know what Will would have wanted. You think he would want me to forget about him and Tabby? To run out and find some other man to love and start a new family? Is that what you think Will would want?"

"Of course not. I," she sighs, takes a deep breath, and continues, "I am not talking about finding another man, or starting another family. I'm talking about grieving their loss, feeling it, finding a way to let go of all this anger, and maybe, finding yourself. I think you need to talk to someone. Someone who can help you navigate this enormous hurt and loss. Someone who can help you process all these feelings in a healthy way so that maybe, one day, you can live a life outside this house with only your anger to keep you company. And yes, I think that Will would want you to find a way to find joy in life again. To smile and laugh and *live* rather than just exist."

"Therapy?" I ask, the disdain dripping from my voice. "You think therapy is going to make the giant hole in my heart…in my *soul* go away? You think therapy is going to make me forget, every single day when I wake up, that I lost everything? That *Justin*," I raged, "didn't steal my world from me?"

"Absolutely not. And no, I do not think therapy is magically going to make all of this go away. What I do think is that talking to someone who can help you navigate this isn't a bad thing."

In the end I had agreed. I had anger in spades, but I didn't have the emotional fortitude to stand up against my mother's tears. Somehow she also managed to broker a deal; when we were together I didn't have to smile or pretend to be anything other than what I was, utterly and completely broken, but I did have to, in her words "Set the bitch aside and behave like a civilized human being." It was hard, because I wanted to scream at the world every second of the day, but when my mother was around I wasn't warm and fuzzy, but I wasn't a raving bitch either.

"So? What is all of this?" my mother asks, peeking in the other two boxes.

"Dishes," I say, absently fingering the corner of one of the cardboard flaps. "I'm supposed to smash them."

My mother looks up from the box she's poking around in and asks, "Smash them?"

I nod and explain what Dr. Whitman said about smashing the dishes against the fence onto a sheet and bringing the whole thing back next week.

"But…why?" My mother sounds as confused as I felt when Dr. Whitman first explained what she wanted me to do.

"She didn't say. She said that grief and therapy were journeys and that she was going to ask me to trust her with harder things, but for now she wanted me to just trust her with broken dishes," I say, shrugging. "I mean, throwing breakables against the fence and screaming my head off while doing it doesn't sound all that bad to be honest." Somehow, admitting this, breaks open a tiny place inside of me where that spark of excitement I felt earlier tries to poke through. I try to smother it, to direct my anger inward and snuff it out, but it's a persistent little thing and I can feel it take hold and stubbornly refuse to be extinguished.

Without my having to ask, somehow my mom knows I need to do this alone. "Do you want me to help you carry the boxes outside before I leave?" she asks.

I consider this, but decide I can manage, and the quicker she leaves the quicker I can start. "No, I'm good. I can do it," I say, and then I surprise both of us by adding "thanks."

My mother makes a noise that sounds like a swallowed sob, but other than that she doesn't draw attention to literally the only kind word I have said to her in six months. Seriously, I am such a *bitch*. She hooks her purse over her shoulder and pauses in front of me, her right hand drifting up as if she is going to cup my cheek. At the last second she snatches it back and clears her throat. "I'll check on you later. I love you Al," and then she turns and walks out, shutting the front door with a soft click.

CHAPTER THREE

I change into a pair of loose cotton shorts the color of blueberries and a well-worn gray tee shirt that says "No Uterus No Opinion" on it and slip on a pair of flip flops. I stare down at my feet and consider that maybe flip flops amid hundreds of shards of ceramic might not be the wisest choice, so I switch them out for a pair of old Keds I find buried in the front closet. Clothing was tough in the beginning. I couldn't bear to open the door to the laundry room, because I knew there was no way I could handle seeing Will and Tabby's clothes, the last tangible remnants of their life, and I couldn't go up to my and Will's room to get clothes because there was no way in hell I could handle walking into the bedroom I shared with the love of my life knowing he would never walk into that room again. In the end, my mother gathered up Will and Tabby's clothes from the laundry room, moving them somewhere else (I have no idea where; I never asked) and transferred most of my clothing from my room down to the family room. She brought over plastic bins with lids, and I've been living out of those for six months.

I adjust the drawstring on the shorts. They sit too low and too loose on my hips. I used to be what was called curvy by the politically correct; the reality was I was about twenty-five pounds overweight. Now though, I'm at least fifteen pounds underweight – all sharp edges and jutting bones.

I carry the boxes outside one by one and set them about ten feet from the fence. I shake out the king size flat sheet I found at Goodwill, and lay it on the ground, careful to line it up tightly against the edge of the fence.

I reach into the box closest to me and grab the boob coffee mug, hesitating for just a second before I hurl it against the fence. It hits the fence with force and makes a clinking noise as it shatters apart and lands with a satisfying dull thud on the sheet in the grass. I choose another mug and repeat the process, this time letting out a "hmph" noise as I throw it. I work my way through four more mugs, my noises growing louder and more defined with each throw. When I throw the seventh one I let loose a scream from deep inside me as I watch it fly apart against the fence. Mug after mug, scream after scream I hurl them against the fence, creating a pile of destruction on the sheet. I finish the first box and move on to the salad plates and bowls. My arm is sore and I can feel the sweat rolling down my spine and between my breasts, but I don't stop. I scream and throw and scream some more.

I think about Will's smile and smash a plate against the fence with a mighty roar. I visualize Tabby and her curly pigtails and I shatter another plate, a sob tearing free from so deep inside of me it feels as if it's been ripped from me. More plates, more memories, more screams, more sobs until I am a sobbing, snotty, uncontrollable mess. I collapse onto my knees, rocking back on my heels and wrap my arms around myself and let my grief free. Deep, wrenching cries of agony that don't even sound human force their way up from the very pit of me and out of my body. I roll to laying, curled on my side, my knees to my chest and my arms wrapped around them. I am hysterical…I can't make it stop even if I tried. I sob and scream until I am gagging, and then I cry some more. Memories flicker through my mind so fast I can't catch a single one. Will, Tabby, Tabby and Will, Will and I, Tabby and I, the three of us…hundreds of thousands of memories spin one after the other and I can't do anything but try and survive it.

I haven't cried in six months. Not the day the police came to my door to tell me about the car crash. Not when I stood there, stoic, as the doctors told me they had done everything they could but had been unable to save my family. Not when I signed the papers to donate their organs so others could benefit from their deaths. Not at the funeral, or the cemetery when we lowered the single casket containing the bodies of both my husband and my daughter, Tabby cradled in her father's arms so she wouldn't be alone or afraid, not later when I was in our house, alone and lonely. Not once. I was afraid that if I started to cry I would never, ever stop. Anger was easier. Safer. More freeing. I embraced the anger and fed it, like a living thing, like fire, stoking it and letting it grow bigger, and fiercer, crowding out every other emotion.

I struggle to find that anger now, to bring it to the surface and use it to smother the tears, to bury the memories, but it's gone. In its place is a depthless cavern of heartbreak and loss and despair that threatens to consume me. I feel utterly and completely broken in a way that feels like I will never be whole again.

I don't know how long I laid in the grass and wailed. Minutes? Hours? The sun is lower in the sky, dusk on the horizon and the air is cooler now. The sweat that soaked my body has long since dried, leaving me shivering.

I don't hear my mom approaching, but I feel her strong arms reach for me and pull me to her. She strokes my hair and whispers in my ear "That's it baby girl. Let it out. Let it out."

She holds me close and rocks me slowly, as if I were a small child again. She murmurs soft words against my head and rubs small circles along my back. She holds me until I am cried out, exhausted and wrung out. Gently, she helps me stand and guides me into the house. Without a word she directs me to the sofa and eases me to sitting, slips off my sneakers and motions for me to lay down. Then she covers me with a soft blanket and smooths the hair off my face.

"Sleep," she says, whisper soft, and I'm already halfway there.

When I wake up hours later, my eyes feel swollen and gritty, and my muscles ache. I have a hollow feeling in the center of my chest, and I feel vulnerable. And sad. Unbelievably, unimaginably, unbearably sad. Anger I could handle. Anger kept me safe from breaking down and allowed me to shut people and emotions out. But this sadness that broke through, it feels all consuming, altering. It's like I left my house with my anger shield and boxes of dishes to smash, and I reentered my house more shattered than the ceramic along my fence.

There's a soft light coming from the kitchen, and I instinctively know my mother is still here. I stand and stretch, my muscles bunching and protesting from being used for the first time in months, and walk woodenly to the kitchen. My mom is sitting at the table, a cup of tea in front of her and a book resting in her lap. She's staring out the window over the sink, and for the first time in months I study her.

My mother, when I was a little girl, was a bundle of energy. She was always rushing around, busy and active. If she wasn't playing with me, she was dancing while she cleaned, or laughing around the table with friends. She was kinetic, always in motion. If someone were to paint my mother in the abstract she would have been a kaleidoscope of colors splashed and swirled across a canvas. Even in my teens and twenties she was like this. I think back and can barely remember a time where my mom was *still.* If we watched a movie, she fidgeted, her leg bouncing, or her finger twirling a lock of her hair. During car rides she would sing at the top of her lungs and wiggle in her seat, car dancing, she called it. I've never seen her so still. It's unnerving. Because if I missed this -this drastic and utter change to her entire being – what else have I missed?

I clear my throat softly and startle her. She whips her head towards me and bobbles the book on her lap, then closes it and sets it on the table. The look she gives me is hesitant – like I'm a wild creature and she's afraid she will spook me. I don't say anything, because I can't. I'm looking at my mother and it occurs to me that not only is she still – she looks *old*.

This is so unnerving. It's like for the past six months, while I was wrapped in my armor of anger, I was utterly and completely blind to everything else going on around me. I needed that anger to protect me from feeling my loss – it was so big, and so unfathomable – it IS so big and so unfathomable – that I couldn't bear to feel even a small part of it. Breaking those mugs and dishes broke something inside of me, something, I'm guessing, Dr. Whitman knew would happen. Instead of letting my grief out, little by little, over weeks or months, everything I had been refusing to feel came rocketing to the surface, like dropping a Mentos into a bottle of Coke. Wave after wave of grief crashed through me and I was powerless to stop it. I tried so hard, but once that first tear fell there was no way to push everything back into the proverbial bottle. But something else happened when the grief forced its way through – the blinders I had been wearing for six months also disappeared.

My mother and I are the same height at 5 foot 7, but where before this I was heavy, she has always been slim. We have the same thick brown hair. Mine is unruly with curls and waves and hangs to just below my bra strap. Hers is cut in a darling pixie that compliments not only her face but her style. I notice now that she has more gray than brown in her hair and wonder when that happened. I see the curve of her spine where grief has folded her into herself, and the lines of sadness and worry etched on her face. I feel like I'm seeing her for the first time after a long absence and it's striking.

"Hey my beautiful girl," she says, softly, patting the chair next to her, inviting me to come and sit.

I move slowly, feeling unsure of my limbs and my body. Everything feels disconnected now, like a marionette held together by strings that are far too loose. I sit and fold my arms on the table and rest my cheek against them, looking at her.

"Can I make you some tea?" she asks.

"Yeah," I say, my voice horse and too soft. I clear my throat and repeat, "Yes. Tea sounds good."

She gets up and moves to the stove and grabs the kettle. She fills it at the sink and places it on the gas burner. I watch as she reaches up to the cabinet where the mugs are kept, and notice she's careful to pick a plain one, instead of one of the dozens declaring me "Wifey" or "Best Mom Ever". My heart squeezes painfully at the sight of them, and I wonder, not for the first time, why I never got rid of those.

"Mom?"

She turns, the mug clutched to her chest, the tea bag string swinging with the motion, "Yeah?"

"I…how…How did you know? How did you know to come back?"

She looks down and then back up at me, "Mildred called me. She heard the dishes breaking and heard you screaming. She was concerned but didn't want to bother you, so she called to ask if I knew what was going on at your house. While we were talking you started crying, and then…well, then I could hear you through the phone. In my fifty-seven years I have never heard something so hideous and heartbreaking. I knew – I knew that everything you had been keeping inside was finally being let out and I just ran. I didn't even shut my front door or hang up the phone. I was still holding it when I came into the backyard."

The kettle starts to whistle so she turns and shuts the stove off, fills my mug and brings it, with a plate and spoon for the tea bag, to the table. I sit up and wrap my hands around the outside of the mug, absorbing the heat until it starts to burn. I move my hands to rest loosely on the table and stay quiet.

"After I got you inside and settled, I hurried back to my house and locked up. I also called Mildred back so she wouldn't worry."

I nod, but I still don't say anything. I'm not sure what to say. I feel so lost right now.

We are quiet for a few minutes and then I venture into dangerous territory by asking "Do you think Dr. Whitman knew this would happen?"

"When you explained what she wanted you to do with those boxes of dishes I was confused. I couldn't figure out what smashing dishes had to do with grieving. But I think I get it now. You needed an outlet, something loud and violent, but safe, to break through that shield of yours and let your grief out. She's been a grief counselor for a long time. I would venture to say that she has seen it all, and likely had a fairly good idea what would happen with that exercise."

"I feel like she tricked me. She didn't ask if I was ready for something like that."

"Ali, I think that was the point. No one is ever *ready* for something like that. Even when the loss is expected, no one is ever really ready. And there isn't a way to prepare for it; you just have to live it. To feel it. To move through it, as hard as it is, until one day you can take a breath without breaking, and maybe the next day you can take two. I have been so worried about you, watching you keep it all inside, so damn angry at the whole world, not letting yourself grieve them."

My eyes fill and I whisper, "It hurts. It hurts so much. I don't want to feel this." I'm crying again. I didn't think I had any more tears in me, but apparently now that I broke the dam my body feels the need to supply me with six months' worth of tears all in one day.

My mom reaches for my hand, and this time I don't snatch it away. I let her curl her fingers into mine and we just sit without words as I cry for my husband and my daughter, but mostly, I think, I cry for myself.

CHAPTER FOUR

The week leading up to my next appointment is brutal. I cry for hours on end every day. I wake up from a dead sleep crying. I cry in the shower. I cry while making coffee. I cry reading about how to dovetail a cabinet. I cry making a sandwich, and while eating said sandwich, which, fucking hell, it's hard to eat and cry at the same time, but somehow I do it. I'm worried I'll dehydrate at the rate I am going.

I try, repeatedly, to call up my anger because I know it's there somewhere, but it's buried beneath all my grief and I can't reach it. I find the only thing I *can* get angry about is not being able to find my damn anger. What a fucking joke that is.

It takes me until the fourth day to smash all the dishes. After the epic unleashing of months' worth of grief and tears, I was afraid of what would come rushing out if I tried again. I mean, I was crying all the time now anyway, but somehow what I experienced at the fence was different. It wasn't just the tears – it was tears and memories and anguish violently erupting out of me in a torrent of emotion. I didn't believe it was possible to survive a repeat of that.

Three days after my meltdown my mother convinces me to try again. She holds my hand in hers as we walk to the fence and stands silently by my side as I take in the wreckage of ceramic I had created. She bends low, and picks up a gorgeous violet bowl, shiny and bright, with almost imperceptible swirls of green and blue. It is stunning. Without a word she hurls it at the fence and lets out a satisfied "HA!" when it crashes and shatters, and then shatters more as it falls to the pile.

She turns to me, beaming and announces, "That was fun."

She picks up another, this one a hideous mix of orange and pink, and hands it to me. I hesitate for a second and then bring my arm back and let it fly. "CRASH!"

I watch as she selects two matching bowls, Elvis in blue suede smiling up from the bottom of them, and launches them, one after the other, giving a little wiggle as they shatter and crash to the ground.

I feel a smile tug at the corner of my mouth, and it's such an unexpected feeling, that I'm momentarily stunned. I don't have time to dwell on it though, because my mom shoves another plate at me and grabs one for herself. She turns to me, a radiant smile on her face and counts down, "Three. Two. One," and then she shouts, "Throw!"

I do as commanded and throw my plate, and as soon as it hits the ground the next one is shoved into my hands. We throw plate after plate, bowl after bowl, my mother turning it into a ridiculous game. She stands in front of me, arms straight up in the air and pretends to be a set of football uprights, and yells "Field Goal!" when I throw my bowl through her arms and it crashes into the fence. She picks up another plate and turns around and throws it, with two hands, over her head backwards, jumping up and down when it hits the mark. She pulls a plate from the box and hands it to me and then takes five steps away from me and starts a ridiculous cheer about needing a basket, kicking a leg up and clapping her hands under them, and then jumping up and down to celebrate like I've just scored the winning point in a game when my plate connects with the fence. She keeps it up until we have demolished every plate and bowl and the boxes are all empty. She's saved the Santa platter for last and hands it to me. I turn sideways and whip it like a Frisbee as hard as I can. It doesn't just shatter – it implodes against the fence.

"Take that you fat, jolly Fuck," my mom shouts. I have never, not once ever, heard my mother say the F-word and it sends me over the edge. I start to laugh. I laugh so hard I can't breathe. I have tears streaming down my face and I have to cross my legs so I don't pee my pants. My mom is laughing next to me, but all I keep hearing is her say "you fat, jolly Fuck" over and over in my head and it just makes me laugh that much harder. I double over, clutching my waist, laughing myself sick, until I tumble, headfirst, rolling onto my back in the grass and keep laughing. At some point my laughter turns to sobbing and I'm laughing and crying at the same time, neither emotion really taking hold, instead, sharing space together and bursting forth simultaneously.

The laughter makes me feel conflicted and guilty. I have spent six horrific months feeling nothing but intense anger, and now, suddenly, in the space of four days I have been inundated with an all-consuming anguish, more powerful than anything I have ever felt, and now I'm laughing so hard I can't stand up. I feel like a raving lunatic. Is this what grief is? The absolute loss of control over one's emotions? Never knowing from one second to the next what you will feel? Because if it is, it fucking sucks.

When I was in college I discovered very quickly that I didn't enjoy being drunk or smoking weed. As a self-proclaimed control freak, I hated how being drunk or high made me feel. I can remember going to my first house party with my roommate at a multilevel house just off campus as a freshman. I didn't drink in high school, despite lots of my friends doing so. I was too concerned with studying and my grades to party. Instead, if I did join in, I was the self-appointed designated driver. However that first year of college I decided that I wanted the entire college experience, and of course that meant house parties and drinking and smoking the occasional joint or bong according to my floor mates.

When we got there, there were dozens upon dozens of people, spilling out of the house across the lawn, and onto the balconies. Inside was loud, and hazy with smoke, people yelling to be heard over the blasting music, and of course, there were several kegs scattered throughout the first level. My friend and I made a beeline for the first keg and waited to fill our red Solo cups. The beer was lukewarm and disgusting, likely because it was the cheapest beer available. I quickly downed the first cup and refilled it.

My friend and I wandered around the party, drinking and refilling our cups like amateur drinkers; that is to say, way too quickly, and by cup four I was finding it difficult to feel my lips and my coordination was a little stumbly. Drink five tipped me over the edge into drunk and I hated it. All I wanted to do was to go back to my dorm and wait for it to be over. I didn't get giggly or silly. I wasn't a happy drunk, chatty and outgoing, flirting with every guy I encountered. I also wasn't a sad drunk like some of the girls, crying in the bathroom over some perceived slight. I was an uninterested drunk – I hated the feeling of not being in control of myself, and all I wanted was for it to be over and to be myself again.

I drank a few more times, and I even tried weed twice, but I never enjoyed it. I didn't embrace the feeling being drunk or high was supposed to provide. Each time I just wanted it to be over. When I was drunk or high I would regret it instantly. I hated the lack of control I felt and just wanted to go back and undo it. As an adult I like the occasional glass of wine, or cocktail, but I also know that one or two are enough to feel relaxed, but not enough to feel intoxicated. Weed, though, I'm all set with weed. It would make my head too confused, like it was somehow full of bricks and weightless at the same time. I detested that feeling.

This is how I feel now. Out of control and uncomfortable in my own skin. All I want is for it to be over. To stop feeling all these feelings and feel like myself again. I hate that I can't regulate my feelings in

any kind of reasonable way. I understood the anger. It
not only made sense, it protected me from feeling
anything else. But this? This all-consuming sadness, the
deep sorrow and unrelenting tears, the hysterical
laughter - I suddenly feel like I not only lost my family
but now I'm losing my mind. How do people do this?
How do they survive this kind of grief? I'm not the first
person to lose a spouse, or a child, or even both at the
same time, but I don't understand how they live through
it. I never wanted to feel this; I mean obviously right?
No one wants to lose their family, no parent should ever
have to bury their child, no one wants to experience
deep and unthinkable grief. But what I really mean is I
don't want to feel, and apparently that is no longer an
option.

I finally stop laugh-crying and roll to my side. My
mother mimics my actions and we lay there,
breathing heavy and look at one another.

"How are you feeling, baby girl," my mom asks,
reaching out and tucking a loose strand of hair behind
my ear.

"Unhinged," I answer, honestly. "I feel like my
emotions are all over the place and I can't get a handle
on myself. It's like breaking those dishes broke
something inside of me and now I have absolutely no
control over anything I'm feeling."

She nods solemnly and rolls to her back. "I know it's
not the same," she starts, "but when your dad left I felt
the same way. I cried constantly. I would go into a store
and some stupid song would be playing over the
loudspeaker and I would have to leave because I would
start sobbing. I would see other couples walking down
the street holding hands or sitting close in a park and it

would hurt so much because I no longer had that. And trust me, my emotions were *all* over the place. Happy one minute, utterly heartbroken the next. I've never felt so unpredictable in my life."

I am speechless. I had no idea she had ever felt this way. It's not something she ever talks about, and I was likely too young to notice.

"How," I take a deep breath, "how did you…what? Get over it?" I hate that I just asked that. I hate that I am even considering that question but I don't know what else to do. It's been six months without my family, but sometimes it feels like minutes, and others like years. I knew I was treating my anger as a shield from others, but I had no way of really appreciating how much it was protecting me from me. Now that it's gone and all I have left is this horrible sadness that feels unendurable, I just want it to stop, and it's only been a few days. I know I can't do this for months and years, but I also know I will never get over the loss of my family. I don't know what to do or how to cope.

"It's not something you 'get over' Al. You get through it. You move forward. You don't move on or get over it. The only way forward is through it. You have to feel it and deal with it and learn to manage it. It hurts and it sucks but it's the only way. I had to let myself go through my grief. I had to let myself cry when I was sad, and laugh myself sick when something was funny. I had to forgive myself for the days I couldn't get out of my pajamas. I had to let myself enjoy the good days. And then eventually there were more good days instead of bad. And yeah, even now, there is still the occasional bad day, but they are so very rare now. I lost someone I loved, utterly and completely. And loss is loss. Yes, there are some losses that are bigger and so much more tragic. Obviously the death of a spouse, or God, the death of a child are so much bigger than a break up. But the grief, the loss…those feelings exist regardless of how the loss comes about. I think losing a child is an entirely different kind of hell. There is no comparable circumstance because I can't imagine anything that could possibly hurt more than that. For some partners though, a break up *is* like a death. Something they didn't see coming, and something they have no idea how to build a life after." She shrugs, "And I think, sometimes, for those people, maybe it's almost worse. The knowledge that the person they love with everything they have, not only doesn't love them anymore, but instead is out in the world somewhere loving someone else."

I hadn't considered that. I hurt on a level I never imagined could exist, knowing that Will is no longer in this world. He had this huge, magnetic personality, and the idea that he doesn't exist anymore is incomprehensible. The thought of things being different, of loving Will the way I do, and having him tell me he no longer loves me but instead was in the world loving someone else causes a new hurt I didn't expect, even knowing the situation is imaginary. And suddenly I'm crying again.

My mom sits up and folds her legs under her. "Allison?"

I feel a shame so deep that I don't know if I can even voice the thought that just went through my head.

"Tell me what made you cry just now," she says, her voice gentle.

"It's too horrible to say. I…I can't. It's," I'm sobbing, a-fucking-gain. "Oh my God, I'm a horrible person."

"You aren't horrible," she insists.

"I am," I hiccup. "I am a terrible human being. Oh my God what is wrong with me," I moan. I hate how I sound, and I hate who I've become in the past four days, and I hate the thought I just had. I want to go inside and get under the blanket on the sofa and sleep until I'm eighty.

"I think I can make a pretty good guess," she says. "And if I am right, it doesn't make you horrible, Alison, it makes you human."

"I would give anything…I would give my life to have Will and Tabitha back. Back with me. But what does it say about me," I am crying so hard now that it's hard for me to even understand what's coming out of my mouth, so who knows how much my mother is able to understand. "What does it say about me that when you were talking about losing the person you love and having them out in the world loving someone else, that I would rather Will be dead? Will didn't leave me by choice, I know that. But the thought of him leaving me because he wanted to, when I love him so fucking much, to go and find someone else, it's almost easier to accept that he's dead. Who thinks like that?"

My mother reaches for me and pulls me close to her, wrapping me up in her arms and gently rocking me while I sob uncontrollably. "It makes you someone who has experienced the worst possible thing in life. It makes you someone trying to navigate your grief. And baby girl, it makes you human. Not every human thought is a generous one. And not every feeling is going to be kind. But it doesn't mean you're a horrible person."

I push into my mom and let her hold me tighter and I realize how much I missed this. I've been so busy protecting myself from the world and from feeling anything, that I forgot how good my mom is at soothing my hurts. How good she is at comforting me. How much she loves me. I was so horrible to her for months and not only did she stay, she loved me anyway. I haven't just been a bitch, I've been a stupid bitch. And of course, this new realization makes me cry even harder.

Once I've cried myself out, I turn to my mom and say "Dad was an idiot."

She laughs and hugs me and says "Don't I know it baby girl. Don't I know it."

I stand and brush the grass off the backs of my thighs and then extend my hand to my mom and help her up. It takes us a few goes, but we manage to shimmy the pieces of ceramic into the center of the sheet. There are way too many pieces to fit into one box, so my mom runs into the garage and grabs an old painting tarp Will had from when we first moved in. We divide the ceramic shards into two piles and place the sheet in one box and the tarp in the other. We carry them through the house and out to my car and slide them side by side in the back seat.

I give my mom the first hug I have initiated with her in over six months and whisper "I'm sorry. I'm sorry for everything."

"Darling girl, you have nothing to be sorry for. Not one single thing. I would trade places with you in a heartbeat if I could take your pain away, but I can't. But

I will always, but always, be here for you. No matter what."

CHAPTER FIVE

I carry the boxes, one by one into Dr. Whitman's office, and place them side by side next to my chair. It's only been a week since I was last here, yet it feels like so much longer. So much has happened in the past week that I feel like a completely different person sitting here now.

I look down at my clothing and think maybe I should have changed. I'm wearing a pair of loose-fitting black cotton shorts, an old yellow Framingham State tee shirt, worn and faded and so very soft from a hundred washings, and black flip flops. My outfit doesn't exactly scream progress, but I'm taking baby steps and I'm pretty sure that that, in and of itself, is progress.

Dr. Whitman opens the door to her office and calls my name. This week she's wearing a bright grass green dress with poofy cap sleeves with crouching tigers on it.

It is glorious in all its absolute hideousness and I find that I love it.

She waits while I bring the boxes into her office and then she shuts the door. Instead of moving directly to her chair, she moves behind her desk and drags out a…table? It's about the size of a four person, round, dining table. Except the top doesn't look exactly like a table should. Its top is similar to a pizza pan, only much larger and the sides go up slightly higher. She has a bottle of adhesive in one hand and a paintbrush in another.

"How was your week?" she asks as she maneuvers the table to where she wants it.

"Brutal, but I have a feeling you knew it would be."

She winks at me and with absolutely zero shame says, "Yup."

She comes around the table and opens one of the boxes. "These are great!" she exclaims. "And there is so much to choose from. You certainly embraced the assignment." She selects a blue shard with a yellow line through it, making me wonder what it used to be. Was it a cup or a mug in its previous life?

She turns, shard in hand and regards me. "Normally," she starts, "this is something I do after a couple of sessions. Obviously therapy is tailored to each individual, but this particular exercise is one I use often – just not this early on."

"Then why?"

She squirts some adhesive onto the base of the table and starts to spread it with the brush. "Tell me, what happened when you started throwing the dishes?" She settles the blue shard into the area she has just treated, hands me the adhesive and brush, and leans down to select another.

I have edited a couple of DIY books recently, so I understand now that she is using the pieces for a mosaic. I consider the boxes full of shards and the size of the table, and I'm glad I went a little overboard when I was shopping. The table is quite large, and it will likely use almost all of the shards to cover it.

"I broke down. Spectacularly. Not just crying, but a complete and utter breakdown. I actually haven't been able to get a handle on my tears, or my hysterical laughter for that matter, since." I brush the adhesive while I tell her this, finding it much easier to be honest if I don't look at her and instead busy myself with something else. "Will you tell me why you had me do that? What the point was?"

She places the piece she is currently holding and nods to the table, an indication she wants me to continue, and moves to her chair, picking up her notebook and opening it to a fresh page. "I should think it was obvious," she states. "When you came last week, you spoke of all your anger. Of pushing everyone away. Anger is most definitely a part of the grieving process, but it isn't the only part. And grief *is* a process. It is widely taught that there are five stages of grief. Denial, anger, bargaining, depression and finally, acceptance. But grief isn't a linear process. It's not even a cyclical one. It's more chaotic than that. People can go from denial to depression to bargaining to anger to depression and back to anger. Depending on the loss, it can take an immensely long time to get to acceptance, and even then, there can be the occasional regression back to anger or depression."

"Ok," I say, acknowledging what she is saying, but still not fully understanding how that is supposed to answer my question.

"Not only did you talk about your anger, but you also embodied it. Every movement and facial expression was a visual representation of how you were feeling. What I didn't hear you say was that you were sad. You didn't cry. You were anger personified." She holds up her hand to stop me, seeing as I was about to object, and continues "I am in no way insinuating that you aren't devastated by your loss. I *am* saying that you were stuck. You can't move throughout the grieving process if you stay mired in one emotion, and never let the others in or out. I have found that this activity is a great way to release emotions that are hiding deep beneath the surface."

Rationally this makes sense to me, but part of me desperately misses that shield that was protecting me from everything I feel now.

"Other than this week, how many times have you allowed yourself to cry since the accident?"

I stiffen, because I hate that word, and so I tell her "I hate the word 'accident'. It feels like it diminishes what happened to Will and Tabby. Like 'oops sorry I killed your whole family but it was an accident...shrug'".

She nods, "Fair enough. What would you like us to call it? Is there another word that you feel fits better?"

There is something miraculous about this woman. That sentence, out of almost anyone else's mouth, would sound condescending. From her it just sounds sincere, as if she truly wants to know what word I would prefer because she cares about how it makes me feel. "I don't..." I start, and then stop and consider how to answer her. "I have no idea. I haven't ever called it anything. It doesn't have a name. On the rare occasion I talk about it I guess I refer to it as 'what happened' or 'the day I lost my family' or 'the day Justin stole my life.'"

"Okay then, how many times have you allowed yourself to cry since that happened?"

"None. Until this week, never. I was afraid – afraid if I started, I would never ever stop." I give a self-depreciating chuckle and say, "I guess I wasn't wrong," as tears flood my eyes.

"Never?" she asks, unable to keep the surprise from her voice and I like that about her too. I like that she's professional, but she's human too. She isn't detached or clinical, and her reactions to the things I say are honest, open and genuine.

"Never," I affirm.

"The hospital? The funeral? The cemetery? Not at any of those either?"

"I couldn't. At first, I was so numb that nothing felt real. After, I was so angry and being angry felt safe, so I fed it and let it protect me."

She considers me for a long moment before saying, "Alright, so in six months you haven't allowed yourself to really grieve, to feel your loss. So what happened when you finally did?"

I concentrate on the little section of the table I am filling in as I recount my week. I take her through the first day at the fence, and the subsequent torrent of tears over the next several days. I tell her about my mom and me finishing the boxes and my hysterical laughter. I tell her about the things my mom told me about when my dad left her and her grief. I even tell her about how guilty I felt when I felt relieved that Will had died rather than leaving me by choice. We discuss how breaking down and breaking through my anger felt, and the new vulnerability I feel now. By the time we finish talking about my week, I have completed about an eighth of the table. I kept to various shades of blue, some with print, and some plain, but I have to admit it looks pretty.

"We are just about out of time, but I have a new assignment for you to work on before our next appointment."

This causes a surge of nerves – I don't feel like the last assignment went too well for me.

"Who is your best girlfriend?" she asks.

"Julia," I answer without hesitation, despite not having heard from her in several months. Something I hatefully forced on her, and that in the end, she had no choice but to accept.

"I want you to have coffee with Julia," she starts. I am about to object when she continues, "with rules." I take a breath and nod.

"These are the rules," she flicks her fingers up as she counts them off. "One – no talking about feelings or how you are doing. Two – no talking about family, hers if she has one, or yours. Three – you can set a timer, but you must stay for at least twenty minutes. Four – you must meet her in public. Coffee at one of your homes does not count."

I blink at her. When she said she had a new assignment for me this was definitely not anything close to what I was thinking she was going to suggest. I figured it would be another exercise that would force me to have another emotional breakdown.

"You want me to have coffee? With Julia?"

"Yes. Coffee. With Julia. And the rules," she confirms.

"Umm, okay I guess. I can ask her, but Dr. Whitman, I treated my friends and family to a lot of verbal abuse, and I don't know if she will even be willing to meet me. I did an excellent job of pushing everyone away with the venom I spewed."

She shakes her head and says "You are looking at it from your perspective. I would bet Julia sees things a little differently."

"What do you mean?"

"Think of it this way, if you were Julia, and Julia were you, and she treated you the way that you treated her, and then she called out of the blue to have coffee, would you meet with her or would you tell her no?"

"I would meet with her. In a heartbeat," I say, with no hesitation whatsoever.

"Right, of course you would. Now, you said terrible things because you were going through the unimaginable. You were too angry to see or feel anything else. Now, you are feeling everything, including, I'm assuming, guilt for how you treated those closest to you. Am I right?"

"Absolutely. I feel awful. I wasn't just horrible, I was wretched. It's weird – I feel awful and guilty, but I also don't feel like running out and apologizing to everyone and embracing them back into my life. I still want the distance. I need it. Even though it's been six calendar months, for me it all feels like it happened yesterday. I can't handle seeing Tabby's playgroup moms or my and Will's couple friends."

"Let's break that down really quick before we wrap up. You are entitled to feel however you want to feel. There is a difference between being unable to feel anything, which is what you were doing, and having feelings, which is what you are doing now. You do not need to 'run out and apologize to everyone and embrace them back into your life.' Do you owe people an apology? I don't know – maybe. Do you need to do it immediately and with everyone? No. The people who love you, who have even the slightest understanding of grief, will likely have not taken the things you said when everything was so fresh and raw personally. As you let people back into your life you will know, based on their behaviors, if they understand or if they require an apology. That is not to say that it's a bad idea to offer one regardless. Just because they understand and know you didn't mean the things you said, telling them you recognize that you hurt them is never a bad thing. It just isn't the thing that requires your focus at this moment. Does that make sense?"

I nod, because it does. I can tell Julia I'm sorry for being a hateful screaming bitch, but if she is the friend I believe her to be, she will blow it off and truly and sincerely not need it. Actually, Julia might be one of the few who would be pissed I even apologized in the first place.

"Good. Now, as for playgroup friends and couple friends, I can't say, because I don't know the dynamics of those relationships, but it is possible that those friendships won't last. If the friendships are predicated solely on you as Tabby's mom, with Tabby in tow, or you and Will as a couple, rather than you and Will individually, then it's likely that those friendships will be ones that do not continue. Does that make sense?"

I nod and feel the tears that were threatening while she was talking start to fall. Tabby will always be my daughter, but without Tabby, am I still a mother? Without Will I am no longer part of a couple, so does that mean I'm not a mother anymore either? I don't have the headspace for something so painful. Not right now. My session is over, and I know this isn't something I can even try and explore on my own. I mentally box this thought up and promise myself I will take it out first thing at my next appointment. I am a quick learner, and if this week taught me anything, it is that if I am going to be forced to confront all of these huge emotions, I need support while I am doing it. I silently congratulate myself on that bit of growth, brush my tears aside, take my next appointment card and leave out the side exit.

CHAPTER SIX

I get back to my car and send my mom a text letting her know my appointment went okay and that I needed a quiet night with no big emotional breakdowns. She texts back that she is going out with some girlfriends tonight but that she would come over in the morning and bring bagels from Hole in The Dough, a great bagel place in town. I give her my order, a cinnamon raisin bagel not toasted with olive cream cheese, which results in her sending back a vomit emoji.

At home I make a simple dinner of frozen tortellini and jarred pesto. I don't have the mental bandwidth for anything more complicated. These days I'm lucky if I manage to eat daily; twice on the rare occasion my mother stops by in the morning to check on me under the guise of "bringing me breakfast". I used to love to cook - before. Before I would make almost everything I could from scratch. Pasta? Scratch. Bread? Scratch. Granola bars and dried fruit rolls? Scratch. Pies and cakes and even ice cream? Scratch. Now, if I can't boil it on the stove or nuke it in the microwave I don't even bother.

I take my bowl to the table and fiddle with my phone. As I eat, I plan out what I am going to say to Julia. I know if the situation were reversed, like Dr. Whitman pointed out, that I wouldn't blink at her request, and rationally I know that she likely won't either. But Negative Nelly rears her head and makes me worried that maybe Julia *will* say no. That she will tell me how badly I hurt her and how she can never forgive me and to lose her number.

I push the mostly empty bowl away and decide to get it over with. I pick up the phone and scroll to Julia's number and press the phone button, my heart beating hard in my chest.

"Ali?" Julia's voice comes over the phone and there's no anger. No hate. Instead I hear worry and I start to cry.

"Al, are you okay? What's wrong?"

"I'm okay. I'm alright. Please ignore the crying. It seems to keep happening lately," I say, feeling exceedingly stupid.

"What can I do? Do you need me to come over?" she asks, genuine concern in her voice.

"No," I say, taking a second to get control of my tears and of myself. "No, really, I'm okay. I, umm, I have a favor to ask. You can say no though I will totally understand if you say no yeah I will totally understand I mean I was so horrible to you and now I have a favor and it's okay if you want to say no," I blurt without taking a breath, my words practically running together. I take a deep breath because I have expelled every last molecule of oxygen in my body with that run on sentence and it demands I replace it.

Julia laughs into the phone and says "Unless you are calling to ask me to help you rob a bank, I won't say no. And even if you *are* calling to ask me to help you rob a bank, I would at least consider it for a respectable couple of seconds before I said no."

And just like that, I know it's going to be alright. And also just like that, I realize, like with my mother, I missed Julia.

"I'm in therapy," I explain, "and my therapist likes to give me homework. She has me making a table during our sessions, which I realize is extremely bizarre without some back story, but anyway, this week she asked me who my best friend is and I said you. So I'm calling to ask you to coffee. With rules."

I hear a noise on the other end that sounds suspiciously like crying so I give her a minute. Lord knows I can't get a handle on my emotions this week, I have no room to judge anyone else for theirs.

Finally she says, "I would love to have coffee with you no matter what the rules are. But wait, did you say your therapist has you making a table?"

I give a soft chuckle and say "Yes. She's unique, and I have only had two sessions with her, but I like her and I'm pretty confident there is a method to whatever it is she is doing. And one of those things was to have me go buy so many plates, mugs and bowls at Goodwill that I could have hosted Thanksgiving for forty people. Then she had me take them into the backyard and smash them into my fence. Which resulted in me having a huge emotional breakdown where I sobbed for about a year in my backyard until my mom came over and took me back in the house. We finished breaking everything together this week, and when I brought the boxes of smashed dishes to therapy today she started me on making a mosaic table. I have literally no idea what the table will do for me but the first part clearly had the desired effect she was looking for, so for now I'm just going with it." I owe her this much but I don't really want to discuss it in more detail than I just provided so I switch topics and say, "So, the rules are I have to meet you in public, it can't just be at one of our houses."

"Okay, that sounds great. There are plenty of great coffee places in town."

"There are more. You aren't allowed to ask me how I am doing or how I am feeling. We aren't allowed to talk about your family, Will or Tabby. I have to stay for at least 20 minutes, but I'm allowed to set a timer. I know that doesn't sound very friendly or appealing but these are the rules she gave me."

"They sound perfect," she says, sounding sincere. "I don't care what we talk about. I'm just thrilled you want to have coffee with me, even if your therapist is making you. I'm the one you picked so I'll just go with that part of it."

I laugh a genuine laugh and say "Always the bright side."

"Absolutely!"

"Does any particular day work better for you?"

"Tomorrow," she says quickly and a little loud. "Sorry. I just…I don't want to wait. I miss you and I can totally do the rules. In fact, I'll come prepared with some nonsensical topic we can discuss. I was watching some cooking show the other day and the contestants had to make Geoduck, which looks like a giant penis coming out of a clam shell. I bet there are other penis shaped things in the ocean. I'll do research!" she babbles, which is what she does when she's excited.

"Penis shaped ocean dwellers?"

"Yup," I can practically see her nodding enthusiastically. "That is completely in keeping within the rules, and besides, now I kinda need to know if there are other penis shaped things in the sea that I never knew about."

"I admit, I kinda want to know now too. Okay, so tomorrow. What time works for you?"

"Eleven," she offers. "Eleven is perfect. Let's meet at MUD. They have great coffee and I have seriously considered offering sexual favors to Valerie if she will give me her recipe for her triple chocolate tart. I have tried like hell to duplicate it and it never tastes as good as hers."

"I will meet you at eleven at MUD with the additional, and newly added rule that you do not sexually proposition Valerie while I am there."

She sighs, "Fine but I'm getting a tart and I make no promises for what I will do after you leave."

"Deal," I say on a chuckle.

We say our goodbyes and hang up. I feel…weird. Weirdly excited and yet, weirdly sad. This was the most normal conversation I have had in six months, yet it also feels completely abnormal. So much has changed in the last week, actually, more things have changed in the last week than have changed in the last six months, and it suddenly feels like everything is moving in fast forward and I'm desperately trying to catch up.

I look up to the ceiling and do something I haven't done once since he died. I talk to Will. Or more accurately, I yell to him.
"I hope you're finding all of this amusing, because I. Do. Not!" I shout, a smile tugging at my lips.

I pull open the door to MUD the next morning at ten minutes to eleven. I like to be early when I go anywhere, which is pointless when meeting Julia because she is routinely twenty minutes late everywhere she goes. It used to be a running joke when we were in our early twenties and meeting up for drinks or dinner after work. I would tell her to meet me thirty minutes before we actually needed to be somewhere, because I knew that way she would be on time for when we were really expected to arrive.

Julia and I have been best friends since we were fifteen. We met when her family moved next door to mine in high school and by the second day I knew she would be my lifelong friend. We went to the same college, were roommates after we graduated, and she is the one who set up my blind date with Will, and then forced me to go when I had adamantly refused every day for a week. We were each other's Maid of Honor, we went through our pregnancies together, and her son Linx is eight days older than Tabitha is. Was. Fuck.

MUD smells like coffee and butter, cinnamon and chocolate and all things delicious. I inhale deeply and I can almost taste the sugar rush. There are only three other customers inside – the midmorning lull before the lunch crowd surges in. I wonder if Julia picked eleven for this exact reason. I figure she did, and it makes me love her even more and feel even guiltier for how I behaved when she tried to support and comfort me when Will and Tabby were killed.

I made an effort today and opted for real clothing, instead of my usual cotton shorts and old tee shirts. I have on a casual summer dress. It's pale pink and sleeveless, made from a gauzy material, with an empire waist and it hits just above my knees. It's looser on me than it was last summer, but it's still a cute dress and it's insanely comfortable. I have on silver ballet flats and my hair is in a thick braid that hangs over my shoulder. I didn't bother with any make-up though. It's coffee with Julia for one, and for two, this is more effort than I have made for anything in months.

I look around and I'm shocked to see Julia is already here, sitting in the far corner, one arm up in the air to signal to me like I might miss her amid all the empty tables. She's bouncing in her chair, and I can't help but smile at how excited she is to see me. Julia is a bubbly chubby blonde, who tops out at about five foot three. Her hair is the most gorgeous mixture of golden honey and white blonde and curls in those tight ringlets that can only be achieved through fantastic genetics and not a salon. She has huge startling blue eyes and a beautiful round face that shows her every emotion. I realize taking in her excitement how lucky I am to have her in my life. After how I behaved, this could have gone much differently. I mean, I justified it at the time, and I could likely still justify it now if I wanted to, but the truth of the matter is that had I simply said "I can't see you right now. It hurts too much and I need time and space," she would have given me that. Absolutely. Instead, I treated her just slightly less horrible than I treated my mother, and she still kept trying. She only gave up when I went weeks without answering her calls, not responding to her texts, and refusing to answer the door when she came over, until I finally did. I wrenched the door open and shouted "Leave me alone!" directly into her face, and then slammed the door as hard as I could. She stopped trying after that, and who could possibly blame her?

I see two coffee mugs and two tarts already on the table, so I skip the counter and go directly to the table. I have a quick internal debate with myself as I make my way over to Julia about whether or not I can handle a hug. I decide that I probably can't, at least not without crying. I feel so fragile and unsure of everything these days, and it's frustrating to no longer be able to trust myself and my emotions. I know Julia and I know she will want one. I also know she won't try and hug me but will wait to see if I instigate one. And finally, I know, without a doubt, that she deserves for me to make that effort.

You're early?" I say when I'm about fifteen feet away, my voice infused with shock and humor.

"I've been here for about ten minutes. I was excited," she replies sheepishly.

She stands as I get to the table and I square my shoulders and reach for my friend. I step into her and give her a hug. It's brief, and despite the fact that Julia holds me tight, she seems to instinctively know I need this to be quick, and she lets go at the exact right moment. When she pulls back her eyes are shining with unshed tears, and I can feel my own eyes start to fill. She flutters her hands in front of her face, smiles wide and cheerfully announces "I'm not going to cry. And you're not going to cry. We are going to have coffee and sexual favors tarts, and I'm going to tell you all about penis shaped ocean dwellers."

I chuckle and move to my chair, making a quick swipe under my eyes to catch the tears that spilled over. I breathe deeply and nod. "Right," I agree with a small smile of my own, "Although, just to say, I love Valerie's triple chocolate tart, but if I were going to offer up sexual favors for one of her recipes it would be her rosemary cranberry bread that she makes at Christmas."

"Oh my God, yes! That bread is amazing and the glaze on top totally makes it worthy of offering sexual favors for the recipe." She takes a sip of her coffee and then turns in her chair and pulls a small stack of papers from her purse.

"What's that?" I ask, indicating the papers with my fork.

"Okay so you know the expression 'fell down the rabbit hole' when people talk about the internet?"

I nod, my mouth full of silky, decadent tart. This is not going how I thought it would. I thought it would be awkward and uncomfortable, my treatment of her in the aftermath of losing Will and Tabby shadowing our meeting. But it's not just that. It's more. Our lives before this were so intertwined that I was worried seeing her would only add to the profound grief I've been feeling the past eight days. I figured I would be anxious to leave the minute I arrived, going so far as to have the timer on my phone set to twenty minutes ready to go in my purse, only needing me to swipe my screen alive and press start. Instead, I find that I don't want to start the timer. I just want to sit here with my friend and pretend for a while that my life is not a tragedy.

"I kinda did that last night. I printed out some of the stuff I found because I wasn't sure I would remember everything." She takes a bite of her tart and lets out an indecent moan. "Oh my God, this is so good. I think I just had a mini orgasm," she mumbles around a mouth full of tart.

"Jesus Jules," I say, taking my own bite and thinking that she really isn't wrong. It *is* that good.

"What? You know I'm right."

"You aren't wrong," I agree, and she beams at me.

"Okay so, do you know what priapism is?" she asks.

"Umm, should I?"

She shakes her head, and says "Okay you know those erectile dysfunction ads that say 'If an erection lasts longer than four hours seek medical attention'?"

I nod and drink my coffee.

"That is priapism. An erection that won't go away. Anyway, there was a minor Greek fertility God named Priapus and he was the God of, like, fruit plants and livestock, but also of male genitalia."

I burst out laughing and I'm so glad I didn't have a mouth full of coffee at that moment, or Julia would now be wearing it. "I'm sorry…what? They had a dick God?"

She nods solemnly. "Yup. The Greeks had a God for everything. In case you are now wondering, because I did, Baubo is the Greek Goddess of the vulva."

I bug my eyes out at her and say, "You're joking." Julia shakes her head. "Nope. She's also depicted as a vulva with chubby legs and a face just above the genital area. No body, no arms, just a vulva with legs and a face."

"I…I literally have no words. That is fantastic."

She takes a bite of her tart and nods in agreement, "Yup."

"Alright so tell me what the dick God has to do with ocean creatures."

"Right, so Priapus is the God of the penis and he is depicted in various ways, but always with a huge erect dick. Like, would be past his knees if it wasn't sticking out from his body." She moves her hands super far apart and emphasizes "HUGE!"

"Like every hero in every novel ever written," I say.

"Oh my God, don't even get me started on that. Just once I'd like to read a book where the hero has a normal sized penis. They are always 'shockingly huge and super thick,'" she makes air quotes with her fingers. "Like, come on."

"Exactly. It's my biggest pet peeve when I edit romance novels. That and the fact that they last forfreakingever. I mean, seriously, what's wrong with writing about a guy who has an average dick and lasts an average amount of time? Let's be honest, do real women actually want to be with a guy who goes for hours?"

"Not me, that's for sure. I'll take my five minutes of actual intercourse and be happy, thank you very much."

I'm nodding along in absolute agreement while she talks but I also recognize we are moving into what has the potential to be dangerous territory, so I get us back on track by saying, "So Priapus has a huge shlong...and?"

Julia snorts and asks, "Did you actually just say shlong?" as she dissolves into a fit of giggles.

I can't help it, I join her. "I did," I say, nodding as I laugh, "I said shlong."

It takes us a minute to get control of ourselves, but eventually we manage. I notice our coffees are empty and go to the counter to get us more. I return with two coffees and two of Valerie's goat cheese tartlets.

Once we are settled again, Julia continues, "Okay, so, animal classifications, if you remember from high school, are broken down into seven parts." She ticks them down on her fingers as she says "Kingdom, phylum, class, order, family, genus and species. There is a phylum called Priapulida, which, you can guess, is named for Priapus, and it's made up entirely of dick shaped marine worms. They are sometimes called penis worms because they very closely resemble a penis."

"This just keeps getting better," I say.

"I know," she beams. "There's also the geoduck, which I already explained looks like a giant penis coming out of a clam shell." She shuffles through her papers and hands me a full color print out of the ugliest thing I have ever seen.

"People...*eat* that?" I ask, horrified.

"Let's not think about that part," Julia says, snatching the paper from my hand. "Pretend I never told you that. Trust me. It's just better that way."

I nod in agreement. It is most definitely better to pretend she never mentioned that disgusting fact.

We drink our coffees and eat our tartlets while Julia tells me about all the other dick shaped creatures she discovered, complete with color photo print outs. When it's time for us to say goodbye I don't even have to think about it, and I wrap her in a tight hug.

"I know you only called me because it was homework from your therapist, but I don't care. I missed you and I'm really glad we got to do this. I hope

we can do it again. I promise to respect your boundaries and any and every rule you want to put on our conversation topics. I honestly don't care if we have to sit like silent monks, I just want to see you again."
I promise to call her, and I mean it. For my mom and me the dishes were the turning point. For Julia and me, it's penis worm.

CHAPTER SEVEN

When I get home from meeting Julia I lay on the sofa, a blanket tucked up under my chin and I cry. Great big racking sobs that make my stomach hurt and my throat raw. I sob into my pillow until my cheek is pressed against a tiny lake of my tears. Guilt consumes me and my heart feels like it actually hurts.

I spent two hours with Julia. Two hours laughing and drinking coffee and having an asinine conversation about worms and clams shaped like dicks, and except for the one brief tangent that could have led us somewhere I couldn't go, I didn't think about Will or Tabby once. For two hours I forgot about my family. I forgot about my grief. I forgot they were gone. I forgot. I forgot. I forgot.

I sit up and hug my knees to my chest, rock myself and whisper "I'm sorry. I'm so sorry" over and over. I feel like I'm dying. I hurt so much and I can't stop the tears that keep coming. The guilt is overwhelming and I hate myself so much right now. How could I have forgotten them? What kind of monster forgets about the death of her spouse and her daughter?

I lay back down and cry myself to sleep. When I wake up it's dark out and I have a headache. I wander to the kitchen and take two ibuprofen and chase them down with a drink of water from the sink. I'm hungry but I don't really want anything specific. I settle on an almond butter and blueberry jam sandwich, and carry it wrapped in a napkin back to the family room. I need to get out of this dress, so I set my sandwich down and quickly change into a pair of gray yoga pants and a navy tank top.

Tucking my feet under me I sit on the sofa with my sandwich and pull my laptop onto my lap. I eat as I stare at nothing. When my sandwich is gone I tap my fingers on the laptop wondering if I am actually going to do this. I take a deep breath, decide to just go for it, open my laptop and start my search.

I find and sign up for an online forum, choosing the username Oizys, the Greek goddess of grief and misery. At least I'm on theme for the day. I make a deal with myself that I do not have to post, I do not have to share, I do not have to reply, but I do need to see. I need to see how others deal with their grief. I need to know how they handle the prospect of a future alone without their partner. I need to see how parents who have lost their children survive the unimaginable. I think, if I am being really honest with myself, I need to know there's hope. Because while I can't imagine ever moving forward, like my mom described, I know I can't go years and decades feeling this absolute and profound, all-consuming grief.

I read for hours, post after post of other people's heartbreak. I cry myself sick at the outpouring of grief I find in the forum. I read the comments too. The replies from other people who have been there, who have survived. I read about a mother who lost her eight-year-old to a senseless act of violence. I can feel her grief like it's a physical thing scraping all of my nerve endings raw. She writes about how the nights are the hardest, times that would have been for homework and dinner, story time and cuddles. She writes about how empty she feels, and how sometimes her arms ache from the emptiness of it all. I know her grief and it burns through me.

I read the comments that others have left for her. Some thank her for sharing her loss, for giving words to feelings they know all too well but can't express. Some offer understanding, their own loss giving them the ability to empathize in ways no one else can. We belong to a club no one wants to join, the price too high, and yet through no choice of our own, we have paid it. I read dozens of comments but the ones I search for, the ones I am desperate for are the ones from parents whose loss is older.

I find them buried in and between the other responses. A father who lost his daughter to cancer four years ago. His wife just had a new baby and while he writes that there are still days where the grief is crippling, they are few and far between, and he is much more likely to smile at a memory of his daughter than he is to cry. I find a response from a mother who lost her toddler when she drowned in their pool, having taken her eyes off of her for just a minute to bandage her other child's scraped knee twelve years ago. She writes about how in addition to grieving the death of her daughter, she had to learn how to forgive herself. She writes about how there were days where she didn't think she could go on, and how the depression and guilt was too much to bear up against. About the day where she tried to take her life to make the hurt and the self-loathing stop. She writes about how it took years but with the help of therapy, her family and her friends, she was able to forgive herself. She admits that it was the hardest, most painful thing she ever had to do, harder even than burying her child. I feel like my heart is bleeding when I read her comment. I miss Tabitha with a desperation I didn't know existed, but I cannot even begin to imagine the hurt this mother went through, having to live with the knowledge that one minute of inattention cost her her child. I think about how strong she had to be not just to survive the loss of her child, but to do the even harder job of forgiving herself. I find myself in awe of her strength and fortitude.

I want to read more but my eyes are tired and starting to burn. I'm emotionally exhausted and I just can't cry anymore tonight. I bookmark the forum so I can find it again and shut down my laptop. I curl up under the covers and as I'm drifting off to sleep I whisper "Good night. I love you both" to the empty family room.

I wake up late in the morning to my phone ringing. It's my mom, and while I am no longer avoiding her calls like I used to, I need a few minutes. I text her to let her know I will call her back in a little bit and I go get the coffee started. I use the bathroom and while I'm washing my hands I look in the mirror, instantly regretting that decision. My eyes are puffy, the whites bloodshot, and I look as exhausted as I feel. Wonderful.

I pour a cup of coffee, sit at the kitchen table, and call my mom back. She asks about how coffee with Julia went and I give her a recap of what I learned. Apparently it does not matter how old you are, penis worms are hilarious at any age.

"I want to tell you something, but you can't say anything, okay? No comments, good or bad. And *no* crying," I tell her.

"I can do that," she says, instantly.

"Mom, seriously. Nothing. Do you promise?"

"Absolutely."

I tell her about the grief forum I found and how I spent hours reading posts and comments. I don't get into specifics, but I do tell her that I specifically sought out comments from parents who had lost their children years before to see how they were managing years later.

True to her promise, my mother says nothing about what I just told her. Instead she says, "I made chocolate babka," although it does sound like she's choking back tears.

"I will be over in twenty minutes," I inform her, and she laughs.

When I arrive at Dr. Whitman's office for my next appointment the following week, she has the table and the ceramic shards set up and ready. Her dress this time is yellow with giraffes and I find that I really look forward to seeing what she is wearing each week.

We exchange pleasantries and then I say, "Before we start, can I ask you a question?"

"Of course."

I wander to the table and finger a navy shard. My eyes fill with tears and my bottom lip is quivering. I swallow hard several times, trying to find my voice. Dr. Whitman gives me time, which I appreciate.

I breathe deep and hold it and then let it out slowly. "Last week," I start, tears streaming down my cheeks, my voice unsteady, "last week you said I wasn't part of a couple anymore because Will is gone."

"Yes," she says, gently, tentatively.

I stare out the window, unable to make eye contact with her. "Does that mean," I choke out a sob, "does that mean I'm not a mom anymore either, because Tabby is gone?" I wrap my arms around myself as the sobs rack my body. I sink to the floor, my legs unable to hold me.

"Oh Allison," I hear Dr. Whitman say.

Suddenly she is sitting on the floor beside me, one hand stuffing tissues into mine, one hand rubbing up and down my back as she tries to sooth me. I pull my knees to my chest and wrap my arms around them, a position I find myself in a lot when the grief is overwhelming me. Dr. Whitman moves with me, turning into my side so she's facing me. As she continues to slowly rub my back she says "When someone loses a spouse, they are no longer part of a couple, because there is no second person to be in that couple with. It is a horrible, painful truth, but it is reality. We call these people widows, or for males, widowers. They aren't a couple anymore, but they also aren't single by choice or through a break-up, and thus the word widow. When a parent loses a child there is no word for it. We don't have a special word because there is no need. A parent is a parent, regardless of if their child is living or not. Let me ask you this. If you had two children, if Tabitha had had a sibling, and six months from now someone asked you how many children you have, how would you answer?"

"I…I would," I swallow hard. "I don't know," I sob. "I don't know the answer. I would have two children but still only one so I don't know. Tabitha will always be my daughter, but how can I be a mother without Tabby?"

"Let me try this a different way. What makes you a woman?"

I turn my head towards her, my cheek resting on my knee "A woman?" I ask, sniffling.

She nods. "What do you feel makes you a woman?" I struggle to answer, staring at her silently.

"Don't think, just answer. Forget about everything and everyone else. Forget about being politically correct. Just tell me, for you, what makes you a woman?"

"Umm, I don't know. I guess the fact that I have boobs and a uterus."

"Okay," she nods, "so if you suddenly found that you needed, God forbid, a mastectomy because of breast cancer, or if you had a hysterectomy, then would you no longer consider yourself a woman?"

"Of course not."

"So why would you think that losing a child makes it so you are no longer a mother?"

I curl deeper into myself and cry harder. I sob for my lost daughter and for all the things she will never be, never experience. I sob for all the moments, big and small, that I will never share with her. I sob as I remember our last day together, her little body sweaty and sandy as she ran on her chubby little girl legs around the playground squealing with delight as only a three-year-old can. I sob with gratitude for the privilege of having been her mother. And I sob with the realization that no matter what, I will *always* be her mother.

"I'm a mother…I'm a mother….I'm a mother," I whisper over and over as I rock my curled body back and forth.

"Yes, Allison. Yes. You are a mother. Nothing can change that. Not even death," Dr. Whitman assures me with a kind smile as I nod.

She gives me time to collect myself, and then directs me to the bathroom where I wash my face with cool water. When I return to the room, Dr. Whitman tilts her head to the table, a nonverbal indicator for me to work on the mosaic. So I move that way and pick through the box until I find a shard that is remarkably shaped like a small purple heart. I turn it over and over in my hand, marveling at the improbability of such a shape resulting from the violent throwing and smashing of ceramic against a fence. I eye the table and decide that it belongs in the very center, so I gently affix it there.

As I work on adhering more of the shards to the table, Dr. Whitman and I discuss coffee with Julia. I dissolve into a minor fit of giggles as I describe, in detail, what a geoduck looks like, and it occurs to me once again that dicks are hilarious no matter how old you are. I tell her about the guilt I felt when I got home, that those two hours felt like a betrayal of Will and Tabby.

"Why?" she asks.

I think the answer is an obvious one so I say, incredulously, "Because I didn't think of them once. For two hours I forgot they existed. For two hours I was happy, and I laughed, and I didn't think of them once."

She raises her eyebrows at me, a clear indication she does not think that that is an answer. She confirms this when she asks, "And?"

I blink at her. "And?" My tone is sarcastic and snappy.

"Yes Allison, And?"

"I…I don't understand. And what? I forgot about them for *two* hours," I say, emphasizing the word 'two'.

She nods. "I see. Tell me, when they were still alive did you think of them every second of every minute of every day?"

"Well, well no of course not. That would be impossible."

She smiles triumphantly at me, like she has just won a game.

"It's not the same thing," I insist.

"How is it not?"

"I don't know, it just isn't," I say, impatiently.

She considers me for a moment and then says, "So before, it was okay to go periods of time without thinking of them. Say, if you were working on editing a book, or if you were having a girls night out. It was acceptable then to just be in the moment and enjoy whatever it was you were doing, without devoting every second to thinking about Will and Tabby?"

I nod emphatically.

"And now, you must think of them every moment you are awake, or it is a betrayal?"

I nod emphatically again.

"Allison, that is impossible. Not only that but it's unreasonable to expect that of yourself. You are a human being, and no matter how much you love them, no matter how deeply you grieve for them, you cannot devote every moment of your life from now until the day you die thinking solely of them. You just told me yourself that when they were alive it was impossible to think of them every second of every day. Now that they are gone it should suddenly be possible?"

"Well," I say, hesitantly, "umm, I mean," I sigh and start over. I hate how logical she is, because of course, when she says it like that it makes total sense. "No, you're right. It would be impossible to think of them every single solitary second from now until I die." I'm nodding now, my head bobbing up and down as I speak, "Of course that's impossible. But I forgot them for two whole hours."

Dr. Whitman crosses her legs, and leans slightly towards me, her face solemn, and says, "I'm going to tell you something that you will not want to hear. It will upset you and you will likely not believe me, but I want you to hear me. Not just listen to my words, but hear them, okay?"

I brace because her warning does not bode well, and I give a tentative nod.

"Grief is a process. We've talked about this. And I've explained that it is not a linear one, or one that follows a set path. Grief is disorderly and unpredictable. But part of the grieving process is the healing process. People, when they speak of grief, they speak of profound sadness, of devastation, of hopelessness and emptiness. All of these words are an attempt to give a name to the feelings associated with a loss so big that there really are no words to describe it. But within that grieving process there is healing. No one can spend their life in a state of utter and total devastation. The human psyche just isn't designed like that. When we experience a loss, when we work through and process those feelings, we are, at the same time, healing."

I want to argue, to yell, to tell her that she is wrong. That I will never heal from losing Will and Tabby. That I will never not grieve their absence. But then I think of those parents on the forum, of the father with his new baby, writing about how beautiful she is, and sharing that, at night, when he rocks her to sleep, he tells her stories she is far too young to understand about the sister she will never know. He writes that the stories make him smile and chuckle in the darkness and that very rarely do they make him cry.

Dr. Whitman watches me closely, likely waiting to see if I am going to break down again or not. I give an almost imperceptible nod, a tiny acknowledgment that I am, for the moment, keeping it together.

"Healing is not the same as forgetting. And no Allison, I'm not talking about forgetting for a few hours or even a few days. I am talking about forgetting entirely. Healing doesn't mean wiping the memory of their existence away. But it does mean that there will be hours where you don't dwell on their loss and that is not a betrayal. It's what is supposed to happen."

I move the box of ceramic pieces out of my way and sit in the chair opposite her. I swallow several times, making sure a fresh wave of tears isn't about to fall, and then I tell her about the forum I joined. I share some of the posts I read, and a lot about the comments I searched out. She asks me questions about things I read and how they made me feel. It's a difficult conversation on top of an already emotionally taxing session, and I'm grateful when our time is up.

"I have a new assignment for you," she says, as we both stand and move to her desk.

"I assumed you would," I say, but I say it with a small smile.

"This week I would like you to once again meet Julia for coffee, with the same rules. Assume this will be a standing weekly assignment. I would also like you to discuss with Julia another friend you might have in common, or if you don't have friends in common, another friend of yours who you could ask to join you both next week. I also want you to sleep in your own bed, once. Just one night"

The tears are instant, and my voice hitches when I whisper, "I can't."

She reaches out and gives my hand a squeeze, nods and says "You can. It will be difficult; of that I have no doubt. And it will hurt, I'm sure. I'm also sure this is important or I wouldn't ask you to do it. It's one of the hard things I mentioned in our first session that you were going to have to trust me with." She squeezes my hand again and says, with force "You can do this Allison. You can."

I nod, not in agreement but because it seems like the right thing to do. I take the card with my next appointment and move to the door. Just as I reach for the handle Dr. Whitman calls my name and I turn to face her.

"When you were reading those posts and comments, what is one word that describes how you felt?"

"Hope," I whisper, the honesty of that one word burns a shame through me as I turn and walk out the door.

CHAPTER EIGHT

I sit on the floor in my pajamas outside my bedroom door that night, trying to work up the courage to go in. I had decided on the way home from therapy to do this part of the homework assignment tonight, partly to just get it done, and partly because if I failed, I had every night for the rest of the week to try again. My mom came over earlier to dust and vacuum the room, and to open the windows to air it out. No one's been in this room in six months, and I'm sure it was stuffy and stale inside. She offered to change the sheets, but I asked her not to. I'm scared of how much it will hurt, but part of me is hoping that Will's scent will still be on our sheets. I haven't smelled my husband's scent in six months, and I miss it desperately. If I am going to have to subject myself to how much this is going to hurt, I might as well get something out of it, and being able to smell Will again will be the reward I give myself for being brave.

I try to come up with a game plan – some kind of distraction to occupy my brain while I'm trying to fall asleep. I momentarily thought about taking a couple of Benadryl, hoping to be drowsy enough to simply drift off to sleep, but decided against it. I thought about bringing my laptop and either working on editing a book, or reading more of the forum I joined, but again I decide against it. Somehow I think Dr. Whitman wants this to be just Will and me.

I stand and reach for the doorknob, my heart thundering in my chest. I swallow back the tears and push the door open. The room looks exactly like I remember it did on that last day, except for the fresh vacuum tracks in the carpet. It's cooler than I thought it would be, but then I notice that at some point my mother must have come back up here and shut the windows, allowing the air conditioning to cool the room, and say a silent thank you to her for that.

"Hi Will," I say, crossing to and crawling onto the bed. I feel stupid, but in one of the posts I read last night a woman wrote about how she talks to her husband all the time. She wrote that it might sound strange, but she tells him about her day, and about the shows she watches, and pretty much just talks to him as if he were right there in the room with her. She said it helps her to talk to him and to think that he can still hear her, that it makes her feel less lonely and less sad when she does it, and I figure it can't hurt to try.

I lay down and pull Will's pillow to me and shove my face into it, breathing deep. I can smell his shampoo and a hint of the cologne he wore and it breaks me. The tears fall hot and fast, and I cry so hard I can't catch my breath. I let myself have that for a while. And I let myself give Will that.

Eventually my tears subside and my breathing quiets and I find myself whispering to my husband in the dark in the bed we used to share.

"Do you remember our first date?" I ask. "I didn't want to go. I had been on so many horrible dates, between dating apps and friends fixing me up with guys they were so sure were 'perfect' for me. I had pretty much given up. Then Julia tells me she has a guy in her office that I am going to love and that she set up a blind date for me with him. I was so angry at her. I flat out refused to go. I wouldn't even let her show me a picture of you. I told her I was done with dating and that if you were so great she should date you herself, but that I was absolutely not going. We fought for a week until she wore me down and got me to agree to go."

I get to the restaurant ten minutes early and let the hostess led me to a table. I let her know I'm meeting a blind date and that I have no idea what he looks like, but that his name is Will. Five minutes later I see her heading to my table with the most handsome man I have ever seen in my life. Five foot ten, maybe eleven, with broad shoulders, thick dark hair and a trimmed full beard, wearing a pair of dark jeans with a dark gray button-down shirt with the collar open. Even though Julia had worn me down and got me to agree to come, I had told her I wasn't dressing up. I was going to wear jeans and a tee shirt and if the guy didn't like it tough. She wasn't having any of that and practically wrestled me into a dress.

When he gets to the table I stand, and extend my hand to him.   "Allison," I say.

"Will," he says, flashing me a breathtaking smile that makes my legs feel like jelly.

I sit back down and try not to sound bitchy when I say "Listen, I'm sure you're a really nice guy, but I've pretty much given up on dating and men in general. Julia didn't give me much choice about coming here, but I'm really not interested in dating anyone right now. Or ever, to be honest."

"That bad?"

"You have no idea. You wouldn't even believe me if I told you."

The waiter comes and asks if we'd like to order drinks. Will orders a Sam Adams, and I order a Paloma. Once he leaves Will says, "Top five?"

I chuckle and ask, "Top five worst dates?"

He nods, "Yup."

"Oh man, it's going to be hard to narrow them down to just five. Okay, let me think."

Once our drinks come and we order dinner, I start to tell him about the top five worst dates I have ever been on.

I tell him about Tom who was, at first glance, pretty perfect. He was handsome, employed, funny and smart. He was a great conversationalist and we had a lot of things in common. Dinner was going fantastic, and I found I was really into him. Until he picked his nose. And I don't mean a quick 'I think I feel something there, let me make sure I don't have something hanging out of my nose' kind of thing. I mean, full on, knuckle deep, digging around in there until he pulled an enormous booger out of his nose, inspected it, and then wiped it on his napkin.

I tell him about Marcus who showed up with his half-sister in tow. Dinner was insanely awkward, but I didn't want to be rude, so I decided to tough it out. Besides, when we were chatting on the app prior to the date he seemed really nice. Things take a turn when his half-sister started to play with a lock of his hair and he seemed unfazed by it. I on the other hand couldn't look away. It was so inappropriate, and he was just acting like it was the most natural thing in the world. And then things went from awkward to so, so much worse. He told me that he and his half-sister, and he continuously called her that, never just his sister, were looking for a third for a threesome. He went on to explain that they have different mothers so it's not weird. That it would only be weird if they had the same mother, but since they didn't, it's okay. They tell me that they have been together for years and decided to spice things up by adding a third and wanted to know if I was interested. I decided 'screw rude' and got up and just walked out.

By my second story Will is in stitches. He accuses me good-naturedly of making these up, and I raise two fingers in a solemn oath that I am not. The waiter comes with our meals, steak for Will and seared ahi tuna for me. Yum.

Will circles his fork at me and asks me to continue. He tells me that he's sorry I have had such horrible first dates, but that this is shaping up to be the best first date he has ever been on. I narrow my eyes at him and then I grin.

For my third worst date I offer up Derrick, a guy my friend Cheryl set me up with. I explain that I'm pretty sure Cheryl actually hated me and that she chose Derrick to set me up with was all the proof I needed to come to that conclusion. Derrick was hot. As in super, unbelievably, movie star hot. He was also a huge, raging dick. First, when the waitress came to take our drink orders, he ordered a beer, and when I tried to order a glass of wine, he told the waitress that I wasn't having wine and instead to bring me a water. Umm okay. He then proceeded to talk about himself nonstop while my eyes glazed over with boredom. When our drinks arrived, he ordered an appetizer for himself, and when the waitress said "And for you, Miss?" he didn't allow me to respond but instead said "Nothing for her." Awesome, guess I'll just sit here and watch you eat, asshole. I wanted to leave, but I had stupidly, stupidly allowed him to pick me up and the restaurant was a good forty minutes from my house. And in a final episode of "This guy is a screaming asshat" when the waitress came to take our dinner order, he ordered a steak, baked potato and a side salad for himself, and then told her I was "all set." When his dinner came he gave me his salad, without the dressing, thank you very much.

Will gapes at me and asks incredulously, "Why didn't you get up and leave? Or better yet, why didn't you ask for a different table and order your own meal and then get an Uber?"

"Because I am a giant, indescribable moron and I didn't want to be rude. I was young and naïve and I didn't want to hurt his feelings."

"I see you got over that," he says teasingly.

"Ha ha," I say.

"How did the date end?"

"He took me home, asked if he could come in, I declined, he called me the c-word, said this is why he never lets a woman order a meal on the first date, and left."

"Jesus. Please tell me that these are in no particular order and that he was the worst."

"They are in no particular order, and he was most assuredly the worst," I confirm.

"Well, cheers to that," he says, lifting his beer bottle.

I clink my glass against his and agree "Cheers."

"Alright, two more. What else have you got?"

"The next one is more annoying than horrible," I tell him.

Will raises his eyebrows and says "I'm intrigued. Do tell."

For my fourth story I tell him about Dan. Dan was the cousin of my friend Avery. Avery swore Dan was the 'best guy ever' and that she was certain I was going to 'fall in love with him' on sight. Avery was very wrong. I drove myself to the restaurant, having learned that lesson the hard way on more than one occasion. Dan arrives and we introduce ourselves. Dan tells the waitress that 'Dan would like a martini, dry, with a twist'. Then Dan proceeded to tell me about Dan's job. Dan is a video game developer, and Dan has a new game coming to market in a few weeks. Dan is very excited. Dan also just bought a new condo and a shiny new sports car.

Will interrupts "Why do you keep saying 'Dan'"?

"Oh, did I not mention that 'Dan' repeatedly and consistently referred to himself as such?"

"No," Will says with a chuckle. "You left that part out."

"Well, he did. Every single sentence started with 'Dan'. I thought about turning it into a drinking game for about a half a second, but then realized I would likely be dead by the end of the date from alcohol poisoning, and I don't like the feeling of being drunk enough to risk it."

Will laughs, and I can't help but laugh with him. I realize that he wasn't wrong when he said this was turning out to be the best first date ever.

The waitress comes and clears our plates and Will asks if I want dessert. I'm comfortably full from my meal, but I'm not ready for the date to end, so I ask to see the dessert menu. All the options look amazing, so we agree to order two and share. We get the Crème Brule with mixed berries, and the flourless chocolate cake with dark chocolate ganache and hazelnut whipped cream. I order a coffee and Will opts for a whiskey neat.

The last story I tell him is about Andrew. I met Andrew in a coffee shop and we started chatting while waiting in line. He asked me to dinner the following evening and I agreed. We met at a very upscale French restaurant that I had been dying to try as I had heard the food was incredible. I point out that while I was excited, the restaurant was one hundred percent his choice. We are led to our seats and given our menus, which are completely in French. This sends Andrew into a mini rage where he rants at me about how this is America and why the hell is the menu in a foreign language. I try to point out that we are at a high-end French restaurant and that the menu being in French is not a surprise. When the waitress comes to take our order he is beyond rude, demanding a 'proper' menu. She tries to explain that she would be more than happy to translate the menu for him and help him make a selection but he is having none of it. His anger escalates until he is swearing at her, creating a huge scene and I'm absolutely mortified. People from nearby tables are staring and whispering, as surprised as I am that a grown ass man is having what amounts to a massive temper tantrum in public over a flippin menu. I apologize profusely to the waitress, as I stand and gather my coat and purse. Andrew rises and grabs me by the arm and demands to know where I am going. I wrench my arm away and tell him I'm leaving, that he is not anyone I would choose to spend my time with and that he should be ashamed of himself for his behavior. He proceeds to shock me, the waitress and the tables around us when he collapses back into his chair and bursts out in tears. I can't even help it, I start to giggle. My giggling makes the waitress giggle, and in turn the other tables join us until we are all laughing at him.

"Oh God, that is the best one in my opinion," Will laughs. "I'm assuming you left?"

"Actually, I didn't. A lovely older couple was out to dinner with their son, Gus, celebrating the fact that he had just passed the bar. His boyfriend couldn't make it to dinner – he was a surgical resident and was stuck in surgery, so they invited me to join them, and I happily accepted. Andrew was escorted out by management accompanied by a round of applause from the other diners. The food was as incredible as I had heard it was, and Gus became one of my dearest friends."

"Gus became one of your dearest friends too," I whisper into the darkness.

I burrow down under the covers, hold Will's pillow tight to my chest, and fall asleep.

CHAPTER NINE

The next several weeks are some of the hardest weeks of my life. I spend a lot of time on the grief forum, reading posts and comments. I search out ones that mirror my own life - the death of a spouse, the loss of a child. I spend an entire night reading posts from the sole surviving spouse, their families lost to them through car crashes, fires, or acts of nature. I read these posts, absorbing their anguish and their grief, and the pain is so severe, so utterly consuming that it feels as if I am bleeding out across the family room floor. I find a post written by a woman who lost her only child and her husband to a teenager driving drunk. He died in the crash that took her family, and I feel a jealousy that is nearly overwhelming. Like me she lost her family but unlike me she doesn't have to live knowing the person who stole them from her is still breathing. I know, on a very deep level, that Justin is someone's child, and that his mother would be grieving as I am if he had died. I also can't bring myself to care. Justin made a selfish decision that resulted in the death of the love of my life and my beautiful three-year-old daughter, and the fact that he walked away with only minor injuries, that he still lives, is an unfairness I can't comprehend.

I haven't been able to bring myself to post my own story, my own heartache. I wouldn't even know where to start. I don't know that I would be able to find the words to describe the depth of pain I feel when I allow myself to consider the finality of their lives. The idea that Will will never kiss me again. That we will never laugh over inside jokes or create new ones. That Tabby will never grow into a surly teenager, or a beautiful young woman, or a mother in her own right. I miss them with a desperation I didn't know was possible, but more, I miss who they would have become. Justin didn't just take their lives, he stole their future, my future. And I'm not sure there are words for the pain that knowledge causes.

I spend hours with my mother, trying to make peace within myself for how I treated her for six months. In the beginning, when I was drowning in grief and anger, lashing out at everyone was the only thing I knew how to do. I needed the release shouting my anger at the world afforded me. It had the additional benefit of pushing everyone away. I needed that distance, to not have the knowledge that their lives were still whole, intact, in my face every time I looked at family and friends. My mother doesn't want or need my apologies, she's told me that countless times. She tells me, repeatedly, any time I bring up my behavior, that as a mother her job is to love me even when I'm at my ugliest, and that given the circumstances, my behavior was understandable. But I know now that it was not.

Grief is not a free pass to be a bitch. There were ways to ask for time and space, to ask that people let me be alone with my heartache, without being a screaming bitch. My mother may not need me to make things up to her, but I need to do it for myself. Since that day at the fence when the anger I was using as a shield crumbled to dust, and all the emotions I had been shutting out came flooding in, guilt was one I hadn't anticipated.

I have coffee with Julia every week, and for our third coffee date we add our mutual friend from college, Lola. Julia sets it up and tells Lola the rules, something she takes very seriously. I find myself looking forward to discovering what new lesson Julia has planned for me. It doesn't escape me that the majority of her conversation topics are in some way penis related. For our second coffee date she entertains me with the top ten animals with the largest penises in relation to their body size. The winner of that particular contest was the barnacle, whose penis is eight times larger than its body. The most disturbing information gleaned from that lesson is that the ejaculate of the blue whale, whose penis is eight feet long, contains a little over five gallons of sperm.

The first time Lola joins us she brings the topic, and there's a few moments of uncomfortable silence when she announces she's going to tell us how to make jailhouse hooch. When it dawns on her why Julia and I are suddenly silent, she looks stricken.

"Oh God! Oh my God, I'm so stupid. I didn't think. I didn't think," she apologizes, clearly horrified at the realization that jail equals Justin and Justin is a no-go topic.

"No," I say. "No, it's okay. Really, Lola, it's alright. Jailhouse hooch doesn't break the rules, and now I find I need to know all about it. It's really okay Lola." I reach over and squeeze her hand, that small gesture reminding me of the woman I used to be.

She smiles at me, but I know it's forced, her embarrassment written all over her face. "If you're sure?"

"Totally," I say, my smile a little shaky, but genuine all the same.

Julia jumps in and says "Let me go get us coffee and some treats and then Lola can tell us about how to make hooch. And just to say, as long as it doesn't require bugs or body fluids or some other equally disturbing ingredients, I'm going to make some and bring it to our next coffee date."

We settle around the table with our coffees and some of Valerie's caramel brownie squares, and I prompt Lola with an "educate us."

Lola takes a deep breath and grins a genuine grin, and I know it's all going to be okay.

"So there are a few ways to make hooch in jail, but the most common way I found is by using multiple layers of trash bags. In order to make the alcohol you need three ingredients, none of which are bugs or bodily fluids," she says, laughing.

"Well thank fuck for that," Julia declares, rather loudly, raising her coffee cup.

"Jules!" I admonish, and dissolve into giggles.

"What?" she asks, like she didn't just drop the F-bomb loudly in public.

I just shake my head at her and turn my gaze to Lola. "Anyway…" I say, indicating she should go on.

"Right so, three ingredients. Spoiled fruit, sugar and yeast. The fruit is typically apples smuggled out of the chow hall."

"They have to smuggle them? They're apples not packets of heroin," Julia states emphatically.

"True," Lola agrees, "But this is also prison, or jail, and not a high school cafeteria. I guess they aren't 'allowed'," she makes air quotes, "to take food from the chow hall. Anyway, they have to hide the apples in their cells and let them rot. I guess this helps with the fermentation or something."

I nod sagely, like I have any idea if this is true or not.

"Prisoners have access to canteen, which is like a little store they can order items through if they have money in their accounts. I did a little research and found some online stores where family members can send their loved ones food packages and shit, and if those prices are any indication of what they are charging in the canteens, then that shit is super crazy expensive. So anyway, for reasons I do not think make a hell of a lot of sense, you can't buy real sugar in the canteen, nor is it available in the chow hall."

"Wait," Julia interrupts. "Why not?"

"Apparently for this very reason. Because sugar is one of the three things necessary to make hooch."

"I'm confused," I say.

Julia nods and says, "Same."

"Right. Same three," Lola says with a grin. "So they can't buy sugar, but they can buy sugary drinks. Which, hello? Makes no sense at all. If the reason they don't have sugar is to prevent people from making alcohol, but prisoners have found that they can just substitute something like Hawaiian Punch or even Sunny Delight, both of which they can order through the canteen, you would think prisons would only make sugar free drinks available."

Julia and I both are nodding in unison, as this really does seem pretty stupid.

Lola takes a bite of her brownie, which most definitely falls in the top five of tasty treats Valerie makes. Then she continues, "So once they have the spoiled fruit, and the fruit juice, they just need yeast. Obviously they can't just buy yeast or have it sent to them, so they need to get creative. Fun fact, the yeast used to make bread is still 'alive' in the bread. So bread works. So do potatoes, something I did not know. Also, apparently the skin of apples contains yeast."

"I'll take 'Things I had no idea contained yeast for two hundred Alex'," Julia says with a smirk.

"Can I just say, that in the last three weeks I have learned that the Greeks had a God and Goddess for male and female genitalia, that there is such a thing as a penis worm, that barnacles have a penis eight times the size of their bodies, that blue whale ejaculate contains over 5 gallons of sperm, and that potatoes and apple skins contain yeast. All things I don't know when I will ever use again, but now I know them all the same."

Lola chokes on her coffee. "I'm sorry," she says, "can you repeat that?"

We have a brief detour while Julia, who I have secretly dubbed the Penis Queen, catches Lola up on all things penis related.

"I don't even know what to say," Lola says, as she dissolves into a fit of giggles and Julia and I join her.

Once we are able to get ourselves under control, because as I have noted repeatedly, penises are hilarious, Lola continues our lesson on hooch.

"So, once they have the three key ingredients necessary, the rotten apples, fruit juice and potatoes or bread are all added to the trash bags and kind of smushed together. Then the bag is tied up, but loosely so that the gas that will be created has room to expand. The bag has to be placed somewhere dark but also somewhere safe where it can't easily be seen. Typically that means putting it way far under a bed or in a footlocker. Now, in order for the fruit, sugar and yeast to ferment, you have to find a way to heat it. So typically that means filling empty soda bottles with warm water and tucking them around and on top of the trash bag. The bag has to stay in the dark for five to seven days, but during that time the bag also needs to be 'burped.'"

"Burped?" I ask.

Lola nods, "Yes. You have to untie the bag and let the air out, loosely tie it again and repeat the process. You also have to keep the water in the bottles surrounding it warm so it can 'cook'. So, anyway, you do this for five to seven days and you know it's ready when you burp it and the gas created fills up the bag in just a few hours, rather than after a day or so."

"I wonder how gross it tastes," I say.

"Well it sounds positively revolting," Julia says. "Guess we will find out, although not next week since I don't have rotten fruit just laying around. So, it will have to be the week after."

"Yay," I say, with little enthusiasm. "Can't wait." I smirk at Julia, and once again we all dissolve into giggles.

True to her word, when we meet for coffee two weeks later, Julia did, as promised, bring hooch. She made one out of apples, Sunny Delight and potatoes, which was absolutely as disgusting as we all thought it would be. She also made a second batch of what she called "high-end hooch" which was made with raspberries, grape juice and bread. This was only slightly less disgusting, but only just slightly.

Dr. Whitman and I meet for four more therapy sessions over the course of the next several weeks. Each session ends with a new homework assignment and with her adding on to previous assignments. I'm still working on the mosaic table, which is turning out beautifully, although I still don't fully understand how making this table is going to help me with my grief. I am currently up to spending five nights a week in the bed that I shared with Will. I still sleep on the sofa the other nights, although I'm not sure why. My time there is limited anyway, two more sessions with Dr. Whitman and I will have graduated to the bed full time. The bed is definitely more comfortable, and I don't cry every time I climb in it now. That isn't to say I don't still cry, I definitely do; great racking sobs that hurt my heart and leave my throat raw and the muscles in my stomach sore, it's just not every time now. I still whisper to Will in the dark, stories from our life together. Sometimes those stories make me cry, but I am surprised to find that there are just as many times that they make me laugh. I think I sleep on the sofa on the nights I'm not required to sleep in the bed as a way to give myself a break. My emotions are all over the place and seem to go from one extreme to the other so rapidly lately that I find it hard to get a handle on them. If I'm not crying, I'm laughing like a lunatic, or feeling immense guilt for having stretches of time where I'm not drowning in profound grief. Every day feels exhausting and I wish I could just take a break and feel nothing for five minutes. Not grief, or guilt, or hilarity, or sadness. Just five, uninterrupted minutes of nothing. Unfortunately, that isn't possible. I mean, okay I guess it is, if I wanted to go the drugs or alcohol route, but those aren't roads I'm willing to travel, so those aren't options open to me. According to Dr. Whitman all I really can do is feel the feelings and manage them as they come. Super.

One of our sessions is spent discussing my job. I used to be able to talk about books for hours – to sit with my girlfriends and a couple bottles of wine and discuss the books we were currently reading. We would fight good naturedly about books we couldn't agree on, those in the 'I loved it' camp versus those in the 'it was the worst book ever' camp, each trying to sway the others to their side. We would make recommendations to one another, our To Be Read lists growing exponentially with every get together. Dr. Whitman asks me about my favorite books and who some of my favorite authors are. I haven't talked about books with anyone since before losing Will and Tabitha, and I get a little bit lost in the conversation. I had forgotten how much joy books bring me, although, I guess when I shut them out of my life that that had been the point – to deny myself the joy they bring me. She asks about the books I edit now and I admit that I no longer edit fiction. That instead I have handed my authors off to other editors and solely edit things like DIY books, books on taxes and financial planning and the like. Books that, for a bibliophile like me, are so dull and mind numbingly boring that there is no chance they could possibly bring me any joy at all. It doesn't surprise me that when our session is coming to an end Dr. Whitman's assignment for that week is to edit a book that will bring me joy to read. And just like with every other assignment she has given me so far, I know this one will be hard. That it will force me to confront feelings and emotions I was avoiding prior to starting therapy. It feels like each week Dr. Whitman rips a little bit more of my emotional Band-Aid off, exposing more of the wound losing Will and Tabitha created.

When I go to Dr. Whitman for therapy session five I'm no longer sure what to expect. Everything about therapy with her is completely different than what I had imagined it would be like when I first agreed to start coming. I know there must be a method to whatever it is she's doing, but I don't know what it is, and I'm not ready to ask – yet. This therapy session is once again, different. We discuss all of the different apps there are now that make it easy to never have to leave one's house. The apps that deliver groceries, the ones that deliver meals from restaurants, even apps that deliver from big box stores, home improvement stores and liquor stores. We live in a world where everything you could possibly want can be delivered via a few swipes of your finger. Everything, that is, except the two things I want most. She guides the conversation until we are talking about food – primarily what it is that I eat now.

I am ashamed to admit that unless it can be cooked in the microwave, or boiled on the stove, I don't have the patience for food. I no longer cook for myself, because cooking is a memory that is tied very tightly to my family. Tabby, Will and I cooked together almost every night, and doing a family activity without my family is something that I don't know if I can handle.

She asks me about their favorite meals. I cry and laugh simultaneously as I tell her that Tabby's favorite food was homemade macaroni and cheese, but that she pronounced it max n geez, a term Will and I adorably adopted. I tell her that Will's favorite meal was my meatloaf with homemade mashed potatoes and gravy made from scratch. My heart squeezes painfully when I recount that after we were married Will told me that he knew the first time I made him that meal that he was going to marry me. I already know what is coming when Dr. Whitman points out all of the hard things she has asked of me so far, and reminds me how far I have come since starting therapy with her. She, predictably, tells me that for this week's assignment she wants me to make Tabby's favorite meal. I don't know if I can do it. I don't even know if I can take the first step to accomplishing this assignment. Dr. Whitman points out that perhaps the first step is asking for help, as she hands me the card with my next appointment on it.

CHAPTER TEN

"I got a new homework assignment from Dr. Whitman today and I need your help. Please," I say when my mother answers the phone. I know I could have asked Julia or Lola and one or both of them would have been more than willing to help me, but for this I knew I needed my mom.

"Of course darling girl," my mom replies instantly. "What are we doing?"

I feel my eyes fill with tears and my chin starts to quiver. Fuck but this is going to be so hard. It takes a few seconds until I can get the words out, and when I do they are strangled by my tears "I have to make max n geez."

My mom is silent for a minute and then I hear a soft "Oh baby. Okay. It's going to be okay."

"Mom," I try to say, but it sounds more like a pained moan.

"I know, I know. But okay. We can do this. We can Al," she soothes. "When do you want to do it?"

"Now," I whisper through my tears. I take a deep breath and then another. Then I say, "I want to do it now, and get it done. If I don't do it now, I don't know if I will be able to do it at all. It's already horrible and I haven't even started. If I let it sit I'll just build it up more and more in my head until it's not just painful, it's crippling."

"Okay," my mom agrees instantly. "I can be over in ten minutes and we can go. Alright?"

"Yeah," I say softly. "Yeah, alright."

We are mostly silent on the way to the grocery store. I'm strung too tightly to say anything, and my mother is treating me like a wounded animal that at any moment might attack. This feels too reminiscent of how things were before I started seeing Dr. Whitman and it only adds to my anxiety.

We pull in and my mom parks the car. Then she turns in her seat to look at me, reaching out to hold both of my hands. "Do you know what we need?"

I pull my bottom lip between my teeth and nod.

"Alright, so we will just go in, get what we need, and get out. Quick and fast, okay?"

"Quick and fast," I agree.

And that's what we do. We go in, we shop, and we get out. And somehow, by the grace of God, I keep it together and do not cry a single tear in the store. The car? That's a totally different story.

We get back to my house and unpack the groceries onto the counter. My mother fills the pasta pot with water and sets it on the stove to boil.

"Why max n geez?" my mother asks.

I busy myself shredding the cheese and answer "We talked about cooking and family favorites today. I told her about Tabby and max n geez, Will and meatloaf," I shrug. "She always comes up with homework assignments I don't understand. This was today's. I am willing to bet anything that next week will be max n geez again plus a night of meatloaf."

She adds the rigatoni to the boiling water. I like to use rigatoni for my macaroni and cheese because I love how much cheese sauce the noodles hold.

"Why both?"

While I've been spending more time with my mom, and she knows about some of the homework assignments, like the night I had to sleep in my own bed, so she vacuumed and dusted the room for me, I haven't explained everything about what Dr. Whitman has been having me do, and she hasn't pressed me for information about my therapy sessions.

"So she does this thing every week. Like, how she had me sleep in my own bed?"

"Yeah?"

"Well every week, in addition to a new assignment, she adds on to previous ones. So I'm up to four nights a week in my bed, and next week I'll be up to five. A few more sessions and I'll be sleeping in my bed full time. She has me meeting Julia and Lola for coffee every week. Last week she had me edit a fiction novel, and since I only edit two to three books a week on average, by next week I'll be back to my normal selection of books. And of course, I'm still working on the mosaic table. So it stands to reason that if she had me make max n geez this week, I'll have to make them both next week. I just wish I understood what the point of it all is."

"Huh. Have you asked her?"

I get out a sauce pan and start the roux I'll use to make the cheese sauce. "No," I say, sheepishly.

"Why not?"

"Everything she asks me to do hurts in one way or another. I think I'm afraid there won't be a reason."

My mother stirs the pasta and asks, "Do you really think it's for no reason?"

I add the milk to the roux and start to whisk it slowly, tears streaming as I remember helping Tabby stand on her stool, the whisk in her chubby little hand, mine resting over hers as we would stir the milk together. I remember how excited she would get to be helping. How she would tell me "Tabby a big girl. I make max n geez," and the tears turn to sobs.

"Ali?" she asks, rubbing my back, "Oh Ali girl, what can I do?"

I shake my head and keep whisking, "Nothing," I continue sobbing, "nothing. Just this. Just be here."

"I can do that. I will always do that," she says, emphatically.

I take a few seconds and then I say, "And no," picking up the thread of the conversation my latest cry fit interrupted, "I don't really think it's for no reason. I'm sure she has one, I think it's more that I am not ready to know what it is yet."

"That's fair," she says as she drains the pasta while I stir the cheese into the sauce. I use a mixture of sharp cheddar and goat cheese, and just a small amount of mozzarella for stretchiness. I mix the cheese sauce into the pasta while my mom greases the casserole dish.

While I pour the pasta into the dish, she gets started on toasting the breadcrumbs with butter in a skillet. The oven finishes pre-heating just as the breadcrumbs finish, so I sprinkle the pasta with the toasted breadcrumbs and slide it into the oven to bake.

I sit at the counter and fold my arms in front of me, rest my head on them and sob into the hollow space created. I'm trying to work out why this hurts more than the other assignments Dr. Whitman has given me. They have all been hard in their own ways, each causing a different kind of hurt. But this one, the hurt is a longing so deep that it feels like a physical pain.

I hear my mom open and close the front door, and a few minutes later open and close it again. She comes in with a bottle that looks suspiciously like red wine. She holds it up and says "I have wine. Well, Sangria, but basically the same thing only better."

I wipe my hands across my face and say, "Mom, the last thing I need is to be depressed, crying and drunk. I think the first two are enough, don't you?"

"I'm not saying we should get drunk. But I think a glass might help you relax a little bit, and that's not a bad thing," she reaches into the cabinet where I keep the wine glasses and pulls two wide bowled glasses down.

We sit at the counter in silence and sip our sangria, each lost in our own thoughts. I don't know what she is thinking, but my mind is a jumble of memories made in this kitchen. Will and I refinishing the cabinets. Will swearing up a storm when he was trying to put up the backsplash and nothing was lining up correctly. Baking with Tabby, flour all over her cheeks and down the front of her shirt. The three of us sharing meals and birthday cakes and ice cream sundaes. A million memories of the three of us made in this kitchen and around this counter flood through me. Tears stream down my cheeks, as I allow the memories to come, and come, and come.

When the food is finished, my mom hands me the potholders and I reach in the oven and the smell is a memory all its own. How many times have we made this meal, my daughter and I? My hands guiding her tiny ones through the steps of creating the sauce and mixing it into the pasta. Her excitement each time Will declares it the best max n geez he's ever tasted. I've heard before that scent is one of the most significant memory triggers, and as I take in the aroma wafting up from the casserole dish, I realize how much truth there is in that statement.

They say you can taste when food is made with love. I think you can also taste when it's made with sorrow, because every bite I eat tastes like ash on my tongue.

CHAPTER ELEVEN

The Friday of the week of max n geez Julia calls me in the morning. Julia doesn't call me – not since the day I slammed the door in her face. We meet for coffee every week, and she has been amazing about respecting the rules Dr. Whitman put in place for those meetings, but she also has never pushed me for more.

"Hey girlie," she says, her voice bright and chipper.

"Hey," I say, a little hesitantly.

"Listen, I was wondering if maybe you would like to come to dinner tonight. Well, not come to dinner exactly, more like go to dinner. I thought it might be nice for you to get out of the house. I was thinking that you, Lola, me and maybe Sasha and Audrey could all go out to dinner. I…"

"I can't," I interrupt her. "I'm sorry, I just can't."

"Oh, umm okay. Yeah. No, I get it. It was just a thought," she sounds sad and I hate that I made her feel that way. It's crazy to think that just a few weeks ago I hurt everyone and anyone I could with the viciousness of my words and didn't even blink. Not just that, but I did it because it was the only thing in my life that made me feel good. Now, though, now hearing that touch of sadness in Julia's voice makes me feel bad.

"Julia, listen, I want to, or I want to want to, if that makes sense."

"Yeah it does."

Julia has been my best friend for almost twenty years, and I feel like I need to explain. After everything I've said to her in the past six months, I think I owe her that much. "It's just, okay, look. I really look forward to coffee with you and Lola. It's nice to feel, I don't know, normal I guess, for a couple hours. But then I go home and feel so unbelievably guilty because for those two hours that we have coffee I forget. I forget to be sad, or to grieve, or to miss them. And then there's Dr. Whitman, who has me doing a lot of really hard things. Like, crazy hard. And she's relentless. Not only does she give me new hard shit to do each week, she builds on all the other hard shit she already gave me. I already feel like an emotional basket case ninety percent of the time. I don't know if I have any more in me right now."

"Oh Ali, I'm sorry. I shouldn't have asked. I just thought, coffee has been so much fun, and I wanted to give you more of that."

"I know, and I love you for that. I love you for forgiving me and for being willing to go to coffee with me that first day."

"There was nothing to forgive," she says.

I give a derisive chuckle and say, "We both know that's not true Jules."

"Do you remember in Sophomore year of college when I was totally stressed over an exam I had coming up, and then that same week Roger dumped me, I lost my wallet and I tripped and ripped my favorite pair of jeans"

I can't help but laugh, "I remember. That was a hell of a week. It was like anything and everything that could go wrong for you went wrong."

"Yes," she says, and I can hear the smile in her voice. "And that very same week, you were trying to be so sweet and brought me a skinny vanilla latte, except when you set it on my desk somehow it tipped over and dumped across my laptop and I completely blew up at you."

"Oh God, I remember that. I'd never heard you say so many swear words in one sentence. In fact, I didn't even know it was possible to string that many swear words together."

"I took everything that was going wrong that week, all my aggravation and frustration out on you. I said hateful, terrible things that to this day I feel awful about."

"Jules," I say softly.

"The point," she interrupts, "is that I was terrible to you and you forgave me, because that is what friends do. They forgive each other."

"I'm not so sure that what you said during a meltdown when we were nineteen is quite the same as my treating you to months of verbal abuse."

"Allison, I think that given the circumstances, you were entitled. Hell, you still are as far as I'm concerned. If you need to vent or unload, I'm here for that, just like

I'm here if you need to cry, scream, breakdown. Whatever. Whenever. I'm here."

"Dammit, Jules you're going to make me cry."

I hear the tears in her voice when she says, "At least you won't be doing it alone."

We are both quiet for a minute, each working on getting control of our tears. Then I make a quick decision and I say, "Okay Jules. Let's have dinner."

"Al, you don't have to. It's fine. I get it. I promise."

"I know. But I guess, if I am going to do hard shit, I might as well do all the hard shit, right? And maybe this way I'll beat Dr. Whitman to the punch," I giggle at that.

"If you are sure? I don't want you to feel pressured or like you have to."

"I'm sure. Just, can you please tell Audrey and Sasha the rules? I think with the five of us no one really needs to prep a topic, but I still need the rules for now."

Without hesitation she responds, "Absolutely."

We make arrangements to meet that evening at six at Junipers, a trendy local steakhouse that has amazing food, and equally amazing cosmos, and say goodbye.

As it gets closer to the time where I need to start getting ready, I get nervous. Every 'first' feels so big and overwhelming, even something as simple as dinner with some girlfriends. I call my mom for a pep talk, which doesn't alleviate all of my anxiety, but it does help some, which, lately, is all I can ask for.

I shower and do the whole, getting ready bit, taking the time to blow-dry my hair and twist it into a chignon at the base of my neck, some loose tendrils falling around to frame my face. I choose a pair of black, wide leg pants that sit low on my hips and are one of the few pairs of pants I own that actually fit nicely. I add a raspberry stretchy tee shirt, and a pair of black flats. I've never been a high heel kind of girl. I find them extremely uncomfortable, and I cannot, for the life of me, find the grace or coordination to walk in them. I do a bit of light make-up, focusing mainly on my eyes. All the crying I have been doing lately has left them perpetually swollen and a little bloodshot. Mascara, eyeliner and shadow aren't much of a disguise, but I'm proud of myself for making the effort, and even I have to admit that it does help some.

I pull open the door to Junipers at exactly six o'clock. I arrived about twenty minutes ago, and used that time to give myself my own version of a pep talk that I could, in fact, have dinner with my girlfriends.

The restaurant is beautiful, all carved dark wood, soft lighting, high backed booths with hunter green leather, and tables with the same leather on the seats of the chairs. My eyes roam the interior until I see Sasha and Julia have already been seated at a table. I'm just about to make my way over when the door behind me opens and I hear Lola's voice. I turn and see Lola and Audrey walk in. Lola looks beautiful in a knee length body hugging dark aqua dress with silver stilettos, her dark blond hair pulled back in a high ponytail. Audrey, at six feet tall and slim, with skin the deepest black, her head shaved bald, and her perfect bone structure, is quite possibly the most beautiful woman I have ever seen in my life. She's wearing a long flowy skirt with a patchwork of patterns, a white peasant blouse and dark brown strappy sandals. On anyone else this outfit would look dowdy and frumpy, but on her it is bougie and hip.

We exchange hugs and then the three of us make our way through the restaurant to the table. I tease Julia for being on time, again. More hugs are exchanged, and there's a small moment of uncomfortableness when Sasha holds on for just a few seconds longer than necessary.

We sit, and the waitress takes our drink orders, cosmos all around. We order goat cheese and artichoke dip with crispy pita chips and three orders of jumbo shrimp cocktail for all of us to share. The conversation is a little stilted at first, but Julia, ever the Penis Queen, saves the day by bringing Sasha and Audrey up to speed on all things penis related.

We laugh as we make our way through the appetizers and our first round of cosmos. For dinner I order garlic crusted sea bass with lemon butter, creamed spinach and a loaded baked potato. I've lost so much weight in the last six months that I can afford the extra calories, and I find that for the first time in a long time, I'm ravenous. Maybe it's the change of scenery. Or maybe it's the fact that it's not food cooked in a microwave. With the exception of very few meals, everything I've eaten in the last six months has been nuked. Whatever the reason, I'm starving, and I decide to take advantage of that fact.

The conversation moves to sex toys as Audrey very excitedly shares about a new vibrator she bought. This is the way with women. The night could have begun with us discussing world peace, and inevitably at some point the conversation would have turned to sex, sex toys, penises or the like. I'm grateful we are on toys and not actual sex, since that would require a violation of the rules.

"You guys have no idea, it's like it's made of magic," Audrey gushes. "I have never, in all my life had an orgasm so intense and so fucking fast. It's a clit vibrator not a G-Spot one, and Oh. My. God. Seriously, it's A..Maz..Ing!"

Lola whips out her phone and demands "Name. Now. I'm going to Google it and order one. Anyone else?" She asks, holding up her phone.

"My phone is in here somewhere," Sasha mumbles as she digs through her purse. "Ah ha! Here it is," she announces loudly as she pulls her phone out.

Julia and I look at one another and dissolve into a fit of giggles. I shrug at her, turn slightly in my chair and reach into my purse for my phone too. Not one to be left out of the fun, Julia does the same.

Audrey gives us the name and we all Google it and order one of our own.

"I feel like you should ask for commission," Julia giggles. "These things are hella pricey, and you just sold four."

"Right?" Lola agrees.

They aren't wrong. It is pricey, but if it is as great as Audrey says it is, then it will be worth it. I haven't had sex in months, and my sex drive appears to have died with my family, but with all the other things changing in my life, I figure it wouldn't hurt to have something on hand should my sex drive decide to make an appearance. Hell, maybe Dr. Whitman will give me the assignment of a self-induced orgasm. This thought makes me giggle, which doesn't stand out as odd since everyone else is laughing along with Julia.

"Hey!" Sasha announces, "check this one out. It claims to be the Cadillac of vibrators" She turns her phone and we all take in the photo on the screen. It looks like it was designed by NASA with a price point to match. "I'm just going to..." she pokes her screen a few times, "there!"

"Did you just buy that?" Julia demands.

"Yup!"

Julia snatches Sasha's phone and reads the description out loud. Unfortunately Julia is also on her fourth cosmo, so out loud also means loudly.

Lola makes wide eyes at Julia and waves one hand up and down signaling for her to take it down a few notches while also whispering "Shhhh, Jules. Not so loud."

The rest of us laugh as Julia whips her head to look around the restaurant then turns back to the table. "Oops," she says, with a shrug, handing Sasha's phone back and draining the last of her cosmo and holding up the empty glass. "Last one for me. Next up after 'Loud Jules' is 'Sloppy Drunk Jules' and nobody wants that. If anyone sees the waitress do me a favor and flag her down so I can order a water and some coffee."

"Did you drive yourself? Do you need me to take you home after?" Lola asks.

"No I came with Sasha, but thanks girlie." She flashes Lola a smile and then turns her attention to Sasha, "You have to tell us how that one is after you get it. I need to know if the description is all that it promises to be."

Sasha holds up her own cosmo and says with a giggle, "You know I will."

We finish up dinner and order dessert and coffee. I opt for the lemon curd cake with blood orange sauce which was, quite possibly, the best thing I have ever put in my mouth. Conversation turns to a popular Netflix series, which I haven't seen, but I don't mind. I sit and listen and marvel at what an amazing group of women I have in my life. They all have husbands and children, and it's so easy to lapse into complaining about what stupid thing their husbands have done, or what adorable thing or naughty, but still adorable, thing their littles have done, but none of them slip even once. Even when talking about the vibrators, everyone at the table knows they aren't going to be using them alone, but not only is it unspoken, it's not even alluded to. They have not only gone out of their way to not bring up their husbands and kids, they have done so without any awkwardness. Anyone listening in on our conversations tonight would assume that every single person at this table is single. And it's one more example of what a screaming stupid bitch I was for months. And how unbelievably lucky I am that I have friends like this who require nothing from me, no big apology, no action on my part to make up for my behavior, just my presence in their lives, even if it came with conditions.

That night when I get home, I'm full of amazing food, delicious drinks and a deep gratitude for my friends. As I walk down the hall I stop outside Tabby's door, and press the palm of my hand to it. I haven't been in here yet, although part of me wants to. Sleeping in the bed I shared with Will hurts, but it also makes me feel a closeness to him I haven't been able to find anywhere else. I can still smell him, and while I know that will fade, overtaken with the scent of my own shampoo and soap, washed away when I am forced to give in and put them in the laundry, I treasure the fact that I have it for now. A piece of Will I will hold on to for as long as possible. I know that if I were to open Tabby's door I would have that too. But just like with Will, I know that the more I take in it, the less of it there will be, and for now the knowledge that it lies beyond this door, waiting for me, is enough.

Instead of opening the door, I press a kiss to it and whisper into the night "Mommy loves you sweet girl." Then I continue down the hall to my room. I wash my face in the bathroom, and change into my pajamas. I brought all my clothes back up to my room a couple of nights ago, no longer seeing the point of keeping them in bins in the family room now that I was back to sleeping in here almost full time. I climb into our bed and shut off the lights. Then I tell Will all about dinner, the girls, the vibrators and the fact that while it took longer than it should, I remembered what amazing girlfriends I have, and that instead of pushing them away, I should have been leaning on them all along.

CHAPTER TWELVE

It's been eight months since Will and Tabby were taken from me, and two months since I started therapy. The mosaic table is complete. Dr. Whitman and I grouted it last week, although I'm not sure what will become of it now. I think about all the things that Dr. Whitman has had me do, and while I do not understand any of it, she continues to give me assignments every session. I've broken dishes to use to make the mosaic table, which also broke through the anger I was using as a shield and let all the grief and tears in. I have weekly coffee with Julia and Lola, which opened up a whole world of guilt and more tears. I'm back to sleeping in my own bed, whispering to Will in the dark, stories from our life together. I'm editing books I love, that I walked away from when I lost my family. I've gone grocery shopping and cooked family favorite meals, the pain from that still lingering every time I walk into the kitchen. I've watched movies with my mother, which was a fairly mild homework assignment in comparison to some of the others. I was at least able to choose movies without any emotional ties to my life and without storylines that would cause me pain. That basically left movies like The Martian and the Saw series, but at least they didn't hurt to watch. Twice she has simply built on previous assignments and not given me any new ones, and both times I was beyond grateful for the small break.

I've continued to spend time on the grief forum, lurking and reading. I've started following a few of the people on there, because their posts put into words so many of the feelings I have, and I want to follow their progress. I want to be able to read how they process their grief and the things they do that help them get through day after day. I also follow them because I hope that for them, they are able to find some kind of peace.

Today when I arrive for therapy I don't know what to expect. It's been a rougher than usual week for me and that is saying something, considering my weeks have been pretty shitty for months. I don't know what else there is for her to ask me to do, and any of the things I can think of I immediately dismiss because no one can be that cruel. Today Dr. Whitman is wearing a long flowy white dress with short butterfly sleeves printed with green, yellow and gold lizards. It's ugly as sin and yet adorable at the same time. She doesn't know it, but her dresses are one of the few things in my life that I look forward to. I love their whimsy and the confidence with which she wears such atrocious articles of clothing. When I was getting ready for therapy today her dresses inspired me to wear a long-loved dress of my own that I haven't worn in quite a while. It's a floor length maxi dress with thin straps, a high waist and a v-neck. It's black with tiny red ladybugs on it, however the lady bugs are so tiny they look more like red polka dots unless you look closely. And it has pockets which every woman knows is literally the best part of any dress.

Dr. Whitman and I make small talk for a few minutes. I tell her that I've had dinner with the girls again, and that I'm so grateful for their easy acceptance of me back in their lives. We talk about the newest book I'm editing and how it's been extremely difficult for me to connect with the storyline because it is about a mother who chooses to leave her husband and two sons to go on a year long journey of self-discovery. I admit that I hate the book and the character. I hate the storyline and can't even connect with the writing, which is something that has never happened to me before. I would give anything to have my family back, and because of that I have this fierce hatred for a fictional character that almost feels visceral.

"How has your emotional wellbeing been this past week?" Dr. Whitman asks me.

"I had some pretty bad moments, a lot of them actually. I didn't know the human body could make so many tears. It's been eight months, but there are days where it feels like it was only yesterday and days where it feels like it's been years. I'm sad all the time, and I feel so empty and lost. I do all of these assignments but I don't understand them. They aren't helping with my grief," I accuse. "Wasn't that the point of coming here in the first place? So you could help me with my grief? I mean, I didn't expect it to go away," I wipe away the tears that have been falling, and run my fingers roughly through my hair, "but I wish it would. I just want it all to stop, and I don't understand how any of what I am doing is supposed to be helping with that," I'm crying in earnest now.

"You have done so much work these past eight weeks. You don't even see how far you have come. When you first walked in here you were so angry at the whole world that you hadn't even cried. I know that for you, crying doesn't feel like progress, but it is. And whether you believe it or not, the assignments I've been giving you have been helping, just not in the way that you thought they would."

"That doesn't even make any sense. And really I don't know that I actually care about that right now. I just know that I don't want to cry anymore," I rant. "I don't want to feel this. I want my old life back. I want my family back," I put my face in my hands and just let go. "I just want all of this to go away."

"Allison, this is the hardest thing you will ever have to do, but you are doing it. Every day that you wake up and get out of bed, and put one foot in front of the other, you are doing it."

"I don't want to. I want it all to stop. I want to wake up and have everything be the way it was. I want to hold my daughter and kiss my husband. This new life that I'm supposedly 'doing' is not *my* life. It's the wrong life."

Dr. Whitman nods in agreement, and then very softly she says, "It *is* your life now. It's just not the one you want. Let's talk about the table for a second. You just said you didn't understand the point of it. Would you like me to explain?"

I don't really. At least not in this moment. In this moment I don't give a fuck about the table, but I feel like whatever she is going to tell me might be important, so I nod begrudgingly. I've learned several things about Dr. Whitman. The first is that she doesn't sugar coat anything. She says it like it is, even if she knows it will hurt me. She's not blunt or unkind when she does it, she's a therapist after all, so she is sensitive to my feelings, but she still tells me what she thinks I need to hear, even if it is hard to take. The second is that when she has something to say, it's important. She asks a lot of questions, and is involved in the conversations those questions create, and she offers guidance, but she very rarely offers her own insight and when she does it is usually profound. She stands and extends an arm at me indicating that I should do the same. We walk over to the table and she says, "Tell me what you see."

I take in the table. The delicate pieces of ceramic, their brilliant colors arranged in such a way that the entire thing resembles the interior of a kaleidoscope. Bright blues and yellows, earthy greens and browns, ruby red, pinks, and whites all arranged in a chaotic pattern around the tiny purple heart I placed in the very center. There are solid pieces, and pieces with patterns that were a part of a whole that are no longer identifiable. Instead the patterns appear abstract and only add to the overall look of the entire thing. "It's beautiful," I say reverently, because it is.

"But what do you see?"

I run my fingers over the top, touching several individual shards before I look at Dr. Whitman, "I don't understand the question. I see a table. I see colors and patterns, and yeah it's pretty, but it's still just a table."

"Do you want to know what I see?" she asks.

"Umm, I guess," I say, shrugging.

"I see a different kind of beauty. Think back to when you bought these pieces. They were plates and bowls, they had a previous life. And what happened to them?"

"I broke them. I threw them at a fence and smashed them to bits."

"Yes. You broke them. Shattered them. And then you took the broken pieces and made them into something different, something useful, and something beautiful." She turns her body so she is no longer facing the table, but is completely facing me. I turn with her and try to process where she is going with this.

"I'm the table?" I ask, sounding skeptical.

She nods and says, "In a sense. Tragedy, loss...they changed you. Broke you in some ways, shattered you in others. You are not the person you were before Will and Tabitha died. Their deaths changed you. You are also not the person you were the first six months they were gone. When you first came to me you were anger personified. Everything about you screamed anger. Not just your words, but your posture, the way you held your body, your facial expressions. Everything. At the time I had no way of knowing that you hadn't allowed yourself to shed a single tear over their loss. What I did know was that you didn't cry, or show any emotion other than anger when you were here. That's why I decided to give you this assignment that day, rather than to wait a few weeks. You needed something that would allow you to let go. Something that would force a release of that anger and let the grief out. But in doing that, you also changed. You became someone else."

I look at Dr. Whitman through my tears but I don't say anything. I feel them slide down my cheeks, but I don't brush them away. Instead, I stand there silently, letting them fall, my face blank, waiting for her to finish.

"When you broke those plates," she gestures to the table, "what would you have said if I told you that the next task was to put them back together exactly as they were?"

"That would have been impossible. I wouldn't have even known where to start."

"Why?"

I don't even think when I reply, "Because there were too many broken pieces. Because there were probably missing pieces. There were slivers and ceramic dust at the bottom of the boxes when I finished the table. That stuff never could have been put back the way it was. It just, well, it would have been an impossible task."

"Exactly. They could never have been what they were. They weren't just broken, they would have had missing pieces, and no matter how much care you took in reassembling them, it wouldn't have returned them to their previous state. "

"Okay?" I say, but it comes out as more of a question.

"But," she says, taking both of my hands in hers, "that doesn't mean they couldn't become something else beautiful. A different version of all the broken pieces."

Dr. Whitman leads me back to our chairs and we take our seats facing one another. I'm crying again, or still, I'm not even sure anymore.

Once we are seated she continues, "Losing Will and Tabitha changed you. But each day you are picking up the pieces of your life, and whether you realize it or not you are putting it back together. It will never look the same as it was, just like those plates will never be plates again. But that doesn't mean that it can't still be something beautiful, even with the missing pieces. It will be different. That's true. And it will be hard. That is also true. But if you let it, if you let go of the guilt you feel for living, for smiling, for laughing, and if you work through the grief like you have been doing, life can still be something beautiful. Just like those plates, with all their broken pieces, became a beautiful table."

I turn to look over my shoulder at the table, not entirely convinced by what Dr. Whitman is saying. I mean, in theory I get it and it makes logical sense. The plates were my life with Will and Tabby. Smashing them against the fence created the pieces of my life after they were gone. The table is my life, in pieces, put back together, different but no less beautiful. It makes logical sense and is a visual representation of what she is saying. But I'm not dishes, and I don't think it's as easy as just picking up the broken pieces of my life and reassembling them.

I turn back to Dr. Whitman and from somewhere deep inside me I find the first hint of anger I've been able to feel since that day at the fence. It's not nearly as fierce as it was in the beginning, more like a tiny spark, but it's an emotion I haven't been able to access in eight weeks and it feels like an old friend, so I grab hold of it as tight as I can and try and pull more of it to the surface.

"I feel like I'm trapped in some horrible nightmare and all I want to do is wake up. I want to scream and yell and throw a tantrum. I don't know how to make everything stop. All I want is for it all to stop. I'm not a table. I'm not fucking dishes. I'm the only one left behind from my little family and I don't want to be here without them." The crying turns to sobs, and I'm so damn tired of crying all the time.

Dr. Whitman gives me some time to get the tears under control. They are still flowing freely, but at least the sobbing has stopped and then asks me gently, "Have you ever considered harming yourself in order to join them?"

I stare at her, dumbfounded. "I...umm...no, actually. That never occurred to me. I want them back, not to join them wherever they are. That's...well, yeah that," I shrug and feel stupid. "It never crossed my mind." I say it like an apology, like maybe it should have. I worry I'm not grieving correctly or something. I didn't cry the first six months. I wouldn't allow a wake, but at the funeral so many others were weeping openly while I stood there, stoic, frozen. I didn't even cry at the hospital when the doctors told me there was nothing else that could be done and that my family was gone. I didn't cry when the transplant facilitator came and asked for my signature on documents that would donate their organs to people who would have otherwise died without them. And it's only just now occurring to me that I did not once contemplate suicide as a means to put an end to my grief and be with my family.

"Am I failing grieving?" I ask with all seriousness.

Dr. Whitman tries so very hard to hide it, but I see the small smile tug at the corner of her mouth when she says, "No Allison. First, there is no such thing as failing at grieving. There's being stuck, which is what you were when you first came here, but that's not failing. People grieve in dozens of different ways. As long as the way in which someone is grieving is healthy, there is no wrong way to grieve."

"But I never thought about killing myself," I wail. I can't stand the sound of my own voice. If I were a character in a book I was editing I would hate me. I cry all the time, I'm whiney, I can't get a grip on my emotions, and I feel like I am exhausting most of the time.

"And you view this as failing?" Dr. Whitman asks, her tone incredulous.

"Well, yeah." I say, stupidly. "I love my family. I miss them like I never imagined possible. I cry all the fucking time, to the point where I'm sick of my own company because of how emotionally unstable I am. I want this all to stop. I want to wake up and have it all have been some terrible nightmare. But even at my lowest points I never once thought of hurting myself to be with them."

She nods and I take that to mean she agrees with me, which causes the tears to flow faster. "Alright. Let's see if I am understanding you. You are failing grieving because you haven't thought about hurting yourself. Additionally, you are sick of yourself because you cry and are emotional a majority of the time. Is that what you think?"

I nod vehemently. Then I share, "Yes. I was just thinking that if I were a character in a book I would hate me. I would probably root against me if I am being honest."

"So with all the books you have read and edited, you've never encountered a character who is grieving?"

I shake my head, but say "No, I have. I remember one where the main character's husband died and she went to work in desperate need of a shower, while still in her pajamas and was fired. And another where her boyfriend or husband, I don't remember exactly, left her and she ate Oreos for breakfast for a week and when she ran out she went to the grocery store in her pajamas as well. But I haven't read any where the main character just cries all the damn time. Who would want to read that? She would be difficult to like, and even harder to root for."

"So you would be more likable if you went out in public in your pajamas?" she asks, and I would have felt like she was making fun of me if not for the sincere expression on her face.

I stand up and pace the room, moving back and forth between the chairs and the window. I need to move. "Okay that's ridiculous. I know that. I sound like a lunatic. But this is precisely what I mean. I am all over the place. I can't get a handle on anything, and I genuinely feel like I'm falling apart."

Dr. Whitman leans forward in her chair and gently says, "Allison, come sit. There's a lot here to unpack and I want to try and address it all before our time ends. I don't want it all to linger until next week and there's a lot to go through."

I sigh because she's right. I just dumped a whole lot on her and clearly I am unable to process it all by myself. And I definitely do not want to wait a week to have the opportunity again.

I return to my chair, grab some tissues to dry my face and then crumple them in my hands.

"Therapy is typically best when the patient talks and the therapist listens and gives input. In the interest of time, how about I do most of the talking and you give your input. Are you alright with that?"

I nod because I have talked enough today, and all I have managed to do was create more confusion for myself. Maybe it will be better if I am quiet.

Dr. Whitman crosses her legs and her face turns very serious. "First, if you were a character in a book, I would absolutely root for you. You see yourself as someone who cries all the time and who is, in your own words, whiny. I see a woman who is dealing with a terrible tragedy with grace and strength. Do you cry a lot? Maybe. But who gets to decide what is a lot? Is there a limit to the number of tears you are permitted to cry for your husband and your child?"

I want to answer, but I don't think she's actually asking me a question. Instead I look down at the tissues in my hand and pick at the corner of one, shredding it slowly into a pile on my lap. My eyes fill with tears, but I'm determined to hold them back for as long as I can.

"Now, if all you did was cry then maybe I would be concerned. But that's not the case. You yourself have told me that there were times you felt guilty because you forgot to be sad for a couple of hours, primarily when you were out with friends. You cry when you are talking about your family, you cry when you are feeling their loss. But that is normal. Especially for someone who was unable to cry for six months. Your first appointment you said you were dealing with your grief by being, in your words, a 'screaming bitch any and every chance you got'. I would probably not have an easy time rooting for that character, because it would be difficult to empathize with her. Are you with me so far?"

I look up from the pile of destroyed tissues and nod. I don't trust myself to speak right now. I want to hear what else she has to say, and at this point almost anything could come out of my mouth.

"I asked if you thought about hurting yourself because you said you didn't want to be here anymore. It was an important question to ask, but it was absolutely not intended to come across as a judgment regarding whether or not you were failing at grieving. And I'll point out, the fact that it never once crossed your mind proves what I said about you being strong." She uncrosses her legs and moves forward to the edge of her chair, "You are not the first person to want to be with their loved ones in an 'I miss them and want them back' sense. That is a normal part of the grieving process. Typically followed by something along the lines of 'If you give me back my husband, I promise to never fight with him again.' Or 'If you give me back my daughter, I will never be impatient with her again.' This is the bargaining stage of grief."

I pluck several more tissues from the box on the table next to my chair. At the rate I am going through them I'm going to have to buy Dr. Whitman a Costco sized box of them to replace the ones I have used.

Dr. Whitman continues, "Now, like I said, when you first came here you were stuck, unable to really grieve. And yes, anger is a stage of grief, but it is not the only stage, and a person can't grieve fully, which includes crying, if they are stuck in one stage." She offers me a small smile. "The activity with the dishes and the fence broke through whatever barrier you had erected and let all your emotions out. You said you thought you came here so that I could help you grieve. But Allison," she leans forward and clasps her hand together between her knees, "you don't need my help to grieve. You've been doing that on your own since our second session. You've been able to cry, to feel the loss, to truly grieve for your family. And you've taken steps on your own to help with your grief. Joining the grief forum and spending time reading posts from others who have suffered losses similar to yours doesn't just help with your grieving process, it helps with your healing process as well. And grieving is hard. It is the most difficult thing you will ever do. Every part of it feels unnatural, kind of like someone asking you to learn how to breathe underwater. The difference is that breathing underwater is impossible, working through grief only feels impossible, but it isn't. It's something you are doing every single day. I'm here to help you live, and to do it without guilt. I'm here to remind you that living isn't forgetting, and that it is okay to still do things that make you happy, even while you are grieving your loss."

I blink repeatedly, her words confusing me. "I don't understand," I state the obvious.

"All the assignments I've been giving you, things like having coffee with your friends, slowly working up to sleeping in your own bed full time, going back to editing books that you enjoy? These were tasks designed to slowly give you back your life, the pieces you shut away when Will and Tabitha died. I can't help you grieve. I can't make your grief go away. I can help you manage some of it, and in our upcoming sessions I will guide you through some ways to address some of the more difficult aspects of it, and I can answer some of the questions your grief brings up, such as when you asked if you were still a mother now that Tabitha is gone, but you are the only one who can do the work that grieving requires. I'm simply here to help you live again."

I'm stunned by her statement. All this time I thought that the whole point of coming to see Dr. Whitman was so that she could help me with my grief. I kept waiting for that magic moment when she would give me the trick or the tool that would make this unbearable pain stop. And every assignment she gave me, I did, but never quite understood how they were supposed to help with my grief. It never occurred to me that her real goal was to show me how to live without Will and Tabby. I mean, now that she has laid it all out for me like this, it obviously makes perfect sense that that is what she has been doing, I just never put it together. I feel a little like she tricked me and also a little stupid for not realizing the whole point of her assignments.

She looks over to the table and asks, "Do you have a space in your home for that table?"

"My house," I correct automatically, then further explain, "it stopped being a home when Will and Tabby died. It's just a house now."

"In your house then." She corrects.

I consider this for a second and affirm, "Yeah, I umm, I do actually. I have a glass enclosed porch that it would actually look beautiful in. I'm just not exactly sure how I would even get it to my house, much less inside. I could probably have Julia ask her husband. He has a truck. Can I let you know next week?"

"Of course," she says, rising from her chair. "Let's get you set up for next week. Also," she moves to her desk, "this week, I would like you to do something for yourself. It can be alone or with friends, but it has to be something you enjoy that you want to do, alright?"

"Yeah okay," I say distractedly, my mind a whirl with all the things she has said, as she gives me my card with my next appointment.

CHAPTER THIRTEEN

When Dr. Whitman gives me assignments at the end of each therapy session, I like to try and do them that same day whenever possible. Part of this is to get it out of the way, and part of it is in case I find the task too emotional and fail, I'll still have several other days before my next appointment to get it done.

I consider the assignment she gave me. It actually doesn't seem all that difficult, especially considering some of the other assignments she has given me over the past several weeks. The hardest part is deciding what it is I want to do for myself. I consider and discard a few options before I settle on something simple but still for me. Dr. Whitman has had me cook both Will and Tabby's favorite dinners, but just like with everything else in my life, until I started therapy, I have been denying myself anything that would make me happy. This means in eight months I haven't cooked *my* favorite meal. Therefore, I decide that's what I'll do. I'll go to the grocery store, get the ingredients I need, pick up a bottle of Sangria, and make my favorite meal.

As I'm driving to the store I add to my plans for the evening. I decide that not only will I make my favorite meal and have a drink, I'll eat while I watch a movie I haven't seen yet, and maybe even have a bubble bath. Dr. Whitman's words from our session today tumble around in my head and I think about all the things she said. It was a lot to take in in the moment and I know it will take me days to process all of it. One of the biggest ones is her saying it's alright for me to live while I'm grieving. I think about the guilt that consumed me the day I got home from my first coffee with Julia. But then I remember coming home from dinner with the girls and instead of feeling guilt, I went to the bed I had shared with Will and told him all about my night. Instead of feeling like I had done something wrong, somehow sharing it with Will in the dark in our bed made me feel closer to him instead of further from him. I don't know if Dr. Whitman has all the answers, but so far the ones she has given me have done nothing but help. It's hard to trust someone I have only just met with the most traumatic part of my life, but it doesn't escape me that in the eight weeks I have been going to see her that there are parts of my life that have improved despite my grief.

I park my car and mentally plan out the list of things I need for dinner as I walk to the store. I get a carriage and start in the produce section, picking up Shiitake mushrooms, cherry tomatoes and snap peas. I stop at the cheese counter to get a wedge of parmesan because there is no substitute for fresh shaved parmesan. Even when I fed my toddler spaghetti, I didn't use that weird gross powdered cheese that pretends it's parmesan. In my personal opinion that is not food, and it is not fit for human consumption. As I'm selecting my wedge, I smile to myself at the memory of Tabby trying to say spaghetti. She would pronounce it 'spetti' which I always found adorable. As I'm reaching for my cheese I freeze, momentarily stunned that this memory made me smile and not cry. I find this confusing and it takes me a couple of seconds to unfreeze myself and continue shopping.

I move to the seafood counter and ask the man behind it for six of his fattest scallops. As I'm waiting I hear a commotion from far away, so I look around. I see a few seniors shopping, and one teenage boy coming up the cereal aisle across from me, but nothing that explains the shouting I thought I heard. Then I realize it's coming from behind me, the boisterous little boy voice shouting "Miss Awi" and I turn, knowing it can only be one particular little boy.

I see Linx, Julia's beautiful three-year-old, his blonde curls bounding around his little cherub face, running full tilt towards me, his arms outstretched. I see Julia hurrying behind him whisper yelling "Linx, stop!" but she's no match for a toddler on a mission. He runs into me without slowing and wraps his arms around my knees, looks up and gives me a huge toothy grin while yelling "Miss Awi".

I react without thinking and crouch down and wrap him in my arms taking in his little boy scent. I haven't held a child since I lost mine, and I had forgotten how incredibly healing the hug of a child can be. But I feel such conflicting and confusing emotions in that moment. Holding him hurts on a level so deep I'm not sure I have felt anything like it, but at the same time it feels like some small part of me is being stitched back together. "Hi, Linx," I say laughing as he looks over his shoulder at his quickly approaching mother and then turns back and giggles at me.

"Al, I'm so sorry," Julia says as she gets to us. "I didn't know you were here until he saw you and took off." She says this while trying to wrestle him back into her arms, but Linx holds on tight and laughs like it's a game. "He wanted to walk," she is explaining quickly, nervously, still struggling to get Linx to let me go, "but he pulled his hand from mine and ran so quickly I couldn't catch him before he made it to you." Linx has given up the fight and Julia picks him up and hefts him onto a hip.

I reach out and stroke one of his curls, "It's fine," I tell Julia. Then I look at Linx and say "You are supposed to stay with your mommy," while giving him a tiny poke in his belly.

Linx giggles and then looks to his mother and announces, "I runned fast!"

Julia looks adoringly at her son and says "You sure did. But you won't be allowed to walk in the store if you do that again Linx. It's not safe to run away from Mommy."

"Miss, your scallops?" The man behind the seafood counter calls to me, and I apologize as I walk over and take the offered container.

"Thank you," I say.

"Miss Awi," Linx says as I walk back towards him and Julia, "I pway with Tabby?"

My heart squeezes and I freeze, unable to put one foot in front of the other. It feels like all the oxygen has been sucked from the room, and I can't breathe. I stare at Linx, unable to say the words that slam through me - 'Tabby's dead'. Aside from the fact that those words would break me right here in the middle of the store, I love this child and I could never in a million years be so cruel as to intentionally inflict harm on him. Not even when I was at my most angry and awful would I have even considered it.

Julia looks like she's been struck. "Ali, oh my God. Ali. I...I..." she stammers, clutching Linx tightly to her. "Oh God. I didn't...I couldn't...I didn't know how..." she trails off, her eyes flooding with tears.

I swallow several times, unsure of what to say. Julia and I are staring at one another, neither able to answer his question. The moment stretches on for so long that Linx becomes impatient.

"Miss Awi!" He shouts, "I pway with Tabby?"

Julia looks down at him, the tears having spilled over and running down her cheeks. Her breath hitches as she swallows a sob and says softly, "No baby."

Linx looks up at her and reaches a hand to her cheek, "Mommy why you crying?"

Julia's eyes dart to me, "I'm so sorry Ali. I just, I didn't know how to explain," she stammers.

I take a deep breath and move forward. I reach out to Linx and run my finger down his cheek. My voice is surprisingly stable when I say "Your mommy is sad because Tabby can't play today."

"She sick?" he asks, sounding concerned.

Fuck this is hard. Every time I think I have felt the worst pain of my grief and loss, some new fresh hell kicks me in the heart. "No baby. Tabby isn't sick, she just..." I swallow back my tears, I do not want to add to his distress. He's already worried about his mother; he doesn't need me to break down too. "She just can't play today."

"Maybe amorrow?" he asks, his mispronunciation just another thing I miss about my own child.

Julia hugs Linx close and promises, "I'll explain. I'll try and help him understand. I'm really so very sorry Al."

Linx squirms in her arms and insists on being put down. She sets him on his feet and reaches for his hand but he's a toddler Houdini and slips from her grasp, dashing the few feet to me and wrapping himself around one of my legs. I place a hand on the top of his head and look down at him. I don't know how Julia is going to explain and I feel a profound sadness at the thought of Linx trying to grasp the concept that Tabby won't ever be able to play again.

"Linx we need to go home now," Julia tells him. "Can you say goodbye to Miss Ali?"

I squat down and give him a tight squeeze, holding him for an extra minute, savoring the feel of his tiny body in my arms. Then I kiss him on his chubby cheek and let him go. He places a hand on each side of my face and gives me a sloppy kiss in return on my own cheek. "Bye Miss Awi," he announces and turns, reaching for his mother's hand.

Julia steps into me and gives me a one-armed hug, whispering in my ear, "I'm so sorry. Are you going to be alright? Do you want me to call your mom or Lola or...." she trails off.

I hug her back and respond, "No. I'm okay. I'm going to finish shopping and go back to my house and do my therapy assignment." My eyes fill but I am determined to not cry. Not in front of Linx.

"Are you sure?"

I nod, surprised to find that I am telling her the truth. "Yeah. I'm sure."

"Okay," she replies, sounding skeptical. "I'll call you later?" she says, but it comes out as a request for permission.

"Yeah," I nod, "call me later."

I look down at Linx and say, "Bye buddy. Be good for your mommy."

"Bye Miss Awi," he waves as Julia leads him towards the front of the store. She glances back at me just before they turn out of sight and gives me a small sad smile.

I take a breath and try and take stock of my emotions. I'm proud of myself and also pretty freaking surprised that I didn't break down crying and not only because of Linx's request to play with Tabby. The kids were born eight days apart, and virtually every memory I have of Linx is him with her, and the reality that that will never be the case again hits me hard. But I realize that the person I feel the worst for in this situation is Julia. The guilt and devastation she felt at Linx's question was written all over her face. I know she feels responsible for Linx running up to me, forcing an encounter I was nowhere near ready for, but more for not having explained to him about Tabby. I don't blame her though. How do you explain death to a three-year-old? They don't have the ability to understand something so difficult. Hell, I don't have the ability to understand it and I'm an adult. For the first time in months my heart hurts more for someone else, and I want to cry for her instead of for me. My heart breaks for Linx too. At three he is so very young, and his biggest hurt should be a scraped knee or a broken toy. He shouldn't be trying to comprehend the forever loss of his friend.

I think again of what a huge mistake I made pushing my friends and family away in the beginning. It's easy to judge myself in hindsight, especially now that the overwhelming anger is no longer my only emotion. I think about how my friends have so easily welcomed me back into their lives, expecting nothing from me but my presence, adhering to rules that I know are restrictive in order to accommodate me. But it's more than that. They love me, they miss me, and they don't hide that fact. Even with this interaction, Julia was clearly embarrassed, felt horrible guilt, and likely was experiencing her own heartbreak for me and for what she was going to have to share with her son, and her primary concern was me. Apologizing to me, asking if I needed her to call someone to support me. I make the decision to do something for them to show them what they mean to me. It feels like the least I can do.

I try to decide if I want to just call it a day and try again tomorrow or if I am going to continue with my plans for the evening. It was a highly emotional therapy session, and while I might not have broken down into a sobbing mess in the store, my encounter with Julia and Linx was also emotional. It would be easy to forgive myself for making the decision that I am too emotionally exhausted to do anything else today. However, this assignment isn't emotionally taxing, and might be the treat I need after the day I have had. Dr. Whitman's words today about grief and healing and doing the hard work echo in my head, and I decide that I am going to continue with my original plan of dinner, a movie and a bath. It feels a little selfish, doing something just for me that I'll enjoy, and I know that I will eventually have to give some headspace to why I feel that way, but not today. Today I am grateful that I have the excuse of an assignment to be a little selfish.

I've made my decision, so I start moving again. I find the risotto and add that to my basket, along with Sauvignon Blanc to make it with. I grab a red Sangria and realize that somewhere out there some poor sommelier would be devastated to witness my plan to pair a red fruity wine with a scallop risotto. I add a pint of Jeni's gooey butter cake ice cream to my basket and then double check to make sure I have everything I need. There's nothing else I need so I check out and drive back to my house.

CHAPTER FOURTEEN

I'm bringing the groceries inside when my phone rings. I quickly place them on the island and dig my phone out of my purse and see that it's my mom calling. I think that maybe Julia called her anyway, but then quickly dismiss that idea. The Julia who was friends with the me 'before' would have absolutely called my mom even though I said it wasn't necessary. She would have viewed it as taking care of her friend. The Julia who is friends with the me 'now' is tentative, worried that she might do something to lose me and wouldn't call my mom, not because she doesn't think it would help me, but because she would be afraid I would be angry at her and cut her off again. I add this to the list of things I need to deal with.

"Hey mom," I say, as I start to unpack the groceries.

"Hi my beautiful girl. I was just calling to see how you are doing today, and to ask what your plans are for tomorrow."

I put the Sangria in the fridge and answer, "I had therapy today which was probably the worst one yet. I think Dr. Whitman took pity on me with her assignment this week because it was such a tough session. She told me I had to do something for myself. It could be alone or with friends, but it had to be something I wanted to do, and it had to be for me."

"I'm sorry it was such a tough session. I try not to ask what you guys talk about, but I am here if you ever need to talk," she says carefully. My mom has been amazing at not asking, and I know that is hard for her. The fact that it was just me and her while I was growing up meant that we were exceptionally close and I pretty much told her everything. I mean, yeah I was a goody goody in high school, and I didn't drink or smoke or even have sex, but I was a teenager, so it's not like I didn't make stupid decisions on occasion, and I always told her about them. After the fact of course. So I know the fact that I keep my therapy sessions private, and typically only share about the assignments is difficult for her. I think about what Dr. Whitman said today and there are a few things I do want to share with my mom, just not over the phone.

"I know, and I appreciate that. Dr. Whitman actually said some stuff today that I do want to talk to you about, but I would rather do it in person."

"Anytime Ali, you know that."

I do know that. And once again I kick myself for being so colossally stupid for so many months. "This week," I tell her.

"Sure," she returns.

I take a deep breath and then I share, "I ran into Julia and Linx at the grocery store after therapy today."

"Shit," she says.

I think I surprise us both when I bark out a short laugh and say "That about sums it up. It was...awful. Linx ran up to me and gave me a big hug, which hurt so much, and then asked if he could play with Tabby, which, there are no words for how much that hurt."

I hear my mother take in a sharp breath, "Oh God Ali. Are you, I don't even know, are you okay?"

"I am. It hurt and it was hard to see him. But honestly, I hurt more for Julia and Linx than I did for myself. Julia hasn't told Linx, because how do you explain death to a three-year-old? And Mom, oh my God the look on her face when he asked that, it was like someone slapped her."

"I can't even imagine. Poor Julia. And oh my God, poor Linx. I don't even know how Julia will explain something this big to a little boy. Are you really sure you are alright?"

I hold the phone between my ear and my shoulder and pick up the produce to put it in the fridge. "I'm sure. I know that sounds like a lie, but I really am. It's bizarre - I cry at the drop of a hat these days. Anything and everything makes me cry, but today in the store I didn't. I couldn't. Not because the tears wouldn't come, because they absolutely would have if I had let them, but more because I didn't want to upset Linx. Julia was already crying, and he was worried about her being sad. I didn't want to add to his distress by breaking down too. It's the first time that I have been able to hold them back actually." I move to the stove and start water for some tea.

"I don't know what to say. I'm proud of you sounds kind of stupid, but still..."

I give a wry chuckle, "It's funny you should say that actually. I felt pretty proud of myself when they left too. Actually, I felt proud of myself for not running out of the store after they left and running to my car to ugly cry. I made the decision to continue my shopping and follow through with Dr. Whitman's assignment. I told myself that after an emotion therapy session and an impromptu run in with Julia and Linx in the grocery store, that it would be totally okay to bail and go home. But then Dr. Whitman's words from therapy today were rolling around in my head and I decided to just keep moving forward with my plans. It's hard, and it hurts, because let's be honest, everything is hard and everything hurts in one way or another, but I think what I am getting from therapy is that I just have to keep going."

I can hear my mother crying and I give her time to gather herself. Lord knows I have needed my fair share of time to control my own tears. After a few minutes I hear her clear her throat.

"Sorry," she says. "I'm just..."

"Mom," I interrupt, "You have nothing to be sorry for. Apparently tears are a new staple in my daily life. I have plenty so I'm happy to share," I joke, trying to lighten the mood.

Thankfully it works and my mom chuckles, "Well aren't you sweet to share," she jokes back. She clears her throat again and asks, "So what are you doing for your assignment?"

"I'm going to make scallop risotto. And I bought some red Sangria. I'm also going to watch a new movie and then I'm going to have a bubble bath." I reach for a coffee mug and drop a maple espresso tea bag into it. I add boiling water from the kettle and let it steep.

"Oh, that sounds lovely, Ali. Good for you. What movie are you going to watch?"

I shrug and then realize that she can't see me. "I'm not sure," I answer verbally. "I figure there must be something new on Netflix I haven't seen yet. I'll probably call Julia too. She said she would call me later but I want to check on her. Oh shit," I announce, remembering the table.

My mother sounds alarmed when she asks, "What? What's wrong?"

"Nothing, I just remembered that I'm supposed to arrange to take the table to the house from Dr. Whitman's office, and I was going to ask Julia if she could ask Ethan to pick it up with his truck. Then when everything happened today at the store I totally forgot. And I don't feel right asking now after our emotional afternoon. Fuck!"

"Okay Ali, it's okay. I have a friend with a truck. I can ask him if that's alright with you."

I'm stunned speechless. My mother has a 'friend' with a truck? A male friend with a truck. I start to giggle, "Mom, are you....dating?"

"Allison Leah Sawyer!" my mother admonishes.

"Oh my God you are!" I lean against the counter and laugh.

"I am not...dating," she denies. "He's a friend. We occasionally have dinner and sometimes we go see a movie or a show."

"That is the very definition of dating Mother," I reply. I take my tea to the island and sit in one of the stools.

"We are not discussing this. I am not dating. I'm too old to date. Now, do you want me to ask him if he can move the table or not?" I can tell she is trying to sound pissy but is failing spectacularly because she is trying to do it while holding back her laughter.

I chuckle and respond, "Yes please. That would be very helpful." I try to sound contrite but I can't keep the humor from my voice.

My mother makes a noise that sounds like a strangled groan, which only makes me giggle more. "Fine, I will ask Henry tonight and make arrangements for sometime this week."

"Henry," I snicker.

"Are you suddenly twelve?" she asks, sounding putout.

I can't help myself, I answer, "Apparently."

"Moving on," she declares. "Now, do you have plans for tomorrow?"

"I have to finish the final edit for one of my authors by the weekend, but otherwise I'm pretty flexible. Why?"

"I wanted to see if you wanted to go with me to the John Singer Sargent exhibit."

"Oh yes, definitely," I say excitedly. "His painting of 'The Daughters of Edward Darley Boit' is my favorite painting."

"Yes, Allison, I know. That's why I asked if you wanted to go with me," she chuckles.

"Oh duh. Well, yes, I would love to go. What time?"

"How about I pick you up at nine thirty. It's about an hour and a half to the museum. Will that work?"

I want to tease her and ask if Henry is coming but I don't. I decide that when we are trapped in a car there will be plenty of time to get the scoop on him. Instead I say, "Sure that will be perfect."

We say our goodbyes, and I contemplate calling Julia to see how she is but decide to wait until after Linx's bedtime. It's five now, so I figure I'll make dinner and watch a movie and call her after. I quickly run upstairs to change, exchanging my dress for a pair of kelly green yoga pants and a fitted black tee shirt with a green shamrock on it. Once back downstairs I stop in the family room and light a vanilla scented candle.

I get out all the ingredients and set about cooking. I let the rhythm of chopping and sauteing, along with a healthy glass of Sangria relax me. As the risotto finishes cooking, I sear the scallops. I plate the risotto, add some of the sauteed vegetables, shave on fresh parmesan and top it with half the scallops. I'm excited to have more than enough leftovers for the next day. Then I take my plate and my Sangria to the family room. I fold my legs under me, my plate in my lap and surf Netflix for a movie. I select a sequel to a murder mystery I enjoyed and settle in.

The food is amazing, the Sangria is delicious, the movie is actually good, and the candle smells great. It's all so bizarrely normal, and nothing about my life has been normal in months. It feels weird, but a good weird. A peaceful weird.

As I sit there I take stock of my feelings. Today was a highly emotional day, and left me with a lot of things I still need to process, but one of the things that I keep going back to is Dr. Whitman saying that her job is to help me live my life again. Eight weeks ago I never would have considered there would be a time in my life where I laughed again. I couldn't imagine feeling anything but that vile burning anger that lived inside of me. It was my constant company for the first six months after I lost Will and Tabby and it protected me from fully feeling the profound sadness their death created. Letting go of that anger forced me to feel everything I had been avoiding, all the sadness and hopelessness and the longing for them. And I wasn't lying when I told Dr. Whitman that I would give anything to make it stop. I feel a hurt so deep I didn't know it was possible for a person to feel, let alone survive. And I have cried more tears in the past eight weeks than I have cried in my entire life. There are days when I feel like I'm drowning in a sea of grief and I can't find the surface in order to catch my breath. It's so completely overwhelming at times and there are no real words or expressions in the English language to fully explain the kind of pain losing a spouse and child causes. But the thing I find shocking is that there are moments where I feel genuine humor. Even with how hard today was, I ended up laughing with my mother on the phone. I'm able to laugh with my friends and genuinely enjoy their company. When I first found I could laugh and enjoy time with my friends I felt immense guilt, another emotion that had been shut off in the aftermath of the crash. I never felt bad for any of the things I said, or more accurately screamed, at the people in my life. Guilt was an emotion, along with absolute devastation and impossible laughter, that I found along the fence line. Shockingly, I seem to have also found moments of peace there as well.

There is no handbook for grief and all the ways it manifests or how to manage the confusing array of emotions that seemingly come out of nowhere like an ambush. If there were I would pay any amount of money in order to buy one. Everything about grief is so complex and feels so chaotic that it's hard to process. It's not just about the loss, which would be bad enough all on its own, but it's also a series of conflicting emotions that it's almost impossible to make sense of them all. Like, how can I have broken down so completely in therapy today and then laugh with my mother? How can I miss Will and Tabby with a longing that I could never have imagined possible and still go out with my girlfriends? How could I have held Linx and hear him ask to play with Tabby, feel the ache of that question down to my soul but still sit here on the couch, eating dinner and watching a movie and feel peace? How does any of that make sense?

I think that when I told Dr. Whitman that I wanted it all to stop, I didn't mean just the grief, although that is at the top of the list. I think that what I really meant was that I wanted the array of schizophrenic emotions to stop as well.

I finish my movie and clean up the kitchen. I refill my glass of Sangria and carry it, along with my phone to the island and scroll through to Julia's number.

"Ali," she answers after the first ring.

"Hey," I reply, feeling awkward. It's been a long time since I was there for anyone else and I'm unsure how to start. "Is Linx alright?"

Julia sighs deeply, "Ali, I umm," she blows out a breath. "You don't have to do this. Check on him and umm talk about this."

God, I loved my friend. "I know. And honestly, I know this won't be an easy conversation, but I think it's something I need to do. Dr. Whitman talks a lot about the 'grieving process' and I think that this is part of mine. Do you mind?" I ask sincerely.

"Jesus Ali of course not. I just don't want to make things harder for you than they already are."

I give a wry chuckle, "Pretty sure that ship hasn't only sailed, it's sunk."

"Fair enough," she sighs again. "It was...rough. I probably screwed it up, because I have no idea how to explain the concept of death to a three-year-old. Fuck, Ali, seriously, are you sure you want to do this?"

"I..No. I absolutely do not want to do this," I reply honestly. "But I think I have to. I don't know. If I told you all the shit swirling in my head you'd probably think I was insane. It's like, I want to get away from my grief because it's too big and too much, but at the same time I feel some crazy need to suddenly confront it head on. I don't know if it was my breakdown in therapy today, or if it was what Dr. Whitman tried to explain after that, or if it was seeing Linx today, but whatever it was unlocked something inside of me and I think I need to do this. And Julia, if I am going to do it, I need to just do it. So don't sugarcoat anything. No euphemisms. Just say it like it is. Can you do that?"

"If you are truly sure," she hedged, sounding more unsure than I felt.

"I'm sure," I affirmed and hoped like fuck I wasn't lying to both of us.

There are several seconds of silence and then Julia continues, her voice soft, "I told him that Tabby got a really bad owie. An owie so bad that the doctors couldn't make her better and that she was in Heaven with the angels." Her voice cracks and I know it is taking everything she has not to break down.

I swallow hard, trying to keep my own voice from cracking as the tears flow freely down my face, "Did he...umm...did he understand?"

"I think at first he didn't. He asked me when she was coming home from Heaven. I...umm...I," I can hear her sniffling on the other end of the phone and I suddenly wonder if I am doing the wrong thing making her relive it. Selfishly I need her to do it; I don't know why, but I need to face this. It feels - I don't know - important somehow. Like a turning point or something. I won't push her to talk if she finds it too hard to share, but as long as she is willing, I know I need to hear it.

After a moment Julia continues, "I tried to explain to him that people don't come back from Heaven. I told him Heaven was a very special place that people go when they die, and that they don't have pain from their bad owies anymore, and no one gets sick and people are happy all the time. So he asked if he could go to Heaven too because then he would get to play with Tabby." She's crying in earnest now, as am I.

"Oh Jules." Everything about this sucks and I suddenly hate Justin even more than I did when I woke up this morning, and I honestly didn't think that was possible.

"Yeah," she sounds defeated. "I'm pretty sure this is where I totally fucked the whole thing up. I told him that only people who die go to Heaven and then I tried to gently explain what dying meant, but for fucks sake how do you explain that? At first I tried telling him that when people get really sick, or get a really bad owie, or even just get really old that their bodies stop working and they die."

This hurts so much. I can't believe this is my life, talking about my daughter in association with death and Heaven. I don't even know if I believe in God anymore, because what God would take my husband and child away? It's all so pointless. And if I don't believe in God, can I really say I believe in Heaven? I mean, I must believe that Will and Tabby are somewhere because I wouldn't talk to them in the night if I didn't believe on some level that they could hear me. I just don't know if I believe in an actual place.

It hits me so hard that I'm surprised I don't double over, when I suddenly realize that I can set aside my hurt and anguish to be there for Julia in this conversation, and not make it all about me. It amazes me but at the same time it feels like a progress I never expected I would ever be able to make. For as much as this entire conversation hurts like hell, I am proud that while I'm not doing it without tears, I am doing it, and that is far more than I ever would have been able to do eight weeks ago.

Therefore through my tears I say, "I think that was the best way to explain it Jules. There isn't an instruction manual for this."

She sniffles some more before continuing, "You would think. Except when you are three apparently a 'bad owie' is relative, as is 'really sick', because he asked why he didn't go to Heaven when he fell off the playground slide and broke his arm. Then he started crying and asked if Ethan was going to leave and go to Heaven too and not be able to play with him anymore, because Ethan has a frickin cold. I screwed it all up and now he's so confused." Julia breaks down sobbing.

I take in a deep breath. This woman has been my best friend for over twenty years and has forgiven the worst of me. I love her like a sister, and I love Linx as if he were my own and I can actually help with his.

I take a second to control my own tears and then steel my spine, gather all my inner strength and say, "Jules, it's ok. We can fix this. Okay? Do you hear me? We can make this better for Linx."

I hear her struggling to get herself under control, and after several hiccupping breaths she manages to say, "Ali this isn't right. I shouldn't even be telling you this. It feels cruel. It's okay, I will..."

"Stop," I interrupt her. "I *want* to help. I *can* help. I lost my way for a long time, and I know I am nowhere near back to being who I was. Hell, I don't know if I will ever even be close to resembling the person I was. But I love you and I love Linx and I *can* do this. Please let me help," I beg.

"Of course, but Ali you don't have to. I can't even imagine how hard this is for you and it isn't your job to fix this. It's supposed to be my job to be there for you."

"No Jules. That's not how this works. I forgot for a while, and I will always be sorry for that, but we are friends and friends support one another through everything. The easy, but most especially the hard. Okay?"

Julia's voice is barely a whisper when she replies, "Okay."

"Okay. So listen, I don't edit children's books, but that doesn't mean I don't know them. I'm a book person - it's not just what I do, it's part of who I am. There are dozens of books for kids of all ages that explain the concept of death and dying in an age-appropriate way. I don't know them all, but there are four that I would strongly recommend."

I gave her the list of the four I know, ones I would have read to my own daughter if the need had ever arisen. We find them together on Amazon and she orders two of the ones that she thinks will help Linx the most. We both cry a little more and trade unnecessary apologies back and forth. I tell her that I have plans with my mother in the morning but that I will call and check on her and Linx in the afternoon.

When we hang up I take stock of my emotional state and decide that it would be completely alright to call it a day. I decide to skip the bath and take a quick shower, put on my pajamas and climb into bed. I curl my body around Will's pillow and sigh deeply. Then, through more fucking tears, I tell Will about my day and fall asleep.

CHAPTER FIFTEEN

The next morning I am up and ready, sitting on my front porch waiting for her when my mom pulls up at nine thirty. It was a rough night full of nightmares that seemed to follow me every time I fell back to sleep. I finally gave up on sleeping at around five-thirty, so I've been ready for hours. Since we are going to a museum I opted for another long dress I found in the back of my closet. Apparently I have an ample supply of dresses I held on to from my thinner days that fit me now that I've lost so much weight on the 'grief diet'. It's not a diet I would recommend to anyone but evidently it is an effective one. This one is a creamy beige with little pink and yellow flowers, wide straps and a ruched neckline across the top of my bust. And of course it has pockets. I opt for a pair of black flip flops because I think they are the most comfortable shoes ever created, and my dress is more than long enough that I could have worn slippers and no one would have been able to really notice. I did my hair in a sloppy bun and did a light dusting of makeup, mostly to cover the bags under my eyes from lack of quality sleep.

I climb into the car and give my mom a quick peck on the cheek. Another first in the last eight months and I once again have a surge of guilt for everything I have put her through. I plaster a smile on my face and vow to make this day a good one. For both of us.

"Morning" I say.

"Good morning my beautiful girl," she replies, then tips her head to the center console as she reverses out of my driveway. "I got you a coffee, and there are bagels in the bag on the floor by your feet. I think I got the coffee right - dark roast, three caramel swirl, three liquid sugar and three cream?" she asks.

"Yes, perfect, thanks!" I reply as I finish buckling my seatbelt and take a sip of my coffee.

"I also got you your disgusting cinnamon raisin bagel not toasted with olive cream cheese, although how you can eat that is beyond me."

I grin, "Umm because it is delicious?"

"I will take your word for it because I don't think I could ever bring myself to try such a culinary abomination."

I laugh, and unwrap her bagel, wrap the wax paper around the bottom half and hand it to her. It's a totally uninspired plain bagel with plain cream cheese. Boring!

I unwrap my bagel, wrap it the same as I did for my mother and take a bite, making a happy noise further driving home the fact that it's delicious. We both are quiet as we enjoy the first few bites of bagel. I contemplate how there are people who separate the sides and eat them individually and wonder what they could possibly be thinking. Part of the joy of a bagel is the yummy cream cheese sandwiched between the sides of a chewy bagel.

"This is bagel nirvana," I tell her. "Chewy, sweet, salty - it literally hits all the right notes. You are completely missing out."

"I'm just fine with that. I don't like olives as it is, so the idea of pairing them with cinnamon raisin is even more, umm, unpleasant."

I shrug and change the subject. "How's Henry?" I ask nonchalantly.

"Allison," my mother warns.

"What?? I'm just being polite," I say, full of mock innocence.

"Bullshit," she chuckles. "You are being incorrigible."

I burst out laughing. "Mom, I'm thirty-four, not six. I don't think thirty-four-year-olds can be incorrigible."

She makes a noise that sounds like "Harumph," and I laugh again.

"You're not going to let this go are you?"

"Nope."

She sighs and gives in, "Fine. What do you want to know?"

I give her wide eyes, which she can't fully appreciate since she's driving, and say "Everything. Where did you meet, how long have you known him, what does he do for a living, when can I meet him? I want to know everything."

"I met him four months ago. He's my friend Bitsy's brother, and he recently moved back to town to be closer to her. His wife Catherine passed from breast cancer about seven years ago. He's four years older than I am and he's a math professor at the university. He loves wine and likes to go to wine tastings to find new ones to add to his collection. He likes to try new ethnic restaurants and doesn't like to go alone, so he's been asking me to join him. Last night we went to this Ethiopian place which was divine. I've never had Ethiopian food before and I absolutely loved it. He's also a fan of musicals, so we've seen several of those. We just went to see Hamilton last week, which was wonderful."

My heart momentarily hurts for the unknown Henry and his loss. I also have a niggling sense of curiosity about how he could lose his wife and be in a place to be ostensibly dating my mother. I mean, granted, I am in a way better place since starting therapy, despite all the tears. I'm able to laugh and have moments of genuine happiness, which still surprise me and leave me feeling guilty, but that doesn't negate the fact that they do happen. But the idea of ever being in a place where I would be able to or even *want* to date again is incomprehensible. I decide I would really like to meet this Henry, if only to see what someone else's life looks like so many years after the loss of a spouse. I also decide that I really like the smile I can not only see on her face but hear in my mother's voice while she's talking about him.

"You like him," I tease. It's an opportunity I can't pass up, because as she has pointed out previously, I'm twelve and apparently also incorrigible.

"He's my *friend*," she insists, stressing the word friend but unable to keep a straight face while doing so.

I take a page from Dr. Whitman's book and just look at her while remaining silent.

She flicks her eyes my way and back to the road several times before she once again sighs and gives in. "I enjoy spending time with him. He makes me laugh, he's exceedingly kind, and we have a lot of things in common. But we really are just friends."

"Is he cute?"

"Allison, he's a grown man. Boys are cute. Henry is..." she searches for the right word.

"Hot?" I ask.

"Handsome," she decides, sounding exasperated.

I chuckle. Then I recap, "So, he's handsome, kind, makes you laugh, you like being with him, you guys go out and do things you both enjoy and do so frequently but you aren't dating? Have you guys even kissed?"

"No!" She says too loud and too fast.

"Why the hell not?"

My mother bites the corner of her lip before admitting, "I'm not sure he sees me as more than a friend. He's never tried anything - not even holding my hand." She sounds disappointed and that sucks.

"Well, have you tried holding his?"

"What?! No! Of course not!" she practically shouts, sounding horrified.

"Mom, it's 2023, not 1823. Women are allowed to make the first move."

"I wouldn't...well, I wouldn't know how. And besides, don't you think if he wanted to hold my hand he would have done so by now?"

I shake my head, "Did you consider he is thinking exactly the same thing?"

"Oh. Well, no actually, I didn't."

"Have you given him any indication that maybe you would like for him to kiss you? Or hold your hand for that matter?" I'm really trying very hard to be an adult here, but I honestly want to laugh. I don't think I ever in a million years ever thought I would be having this conversation with my mother. My daughter, yes. And that thought makes my heart squeeze. HARD. It hurts so much to know I will never have these moments with Tabby. Teasing her about a boy and watching as she gets flustered while her cheeks turn an adorable shade of pink. But today is about my mother and I, so I say a silent 'I'm sorry baby girl. I love you so much but I owe Ama a good day and that is what she is going to have' and set my own heartache aside. I take a second to revel in the fact that I did in fact do just that, and decide this is something I will unpack later with Dr. Whitman because I have about a thousand different feelings about it, but not all of them are bad.

She considers this for a minute and then admits, "I don't know." She pauses and then continues, "No, that's not true. I do know. I haven't. In fact, I'm pretty sure I have made it very clear that I am only looking for a friend and nothing more."

"Mom, why? Clearly you like him. Why wouldn't you want to let things happen and see where it goes?"

"Because what if he's not interested? What if he only wants to be friends? This way I don't embarrass myself and lose my dinner and musical partner." She sounds like she's fifteen and I think it's so cute. It's also a little scary to think that no matter how old we get, we are all fifteen when it comes to fearing rejection from the opposite sex.

I reach over and give her hand a squeeze and encourage, "Mom, I'm willing to bet that he feels the same and is just as worried as you are. How about this?

Why don't you guys come to dinner at my house tomorrow night so I can see how he is around you and then I promise to give you my very honest opinion about if he is interested in more or not?"

"Al, I don't know."

"Why? He can bring the table, and dinner can be my way of repaying him for the favor. It will be very low key."

She thinks about this and then agrees, "Actually, that might be perfect. Okay," she says, nodding. "Let me call him when we get to the museum and I will ask him."

I do a mini internal victory dance and grin at her. Then I marvel once again at how much my life has changed since I started seeing Dr. Whitman. It occurs to me that it happened so slowly that I didn't really notice it until she pointed it out, but I am in fact, living again. I definitely still have times where the guilt about that fact is overwhelming, but I'm even learning how to forgive myself for that.

We ride in silence for a little while before my mother hesitantly asks, "How are Julia and Linx? Is it okay to ask that or would you rather not talk about it?"

"No it's okay. I called Julia last night and the whole conversation was so fucking sad. But do you want to hear something really strange?"

"Okay?"

"I cried - obviously. I mean we were talking about how she explained the idea of death and Heaven to Linx because of Tabby, so of course I cried. But the weird thing was I mostly cried for them. It was so hard on Julia. She was so worried she messed it up and she was just so devastated that she made it harder for Linx to understand. And oh my God Mom, the idea that this little boy had to try and understand the idea of gone and not coming back was just heartbreaking." My voice is thick with tears, so I swallow a few times and take a couple of deep breaths through my nose. Once I'm sure I can keep going without crying I say, "I helped her find a couple of age-appropriate books on Amazon that will help Linx better understand."

"I can't imagine how difficult it was for Julia. It's hard because she has to explain the idea of never coming back without scaring him into thinking that any time she or Ethan leave they aren't coming back too."

"Exactly! Like, I guess she told him Tabby got a really bad owie and the doctors couldn't make her better, which in theory is as good an explanation as any, except then he didn't understand why he didn't die when he broke his arm. She also told him sometimes people go to Heaven when they get really sick and their bodies stop working, and of course Ethan has a cold so that freaked him out too."

"Oh geez. Poor Linx"

I nod my head in agreement and blink away the tears that have pooled in my eyes. "I think once she has the books it will at least make it easier to explain. I also think that once he actually understands it will be harder because, well, because then he will understand."

"Yeah," she agrees, and really there's not much more to say other than that.

We are quiet for another few minutes, each of us lost in our own thoughts. I let my mind wander and I'm surprised at the direction it takes. I don't follow the Linx and Heaven and death and dying thread that would have been so familiar to travel. Instead I think about how so many parts of my life are divided into befores and afters. Obviously the big one is before Will and Tabby died, and after. But there's also before I started therapy and after. There's before when I was pushing everyone away, and after when I was lucky enough to have my mom and friends welcome me back into their lives without expecting anything from me. My friends even went so far as to adhere to the rules set by Dr. Whitman without making it awkward or uncomfortable. There's before when I shut out anything that might bring me joy, to after where I am not just doing things that Dr. Whitman assigns me that bring me joy, but am doing things on my own, like dinner with the girls, or this outing with my mom, that also bring me joy.

"So you know all those assignments that Dr. Whitman gives me and builds on each week?" I ask, breaking the silence.

"Yeah?"

"I kind of had a major meltdown in therapy yesterday and one of the things I cried about was not understanding the whole point of the assignments. I told her I didn't understand how they were supposed to help with my grief since I basically cry constantly and feel like I have absolutely zero control over my emotions." I go on to explain everything Dr. Whitman told me about her role in my therapy and about the purpose of the assignments and what the table is supposed to represent. I explain that every one of those assignments, except the smashing of the dishes, was not designed to help me deal with my grief, but to slowly get me back to living my life.

My mother nods and says "You know that actually makes a ton of sense, because once you let go of your anger you were able to really grieve. And I don't think anyone can teach you how to do that since there isn't really a right or wrong way to feel grief. It just kind of happens, ya know? But then I look at all the things you have back in your life since you started seeing Dr. Whitman, and it makes me so happy to see you smile and laugh again, to see you get out of the house and do things, and just to see you have moments of genuine happiness. And I hope that you know that doing those things in no way takes anything away from your feelings about Will and Tabby."

"It's so weird. Like, when they first died, I was convinced I would never have a single moment of happiness ever again. It wasn't even something I could fathom..."

"Of course not. At first, it's too new and too big and just...too everything," she agrees.

"And then I was so freaking angry I couldn't get out of my own way to do anything or feel anything but fury. I don't necessarily want to go back to that time, but I won't deny that having that intense anger kept me from feeling this horrible sadness, and sometimes I miss it," I admit honestly.

She nods in understanding, "I get that, I really do."

"It's kind of sneaky of her actually. She sort of tricked me into living without telling me that's what she was doing."

My mom starts to laugh and agrees, "I suppose she did. And I don't think I'll ever stop being grateful to her for it."

"She's mentioned a few times that part of the grieving process is the healing process and I honestly thought she was full of shit when she first brought it up.

Like, how the fuck do you heal from something like this? She said it just happens naturally, and I thought there was just no way..."

"Except?"

I shrug, "Except I think she was right. And I don't know how I feel about that. I mean, I know I feel horribly guilty but at the same time, I feel a sense of relief that there is more in my life right now than just being pissed off at the world, or soul crushingly sad."

We pull into the museum parking lot and as she looks for a spot to park my mom asks, "Why do you feel guilty? Truly, Ali, why? Because I honestly believe that Will and Tab loved you so much that they would be so happy to see you finding a way to go on and do it with a smile. They would want you to be happy. I told you that before. When you love someone that's what you want for them."

"I have grown enough over the past several weeks that logically I know that. But I still feel like I'm betraying their memory by being happy without them."

My mom parks and shuts off the car. Then she turns in her seat and gives me her full attention. "Listen really closely to what I'm going to say, okay? You didn't walk away from them in order to selfishly live your life without them like your father did. You didn't choose to 'be happy without them' by cutting them out of your life. They died. They can not be in your life. Healing from their loss and going on to live a life where you can be happy in their absence is healthy. But it's more than that - it's a huge responsibility."

I can't help the look of confusion that crosses my face. "A responsibility?" I ask.

She nods in confirmation, "Yes, one thousand percent. You have a responsibility to both of them to live a full and beautiful life not just for you, but for them. They are counting on you to live for all three of you. To embrace the joy and happiness they can no longer experience. You are the one still here, and you owe it to them not to waste the life you still get to live."

I had never considered this. I spent so much time shutting out anything that could make me happy, and then so much additional time feeling guilty about doing things that did, like I was in some way betraying their memory by being happy when they couldn't. It never occurred to me that I was dishonoring them by wasting my life by not actually living it. This thought makes me profoundly sad and fills me with far more guilt than I think I have ever experienced in my life.

"Oh my God that makes me feel so guilty," I say, my eyes filling with tears and my voice thick. "I never thought of it like that. I was so busy worrying that I was dishonoring them by living that the idea that I was actually doing it by wasting my life never occurred to me. Also, can I just add that I feel really easily swayed by other people to see their side without much work and it's fucking annoying. It makes me feel like I lack any kind of conviction, " I pout.

My mother chuckles and brushes away the tears on my cheek with her thumb, "Easily swayed?"

"Yeah," I nod. "Okay, so anytime I am utterly and completely convinced of something, you or Dr. Whitman come in with this super annoying logic, and suddenly I'm like 'Oh yeah that makes total sense' and just end up changing my mind and agreeing."

"So you are annoyed that we are logical and that when we point out the logical things that you might have missed in your anger, and sadness and guilt you realize we are right?"

"Yes."

"Makes sense," she laughs. "But seriously Ali, you aren't dishonoring them. You are grieving and trying to navigate this new life without them. Do you owe it to them to live a beautiful life? Yes absolutely. Would you be dishonoring them if you spent the rest of your life never actually living? Yes again. But I didn't mean to make you think you were doing that *now*. Okay?"

I dig in my purse for some tissues and open the visor to dry my eyes and check my makeup. I say a silent thank you to the makers of waterproof mascara for the fact that it is not running in rivers of black down my cheeks. I remember my promise I made to myself to make this a great day for my mom, give her a bright smile and say "Okay," and mean it. "Let's go see the daughters," I say, excitedly.

"Let's," my mom replies with her own smile and a squeeze of my hand.

CHAPTER SIXTEEN

We have a wonderful time at the museum. We spend a considerable amount of time viewing the John Singer Sargent exhibit and then move from room to room taking in the other paintings and exhibits on display. The conversation in the car had turned a little heavier than I had wanted for our day out, so I make every effort to keep the conversation light for the rest of the day. We spend a lot of time talking about art, but also about Henry, my mom's friends from her bridge club, what book they are reading in book club, and joking around. She did call Henry and he agreed to pick up the table the next afternoon, which I called Dr. Whitman to arrange, and to stay for dinner in exchange. My mom helps me plan out the menu since it's been a while since I've cooked for anyone besides my mother and myself, and let's be honest, except for the few meals I cooked because Dr. Whitman made me, I haven't truly cooked anything in months.

We stop at a really cool sandwich place around the corner from the museum for a late lunch, early dinner and then head home. My mom drops me off at just after five and we make plans to go to the grocery store after her garden club meeting in the morning. I let myself into my house and go upstairs to change. The house is so quiet without my family, and it just makes me feel more lonely. I contemplate, not for the first time, the idea of getting a pet of some kind. The first time I considered it was after two weeks of therapy, but I dismissed it because too many things in my life were changing too fast for me to want to take on another unnecessary one.

Now I think about it again. Having a kitten or a dog won't take away the ache that I have over the loss of my family, but it would be nice to have some company at night when everything is so silent. I mean, I realize a kitten or a dog isn't exactly going to be a great conversationalist, but the not being completely and utterly alone would be nice. I decide that I will make time this week to go to the shelter and find an animal who needs me as much I need them.

I pad back downstairs in a pair of aqua yoga pants and a gray tank top with 'No Thanks' scrawled across the chest. I pour a glass of Sangria and send Julia a text checking on how Linx is doing today. She responds letting me know that it was a rough day filled with lots of questions, but that the books should be arriving tomorrow, and she is crossing her fingers that they help answer them. I tell her I'm here if she needs me and to please call me if she does. I text her again and let her know that I decided to go to the animal shelter to look for some company sometime this week and ask if she

and Linx might like to come with me. I
thought Linx might like to help me pick a new friend so
I would be less lonely. She texts back heart emojis
which I take as a yes.

I pace the downstairs and find I have a new emotion
to deal with - boredom. I feel restless and unsure what
to do with myself. I have a book I need to finish editing,
but that won't take long, and honestly I don't feel like
doing that right now. I hate the book so much and I
know I need to get it finished, but I'm not in the
headspace to deal with it right now. I promise myself I
will do it first thing tomorrow morning and just get it
done but not tonight. I could read a book for pleasure or
watch a movie, but I quickly dismiss those as well.
I decide to check the grief forum and see if there are
any updates from the people I have been following.

The dad with the new baby posted that the
anniversary of his daughter's death is coming up and
that he and his wife will be spending the day
volunteering at the pediatric cancer ward of the hospital
she passed away in. He wrote that he will be dressing
up as Batman, and his wife will be Wonder Woman,
and they are going to bring stuffed animals and treats
for all the children. I cry, not because I am sad, but
because I'm so moved by the idea that they are taking
the very worst day of their lives and spending it by
bringing joy to children suffering from the same illness
that their daughter died from. It's so beautiful and it
moves me so much that I decide to comment.

*1803 Oizys replies: I lost my husband and three year
old daughter to a car crash just before Thanksgiving. I
joined this group a few weeks ago because I needed to*

see how other people with similar losses survived a grief that feels unsurvivable. Your posts are one of the ones I follow. I think when I first started reading them, they gave me hope that there might be a time where I would smile when I thought of my daughter rather than cry all the time. I love reading about your new baby and the joy she brings you and your wife. I think the part that hits me the most is that despite your loss you have joy and I love that for you both. I haven't been able to bring myself to share my own story yet, or even comment on other people's posts, so I hope I'm doing it right. I wanted you to know that what you share makes a difference and to thank you for sharing feelings and thoughts that are so personal and private. I also wanted to tell you that I think what you and your wife are doing on the anniversary of your daughter's passing is the most beautiful and selfless action I can imagine. It's a beautiful tribute to your daughter and I guess I just wanted you to know that.

I post it but feel kind of stupid. I edit the written word for a living and no matter how many times I edited my post I couldn't find the right words to really tell this stranger what his words and his story means to me. I sigh and shut my laptop, hoping that despite the difficulty I had finding the actual words I wanted, that this stranger understands what I was trying to tell him.

I think about the different milestone days that are coming up. It's July now, which still amazes me. I lost so much time when I was in my anger fog, that I didn't even realize how much of the calendar year had passed when I came out of it. I didn't even notice that I missed grieving the big holidays of Thanksgiving and

Christmas as well as our wedding anniversary in December, something I think I am now grateful for. I don't think it will be easy this year, but I certainly think I am far more equipped to deal with them this year, especially knowing I can and will lean on my mother and my friends for support and comfort. I think about how Will would have celebrated his thirty sixth birthday in August, and Tabby would have turned four at the beginning of October. Then there is the first anniversary of their deaths in mid-November which is likely going to be the most brutal of all. I think about the man from the forum and wonder if there is anything I can do to honor their memory rather than spend these days drowning in my grief.

When Will and Tabby died, I signed papers in the hospital to donate their organs. So much about that time period is a blur, but I remember that moment with perfect clarity. The transplant coordinator came and brought my mother and I to a conference room and discussed the different types of donations I could authorize. For me, this wasn't as difficult a decision as I would have thought prior to being in that position. Knowing that out there somewhere were children and loved ones whose families were desperate not to be in the position I was in now and knowing that Will and Tabitha could help change lives - that parts of them could go on living - I stoically signed the papers without a second thought. My only stipulations were they couldn't take their eyes or skin. I donated their hearts, lungs, kidneys, livers, pancreases and small bowels. I also donated bone marrow from both of them. Then I walked out of the room and let the anger take hold.

It brings me comfort now to know that somewhere out there a husband is able to take his wife dancing because he got one of Will's lungs. Somewhere a mother is cuddling her toddler who is still alive because he has Tabby's liver. There are so many people out there right now who are living with parts of Will and Tabitha in them, and while it hurts me desperately that they are no longer part of a whole, I do get some peace knowing that pieces of them go on.

This is just another example of how nothing in my life makes sense. Given how I spent so many months so fucking angry I literally couldn't function, and then spent weeks sobbing uncontrollably at the drop of a hat, it doesn't actually make sense that donating their organs brings me peace. In fact, with the way I've handled their loss, it feels like the opposite should be true. That the idea that parts of them are out there somewhere living on in someone else's body without me should break me. That some other woman might be the one listening to Will's heartbeat when I can't, should be unbearable, especially given my reaction the day my mom and I finished breaking the dishes at the fence and she brought up grief from a breakup. My first reaction was that I was grateful that Will had died and not left me, but I'm okay with the knowledge that his heart is loving someone else, which makes absolutely no sense. Grief is a confusing bitch.

I close my laptop and wander to the kitchen. It's too early for bed and I need an outlet for this restless burst of energy I've had since returning from the museum, so I decide to bake. I figure it can be dessert for tomorrow when my mother and Henry come for dinner. I'm an excellent cook, but I'm an even better baker so

I decide to bake something with a visual wow factor.
I spend the next two and half hours making six of the
most beautiful mini lemon basil tarts with a flaky
buttery shortbread crust. I decorate the top of each with
a candied lemon slice and prepare fresh basil leaves to
top them with when I serve them. Then I take a picture
and text it to my mom. No vomit emoji in response this
time - instead she sends back about twenty heart eye
emojis, which makes me laugh.

I clean up the kitchen and go upstairs, stopping at
Tabby's door to press a kiss against it and whisper
goodnight to my daughter. Then I head to mine and
Will's room. I take a quick shower and then climb into
our bed. I tell Will all about Henry and my mom and
how adorably insecure she is about whether he likes her
or not. I miss my husband, but I've found that talking to
him like this at night has become a ritual that makes me
miss him just slightly less.

I get up at seven and go through my morning routine
in the bathroom and then head downstairs to make
coffee. I take my cup and my laptop to the kitchen
table and spend the next few hours finishing up the final
edits on the book and send them to the author, so
grateful to be finished with it. I know Dr. Whitman
wants me to continue editing fiction books, but I realize
now that I will have to be slightly more aware of the
premise of a book before I agree to work with the
author, especially if I have never worked with them
before. I have a new book I've been waiting for from an
established author waiting for me in my inbox. The
book is a psychological thriller and I'm excited to get
into it, but I know that with this author once I start the
book I won't want to stop, and I have plans with my

mom this afternoon. I have coffee with Julia and Lola tomorrow, but after that I'm free for the whole day, and I mentally plan out another 'me' day involving take out, baked goods and this new book. Dr. Whitman would be so proud.

While I'm waiting for my mom to show up I send Julia a quick text asking if she and Linx wanted to meet me at nine tomorrow at the humane society. My phone rings seconds later...

"Hey Jules."

"I hate you. I just wanted to tell you that," she says laughing.

I laugh too and say, "Let me guess, Linx wants a pet because you mentioned helping pick one out for me?"

She groans, "Yes and since I'm feeling super guilty about fucking up the whole Heaven explanation I'm probably going to give in, and the kid is going to end up with a pet pig or some other insane choice."

"Oh Jules, you didn't fuck up the Heaven thing," I try and reassure her. "Did the books come yet?"

"They are out for delivery now. And I did fuck it up, but its okay. I'm a mom, I fuck a lot of things up."

"If only they came with instruction manuals, right?"

"I looked," she jokes, "Amazon didn't have one of those."

"Write one," I suggest, "You'd make millions."

"Unfortunately I think I would have to title mine 'How to fuck up your kid in 10 easy steps'"

"Total bestseller. I'll even edit it for you."

"Awesome! I'll get on that. Should only take me about twenty years or so for conclusive evidence my manual is effective. Seriously though, have you thought about what you are going to get?"

"I'm not sure actually," I say. "Honestly I think a dog would make a better companion, but then I worry that might be a bigger commitment than I'm ready to make. On the flip side, it would be nice to have another reason to get out of the house. I mean, dogs need to be walked right?"

"They do," she agrees. "But I don't think you are giving yourself enough credit for how far you've come if one of your reasons for getting a dog is to have another reason to get out of the house. You should get a dog because you want the company, not because you don't think you're doing enough."

"Thanks," I reply, and mean it. "A dog sounds nice. But kittens are so fluffy and adorable," I gush. "I just can't decide."

"You could get one of each," Julia suggests, unhelpfully.

"Definitely not," I say, chuckling. "But thanks."

She laughs and agrees to meet me at nine tomorrow. We say goodbye and hang up just as my mom walks through my front door.

I update her on my plans with Julia tomorrow morning, and my mom puts in her vote for two white kittens.

"I'm not getting two pets," I tell her, like I just told Julia. "One is enough company."

My mother gives me a knowing look, which has never, in my life, boded well. This means I will likely come home tomorrow with two pets. Lovely.

We head to the grocery store and pick up the ingredients for dinner. My mom lets me know that Henry will be over at five with the table, so we plan to eat around six. When we get back to the house she helps me dust and vacuum, and we move a few items Will and I were storing on the porch to the basement.

"Do we want to eat out here tonight? On the new table? We got stuff to make the room pretty, we might as well use it," She suggests.

"Sure," I reply. "That would be nice actually." I love this room. All three outer walls are floor to ceiling glass, and the wall between the porch and the kitchen is made up of French doors. The wall across from the kitchen is made up of glass panels that can be slid into one another in order to open up to the patio beyond, where there are four Adirondack chairs set up around a stone fire pit. The ceiling and floors are white wooden planks, and there is a cream-colored chunky jute rug on the floor. Will and I hadn't gotten around to furnishing this room yet, so it's literally the perfect spot for the table. I have chocolate brown tight weave rattan chairs in the basement that would be perfect around the table, and my mom and I stopped on the way back from the grocery store to pick up chair cushions for them. I opted for a shade of very pale teal because I thought it would look beautiful with the vibrant colors of the table. We also picked up several strings of fairy lights and ran them back and forth along the ceiling and around the top of the windows. Then we drag the chairs up from the basement and wash them down and put the new cushions on. It looks so magical and I am actually excited to eat out there. We decide not to open the glass to the patio because no one wants to eat with mosquitos, but we do flip on the gas in the fire pit because it looks pretty when it's on.

"Do you want to go turn the grill on so it can heat up?" I ask my mom.

"Sure. Why don't you start slicing up the peaches so I can grill them when the grill is ready. This way they can cool down before we add them to the salad," she suggests. "Oh! And get the pork chops in the marinade too."

"Sounds good. Do you want to candy the pecans when you come back in, or do you want me to do that part?"

"I'll do it."

"Okay." We each go off to do our respective tasks. I slice up the peaches into wedges with the skin on and toss them in a tiny bit of oil. Then I make a marinade of olive oil, brown sugar, brown mustard, garlic, lemon juice, Worcestershire sauce, paprika, apple cider vinegar, onion powder, thyme and parsley and massage it into the pork chops and then leave them to continue to marinade. I prep the rest of the ingredients for the salad while my mom makes the candied curry pecans. She grills the peaches while I clean up the kitchen.

Henry arrives just before five and after introductions, easily carries the table onto the porch with no help from us.. Henry looks nothing like I expected. I don't know exactly what I expected, but it definitely isn't this man. Henry is gorgeous. Not that my mom couldn't land a gorgeous man, she is beautiful and absolutely could. But Henry's brand of gorgeous is absolutely not what I would have thought my mom would go for. He's at least six foot three and has to be over two hundred pounds of what looks like pure muscle. He's got wavy salt and pepper hair, a thick salt and pepper beard, two full sleeves of tattoos and pierced ears. He's wearing jeans that hug his thick muscled thighs like they were custom made for him, and he has on a tight black tee that clearly shows the defined muscles of his broad chest and flat stomach. He does not look like a math professor who likes wine, ethnic food and musicals. He looks like a biker who eats meat at every meal and drinks beer. I'm now concerned not only with my choice of dinner, but also my dainty desserts that I made with a completely different Henry in mind.

I try to be surreptitious in my observations of how Henry interacts with my mom, but it must be coming off as awkward because my mother keeps giving me wide eyes, so I decide to tone it down. I do notice that he's very attentive to her, pouring her wine, carrying the chops for her to the grill, standing close to her at every opportunity. Yeah, he definitely doesn't see her as just a friend and she just needs to give him the smallest indication she's interested and he'd go for it.

While they grill the chops and I sneak glances at them from the window, I finish making the salad. I add arugula, the grilled peaches, blueberries, the curry candied pecans and goat cheese to a large salad bowl and dress it with a homemade honey vinaigrette.
I slice up thick slices of fresh sourdough that I baked this morning and put them in a bread basket. I set the table with plates and silverware, cloth napkins and the food. I also add a crock of butter and a bottle of wine that Henry brought. They finish the chops and we all sit down at the table.

"This looks delicious Allison, thank you," Henry says as he picks up the platter of chops and passes it to my mother so she can serve herself first.

I add salad to my plate and pass it to Henry. "Thank you. I hope the chops and salad are okay. I thought that since it was warm out a heavy meal would be too much."

He serves himself salad and passes it to my mother and says, "I love salad, and this isn't one I've had before. The grilled peaches and the goat cheese are going to be terrific together."

We finish passing the food around and start to eat.

"Did you make this bread Al?" my mom asks, spreading a healthy smear of butter across the top.

I nod and confirm, "Yeah this morning. I got a starter from Sasha a few days ago and I thought it would go great with dinner."

"It's delicious," she said.

We continue to make small talk throughout dinner, and I find I really like Henry, but even more, I love how he is with my mother. He clearly adores her, and I don't understand how she possibly could have missed it.

Henry tells me about the different wines he collects and about some of his favorite ethnic foods. He tells me he loves food but is a hopeless cook, so he spends a lot of time eating out. He tells me his current favorite is Indian and my mother jumps in and raves that I can make pretty much anything and that I'm an amazing cook. I nod in affirmation that I can cook pretty well and admit that cooking different ethnic foods used to be a favorite pastime of mine. I invite them both back to dinner next week, and promise Henry an authentic India spread, which they both excitedly accept.

"What do you do for work Ali?" Henry asks.

"I edit books," I answer, and I can't help but smile. Books make me smile.

My mother beams at me. I know she is enjoying seeing me having a normal conversation with someone who isn't her. I mean, I've had normal conversations recently, with Julia and Lola, with the girls at dinner, even sometimes with Dr. Whitman, but my mom isn't there for those so this is kind of a new new normal for her. I was worried she was feeling left out since she's been fairly quiet while Henry and I monopolize the conversation, but now I realize she is watching me and getting immense joy from it.

"I'm a big book nerd," Henry admits. "I probably read two or three books a week. What kind of books do you edit?"

"I love that!" I gush. "Umm I edit fiction usually. What are your top five favorite books?"

"Any authors I might know? And only five? That might be too hard to come up with. Do series count as one book?"

I laugh and say, "I definitely count a series as one book. And yeah you might depending on what you read. I have a couple of New York Times Bestsellers I edit for. Do you know Anthony Jakesam?"

"I've read all his books. I would put his zombie apocalypse series in my top ten. You edit him? That's amazing. And top five would be Connelly's Harry Bosch series, Weir's Project Hail Mary, Kerouac's On the Road, Krakauer's Into Thin Air, and Dumas's Count of Monte Cristo. Yours?"

We continue having two conversations at once while we finish dinner and the bottle of wine. I could talk about books for hours, and while I know my mom is enjoying watching me, I feel bad she's being left out of the conversation. She might go to book club every week, but it's more of a social activity for her than about an actual love of books. I move the conversation to musicals and my mother instantly becomes animated and involved in the conversation. I watch as she beams at Henry when she talks about their outings, and I want to laugh at how oblivious they both are to the other person's attraction. I believed her when she told me that she was giving him 'I just want to be friends' signals, but clearly that's not the case. Neither of them are being subtle in the slightest, but somehow they are both missing it. It takes everything I have not to burst out laughing.

We clear the table and I take the tarts out of the refrigerator and top them each with a fresh basil leaf. I make a pot of coffee while my mom puts the leftovers away and then we all take our coffees and the tarts back out to the table. My mom and Henry rave about how good they are, and even I have to admit they are not wrong. These aren't tarts I've made before, but they are definitely going on my list of things to make again. I would bet almost anything they would be a hit at MUD and add to my ever-growing list of things I want to do - bake a batch and bring them to Valerie to try.

The evening winds down and after dessert and coffee we move to the foyer to say our goodbyes.

"Thank you so much for bringing over the table," I tell him. "And don't forget dinner next week. I'm excited to try out some new Indian recipes."

"You're welcome. I'm happy I could help. The table is beautiful Allison. Your mom didn't tell me anything about it except that you made it, and it's beautiful. You should be proud of that."

I smile at that since he must know that there is clearly more to the story seeing as he picked the table up at a therapist's office, but he doesn't ask and at the same time makes sure I am aware that my mother didn't violate my privacy by telling him what that story was, "Thank you. It was a lot of hard work," I say, the understatement of the century.

My mom gives me a hug and demands I send pictures of whatever I end up picking at the shelter. I hug her back and promise to send a photo of the one animal I select. She laughs and says, "We'll see," which makes me laugh.

I give Henry a brief hug and thank him again. After they leave I send my mom a quick text telling her that I think Henry is great, and that I also think they are both oblivious to how the other is feeling. I assure her that after observing them both for just a few hours that there is definitely something between them, and that I'm not sure how either of them is missing it. I tell her that it would seriously only take a simple touch on his hand to move things along and that I think she should be brave and go for it. My mother, ever the fan of emojis, sends me back a kitten and a dog. I burst out laughing.

CHAPTER SEVENTEEN

"Miss Awi," Linx yells as Julia lifts him out of his carseat and puts him down in the parking lot of the shelter. "Miss Awi, I get a pet!"

I squat down and stretch out my arms and Linx runs into them, making us both giggle. "Me too!" I tell him. "Are you going to help me pick a new friend?"

He nods solemnly and says, "You need a fwend so you not lonely acause Tabby and Mr. Wiwl went to Heaven."

My heart squeezes and I blink hard to prevent any tears. I hear Julia make a soft gasp. I take a deep breath and nod at Linx, "You're right Linx. So let's go see what they have, okay? I bet we both are going to find the perfect new friends," I say, standing and taking his hand. The three of us make our way inside, where we are greeted by the bubbliest human being I have ever met in my life.

"Hi! My name is Candi! Welcome to A Second Home! We are so excited to have you!" Candi speaks in exclamation points and after only three seconds I'm grateful I only have to spend a limited amount of time with her because that would get old fast.

"Mommy! She has bwue hair. I want bwue hair too!" Linx exclaims.

Julia laughs and says, "Maybe another day okay buddy? We need to pick some new friends for you and Miss Ali today."

Candi does indeed have blue hair. It's in two long braids like Heidi, right down to the sweet little bows tied at the ends. She also has at least ten earrings in each ear, and multiple facial piercings. She's all of five feet tall and maybe ninety pounds of exuberant energy.

She claps her hands together and announces, "How exciting! What's your name?"

"Winks," he says, proudly.

Candi sends a questioning glance to Julia, who says "Linx." Candi nods.

"So Linx, do you know what kind of new friend you want?!"

Linx nods his head and says, "A cow."

Julia and I burst out laughing and Candi giggles. "I'm sorry buddy! We don't have cows here! But we do have kitties and doggies and a few other friends!"

Candi leads us around the facility where we meet kittens, cats, puppies and dogs. She also shows us a few rabbits, a couple of birds, an iguana, a descented skunk, three ferrets, and a pot belly pig. Linx instantly falls in love with the pot belly pig and I whisper to Julia that she totally jinxed herself with her sarcastic pig comment. She elbows me and whispers back that she hates me.

"Mommy, I want the piggy!" Linx exclaims excitedly, while laying his head on the pig's belly. The pig snorts in response.

"Umm, Linx, honey, I don't think a pig would be very happy living in our house. Maybe we should go back and look at the kittens," Julia says, a hint of desperation in her tone.

Candi pipes in with "Oh no! A pot belly pig is a great house pet! They love being with people and Wilson here is housebroken! Aren't you Wilson?" She croons at the pig while scratching him behind his ears.

Julia and I look at one another and exchange a silent 'Oh shit, now what?' look.

"Linx," I say, "wouldn't you rather have a nice kitty who can sleep in your bed? A pig is kind of big to sleep in bed with you."

"Wison can sweep in bed with me. I'm wittle."

Julia crouches down in front of Linx and tries to reason with him. "Linx baby, Wilson is really big. I don't think Mommy or Daddy could pick him up to put him in bed with you, and he wouldn't be able to jump up there on his own. A kitty could jump up and sleep with you much easier."

"Oh! Pigs can climb stairs! You just need a set of bed steps and they sell them on Amazon! And then Wilson could totally sleep in bed with you Linx!" Candi puts in helpfully. Julia shoots daggers at her and I'm positive that this is one of those 'if looks could kill' situations.

"YAY!" Linx shouts and rolls over on his belly to lay down next to Wilson. Wilson wiggles his fat body closer to Linx and shoves his snout in the little boy's neck and snorts again. Julia is fucked. She's going to go home with a pig. I don't even try to stop it when I start to laugh. I laugh until there are tears streaming down my face while Julia just stands there looking helpless.

I sling my arm around her shoulder and whisper in her ear, "Ethan is going to divorce you."

She just bites her lip and nods vigorously. Then she starts to laugh too. "He is totally going to divorce me."

Candi clips a leash on Wilson's collar and hands it to Linx. "Come on Wison. We need to help Miss Awi find a friend too." He gives Wilson a gentle tug and pig and boy walk together to the door to the next area. "I think Miss Awi would wike the skunk." He tells Wilson.

"Umm Linx? Miss Ali is not getting a skunk." I call after him.

We spend the next half hour looking at the different available animals again, and then I spend an additional twenty minutes convincing Linx I did not, in fact, want a pet skunk. I did, however, really want a dog/cat bonded pair that we met. Apparently my mother was right that I was indeed going to get two new friends. Felix is a three-year-old blue Great Dane and Oscar is a three year old Russian Blue. They have identical coloring, and Oscar looks like a mini Felix in cat form. They are adorable and I decide I want them. I want them more when I find out that they were adopted together at eight weeks old by a couple who passed away six weeks ago in a boating accident. Because they are a bonded pair they really need to be adopted together, and apparently no one who has visited the shelter has shown an interest in adopting a dog the size of a horse and his mini me. For me it was love at second sight and their story only made me more sure. Like me, they lost their entire family in the blink of an eye, and I feel very strongly that they need me just as much as I need them.

Julia and I fill out the adoption paperwork, me excitedly, and her very begrudgingly. She hands hers to Candi and then turns to me and says, "When Ethan asks for a divorce, I hope you know that Linx, Wilson and I will be moving in with you."

I laugh and nod, "Yeah, I know."

We both know it's a joke though. Ethan is a total pushover and would adopt eighty-seven pot belly pigs if that's what would make Julia and Linx happy. That man lives and breathes to make them happy, and if Wilson is what is going to do that, Ethan will totally roll with it. It's why Julia didn't even bother to check with him before filling out the paperwork. Because she knows without a doubt that her husband won't even blink at the new addition to their family.

We each load up our new friends into our respective cars, Candi lending me a kitty carrier for the trip home. I follow Julia to the pet supply store where I buy two giant dog beds, one for upstairs and one for downstairs, a new collar and leash, dog and cat food and water bowls, the one for Felix on an elevated platform per Candi's instructions, along with dog and cat food. I also buy a litter box that magically cleans itself, a scratching post, my own kitty carrier and lots of toys for both of them. I wasn't going to buy a dog crate, since Felix is three and housebroken, but Candi said that crates can make dogs feel more secure, and that having it doesn't mean I need to close it, so I buy one of those as well.

Julia and I decide that coffee today is likely not going to happen today, so she gives Lola a call and tells her about our outing this morning and Lola cracks up when Julia gets to the part where she jinxed herself into a pet pig. Lola asks if she can swing by each of us to visit and meet our new friends later in the afternoon and we both agree.

I take my new friends back to the house and bring them inside. I lock Felix and Oscar in the sunroom while I make multiple trips in from the car with my haul. I text my mom and tell her to come over and then go about setting everything up. I leave Felix and Oscar in the sunroom for now, although they are curled together in a streak of sunshine, sound asleep, and don't even notice that I didn't open the doors. I watch them through the doors for a few minutes and love how easily they felt comfortable enough to fall asleep.

"Al?" I hear my mom call from the front door.

Felix lifts his head and woofs at the sound of my mom's voice but doesn't get up. Instead he gives Oscar a lick and settles back down.

"Kitchen," I call back and start heading her way.

"What did you get? Please say a kitten," she pleads excitedly. I have no idea why my mother hasn't gotten her own kitten. She's mildly obsessed with them but has never owned one.

"I got a kitten," I confirm and her whole face beams. "I also got a dog," I add.

"What? Really?!" she claps her hands together and announces, "I knew it! I totally knew you'd end up with two pets!"

I nod. "Well, you were right. But I had to, they are a bonded pair whose family died six weeks ago. No one wanted them, probably because Felix is the size of a pony, but I fell in love with them almost instantly."

My mom swallows and asks, "A pony?"

I nod, "Felix is a Great Dane and Oscar is something called a Russian Blue. They have the exact same coat coloring, and they are so cute together."

"Felix and Oscar?"

"A true odd couple for sure. Want to see them?" I ask and she nods. I led her to the French doors to the sunroom and open them. Felix lifts his head and thumps his tail, waking Oscar. Oscar stands, stretches and wanders over to us. He weaves in between our legs and purrs. My mom crouches down to give him scratches behind his ears. The second she touches Oscar, Felix gets up and lopes over, not in any kind of aggressive way, but definitely in an 'I'm watching to make sure you don't hurt him' kind of way. My mother coos at Felix and slowly extends her hand, which he butts with his big head.

"Who is a pretty boy?" She asks, directing her question at neither one of them specifically. Felix licks her face and Oscar stretches his butt up at her. "They are terrific Ali. And beautiful."

"They are way better than what Julia ended up with. And definitely way better than what Linx wanted me to actually get."

She giggles and lays down on the floor with the animals. They climb on and over her, lick her and rub against her. "What did Linx want you to get?"

"A descented skunk," I say, lowering myself to the floor. Felix gives up on my mom and comes and lays down next to me, putting his big heavy head in my lap. I pet him and wonder if he feels as sad inside at the loss of his family as I do. I lean down and rest my forehead on his head and sigh.

My mom laughs and says, "Oh my God. Gross!"

"Yeah it took about twenty minutes to convince him that wasn't what I really wanted. He was extremely insistent. When I told him I wanted Felix and Oscar he walked around them with his chubby little finger on his chin and asked them if they were going to be good friends to me and help me not be so sad. He then felt the need to explain to Candi, with an I, the bubbly shelter employee who spoke in exclamation points, that Will and Tabby went to Heaven from bad owies and that I was sad so I needed new friends. It was hard to hear how matter of factly he stated it."

My mother rolls up to sitting and says, "Oh Ali. I'm sorry."

"I thought it would be awkward when Linx said that, but despite her extremely annoying personality Candi handled it far better than either Julia or I could have in that moment. She got down on Linx's level and told him that Felix and Oscar's family went to Heaven too, and that they needed not only a new friend, but really needed someone who could take care of them and love them. She told him that Mr. Stinky was really happy at the shelter, but that Felix and Oscar were really sad and needed a family. Linx instantly declared I could have them instead of the skunk."

"God that little boy. And wow Candi did great! So what did Linx get?"

"A pot belly pig," I deadpan.

"Shut up."

"Seriously. His name is Wilson and I'm pretty sure it was love at first sight for both of them."

"Julia actually let him get a pig?"

I chuckle and say, "It wasn't really a matter of 'let'. Linx really didn't give her the option of saying no. He just sort of declared he was getting the pig so it could sleep in his bed. Julia tried to argue for a kitten, but it obviously wasn't effective."

"Aren't pigs...I don't know. Dirty?"

"Apparently not. Pot belly pigs are great pets I guess, and Wilson is even house broken. He walks on a leash too. They were kind of adorable together to be honest."

"I wonder what Ethan is going to think."

"Julia promised to text me when he got home and let me know how he reacted. But honestly, I don't think he's going to care. If Linx is happy and Julia is happy, then Ethan will be happy."

"True," she agreed and then she started laughing again. "I want to meet Wilson. Can you text Julia and see if she's up for company?"

"Sure but first can we have a couple of conversations?"

My mother looks nervous. "Are these conversations I'm going to want to have?"

I laugh and say, "One of them yes, one of them, maybe not."

"Great," she sighs. "Let's do the yes one first."

"Okay. Why don't you have a cat?"

"What?" she asks, clearly startled by the question. She probably thought I was going to ask about Henry. I totally am, but that's the maybe not conversation.

Why don't you have a cat? For as long as I can remember you have been obsessed with kittens, but you've never had one. How come?"

"I don't know actually. I've thought about it, I guess, I've just never done anything about it. But," she strokes Oscar down his back, "I don't know, maybe now I might. Oscar is so sweet. It might be nice to have a cat of my own."

"Well..." I say, "when we were at the shelter today, I might have found a cat that I think is pretty perfect for you. I actually thought about just adopting her for you, but I kind of had my hands full."

She picks Oscar up and settles him in her lap, "What makes her perfect?"

"She's eight, so she's going to be harder to place because she's older. Her family had a new baby and decided they didn't have time for her anymore, so they dumped her at the shelter. She's sad and lonely and confused. They have trouble getting her to eat or interact with any of the shelter staff. She's also gorgeous. She's a white dainty long haired cat with the bluest eyes I've ever seen. Her tail is so fluffy it could be used as a duster. But it's her name that is going to seal the deal for you," I say.

"Oh my heart. What a shit family. That poor kitty." Her eyes tear up and I know I have her. The name will just be the icing on the cake. "What's her name?"

"Princess Diana," I tell her, and I totally know what she is going to say next.

"I think I'll go there tomorrow and make my own new friend."
I do a mini internal victory dance for my mom and the sad Princess Diana. Princess Diana doesn't know it yet, but she hit the new mom motherload.

"I really like Henry," I tell her.

"Yeah?"

"Mom, he's great. He's also absolutely nothing like I pictured. I pictured a tall, skinny, nerdy guy with glasses and a dry sense of humor. I did not picture an older and hotter version of Jax Teller, complete with tattoos and a beard."

She blushes up to her hairline. "I told you he was handsome."

I chuckle, "Mom, that man is *not* handsome. He's hot as fuck."

"Allison!" she chastises.

"He is!" I exclaim. "He's also really nice, extremely interesting, and so freaking into you that I have zero clue how you could have possibly missed it. And he's just as blind, because you might think you're playing it cool, but the fact that you are equally into him is just as obvious."

She slides her eyes to the side and bites her lip and if possible blushes even more. "What?!" I demand.

"He kissed me," she mumbles.

"What?!" I screech startling Felix and Oscar. Oh God, my mother is right. I am twelve.

"After we left here he drove me back to my house and walked me to the door. I did what you said and brushed my hand against his on the walk up to the house. I was so freaking nervous I almost threw up. But when I brushed my hand against his he kind of turned his hand and held mine. When we got to the door he kissed me." She looks so dreamy, and it's so adorable. I feel happy for her but as I search my feelings I find that I do not feel sad for myself, I don't feel jealous, in fact, I don't feel any negative feelings. I'm not sure what this means or even how I feel about what it could potentially mean. I add it to the ever-growing list of things to discuss with Dr. Whitman. The good news about this list I keep adding to is that none of it is really super painful and it will certainly help avoid any huge emotional breakdown in my next therapy appointment. It feels a little bit like housekeeping - just a long list of little things that need to be addressed. I mean, I know we need to discuss Linx and the whole Heaven conversation, but I've discussed that repeatedly with Julia and with my mom, so I'm hoping I'll be okay discussing it with Dr. Whitman.

"Mom! That's so great! I totally knew you guys were into one another. So, what does this mean now? Are you officially dating? Did he spend the night?"

"Oh my God Allison, no! Of course not! He kissed me at the door and then went home. We talked last night and yes, we both have feelings for one another. We decided to date and see how it goes. But we also agreed that jumping into bed isn't a good idea so for now that's not going to happen."

I sigh, "That's disappointing."

She chuckles and says, "I'm sure you'll get over it. Now can you please call Julia so I can go see Wilson?"

I sigh again and call Julia.

CHAPTER EIGHTEEN

I get back from Julia's around one. My mother fell in love with Wilson about two point three seconds after meeting him. Linx was thrilled to be able to introduce Wilson to my mom, and Wilson seemed to have made himself very at home with his new family. Lola showed up at Julia's while my mom and I were there and we had coffee and watched while Linx attempted to teach Wilson to play fetch. There was a lot of laughter and frustrated little boy grunts but very little fetching. Lola followed me back to mine and stayed for a few minutes to meet my new crew before heading home. I spend some time bonding with Felix and Oscar, and then take Felix for a long walk. He walks great on a leash and was really happy to walk around the neighborhood.

When I get back from walking Felix I take my laptop to the sofa and dive into the new book in my email that I've been eager to read. I edit for a few hours and don't even notice the time passing until my stomach starts to growl loudly. I stop and feed Felix, let him out into the backyard for a potty break and order some take out Chinese. While I'm waiting for my dinner to arrive I whip up a quick batch of oatmeal chocolate chip cookies and toss them in the oven to bake. I check on Felix and Oscar and find them on the downstairs dog bed. Felix curled up in the bed and Oscar curled up on top of Felix, both of them sound asleep. I smile at them and sigh contentedly at my decision to adopt them.

As I'm cleaning up from the cookies my phone rings and I see that it's Julia. I can't wait to hear how Ethan reacted to the addition of Wilson.

"Are you, Linx and Wilson homeless?" I tease.

She laughs and says, "Nah, he took it like a champ. Actually, he didn't seem all that surprised, which I found really disappointing. I mean after seven years together I get that I'm not a font of mysteries, but I bought a fucking pig. Not even a pig, it's a damn house pig. Doesn't that at least warrant a raised eyebrow and the threat of divorce?"

"If it makes you feel any better I would absolutely have threatened to divorce you."

"Thank you."

"What are friends for? So he really had zero reaction?"

"Literally none. He got home from work and Linx ran to meet him at the door, Wilson following right behind him. Ethan picked him up, looked down at Wilson, looked at Linx, then at me and fucking grinned. Then he proceeded to sit on the floor and play with the pig while he and Linx giggled their heads off. I had a whole spiel prepared about boys and their pigs and everything."

"Boys and their pigs?" I asked, laughing.

"Well I took some liberties with the whole 'boys and their dogs' thing," she defended.

"Obviously," I replied.

"Yup and it was all for nothing. I mean, after the initial introduction he had some questions, but they were more along the lines of 'how do we take care of Wilson' and not 'do I need to have you committed'. I told him I was disappointed that he didn't at least ask if I was insane."

"He knew that when he married you. I don't think he needs to ask a question he already knows the answer to Jules."

"Ha ha. That's exactly what he said," she pouts.

I laugh and say, "Sorry. Really sorry, but also so very true."

She makes a hmph noise and then I hear her call "Okay be right there. Hey Al? I have to go. Apparently Ethan and Linx taught Wilson a trick that I have to see. I'll talk to you tomorrow, okay? Oh! And before I forget again, thank you. Those books were amazing. They helped so much and I meant to tell you this morning but I forgot."

"You are very welcome. I'm so glad they helped. Okay text me tomorrow. Enjoy the piggy show!"

With perfect timing, we hang up as my food arrives and I take a container of veggie lo mein and some chopsticks back to my laptop and work on the book some more. I have a pretty good track record for guessing how successful one of my author's books is going to be, and I know for sure, without a doubt, that this one is going to be a bestseller and do it quickly. The timer for the cookies beeps and I transfer them to a cooling rack. While I'm waiting for them to cool I decide to take a break from the book and check the grief forum. There's a five on the little envelope in the corner so I click on it. It takes me to the post I commented on the other night and I see there's a reply from the dad, whose username is InsomniacCoffee, plus four other responses to my comment.

1353 InsomniacCoffee: I'm so sorry for your loss. I'm glad that you found this forum. I know when our daughter first passed away, my wife and I found a lot of comfort doing exactly what you are doing now - reading the stories of others who had been where we found ourselves. We were fortunate, and I use that term very loosely, that we knew what was coming. It certainly doesn't change the loss, or the level of grief, but the ability to say goodbye, to know it was going to happen, while horrific during, was a blessing after. I'm sorry that you didn't have that. This is the second year we are doing something on the anniversary. The first several we always went to the cemetery, but then just spent the whole day being depressed and crying. I know when you lose someone you love everyone has advice, most of which is unwanted, but I'll give you some unsolicited advice anyway. Advice I wish someone had given us - do something on the anniversary. Something special that you had on your family bucket list, or something that you can do to give back in their name. Whatever you choose, do something. Don't sit at home and wallow in your grief. It's a horrible day but I promise that doing something "with" them or for them honestly makes a huge difference in how horrible the day actually is. Also, we are all here whenever or if you are ever ready to post your own story.

The other four responses were from people whose usernames I don't recognize but who all offer some variation on the same advice - do something on the day of the anniversary. One woman posted that every year on the anniversary of her husband's death, going on ten years now, she volunteers at a soup kitchen her husband volunteered at every other Sunday while he was alive. She wrote that she has been remarried for six years, and her new husband joins her to honor her husband who passed away. A mom who lost her teenage son to suicide volunteers once a month at the suicide hotline and always makes sure to schedule herself on the anniversary of his death. There's also a woman who posted that she and her fourteen-year-old son spend every anniversary of her husband, his dad's, death checking something off their family bucket list. They take a photo of the dad and bring him with them. So far they have gone to Blue Man Group, The Aerospace Museum, a cruise to the Bahamas and an African safari. She said they even take vacation photos of themselves with his picture so they can feel like he's "with" them. She said that celebrating their family makes the day something they look forward to as a way to honor his memory rather than something they dread. The last person to comment said that she's had nine miscarriages and has never been able to successfully carry a child to term. She said that on the anniversary of every miscarriage and the anniversary of every due date she and her husband rocks babies in the NICU. She said that most of the babies they comfort are drug babies who end up in the foster care system, and that after nine miscarriages and a lot of therapy and time since the last one, that they are finally in a healthy place mentally and have signed up to be foster parents. They are hoping to adopt one of those babies abandoned in the NICU by parents whose addiction illness makes them unable to be parents.

I cry as I read these, and Felix comes and sits next to me and puts his head in my lap. I absently pet his head and marvel at how lucky I am that no one who went to that shelter noticed how sweet and loving Felix is. Oscar, not wanting to be left out, jumps up on the sofa next to me and lays down up against my thigh, his purring soothing me. I pet both of my new family members while I try to think of a way I can honor my family on the anniversary of their death. They didn't die of cancer, or suicide or spend time volunteering somewhere I can take over. Nor did we ever really have time to make a family bucket list I could do on my own in their memory.

I remind myself that I still have time, and I already have it on my list of things to discuss with Dr. Whitman when I have my next appointment, so I box it up, and set it aside. I get up and grab a mug of hot chocolate, four cookies, because yum, and go back to the sofa and the book I'm editing. I get sucked in and before I know it it's after midnight. This book is a winner in so many ways, and I'm desperate to get to the end, but I'm tired and I know that the editing will suffer if I don't stop now.

I let Felix out for one more potty break and shut down the downstairs. I head upstairs and the animals follow behind me. I stop at Tabby's door and press a kiss to it, now a nightly ritual. I take a quick shower and walk back into the bedroom to find Felix and Oscar curled up in the middle of the bed. I chuckle and walk over to the bed, hands on my hips.

"Guys, this is not the plan. Felix, you have a doggie bed over here." I call him repeatedly and he finally lumbers to standing and jumps off the bed. I get him settled in his dog bed, Oscar moving from the bed to where Felix is, and then I climb into the bed alone.   I tell Will all about my trip to the shelter, and whisper introductions to him and Felix and Oscar. I tell him that I absolutely love whoever named them because they did so spectacularly. I mean, really? What else could have possibly been more perfect? I crack up when I tell him about Linx and Wilson, and then laugh even harder when I describe Julia's disappointment at Ethan's non-reaction.

"I kept trying to imagine how you would have reacted to the same situation, but I feel like I would have been just as disappointed as Julia. I'm not so sure you would have reacted any differently than Ethan did," I tell Will.

I tell him about the comments on the forum and how I'm trying to think of something to do on the anniversary of their passing to honor them but that I'm having trouble coming up with ideas.

"I wish you could help me come up with something, but if you were here I wouldn't need to do that would I?" I feel the tears come and let them fall. I curl into a protective ball and sob. I hear unfamiliar movement and for a moment it scares me, but then I hear the jangle of Felix's collar and remember I am not alone now. I bounce a little as Felix jumps up on the bed. He pushes his nose into my face, licks my cheek and then lays down next to me as close as he can get. I realize he heard me crying and came to comfort me which only makes me cry harder. I wrap my arm around him and sob into his fur. I feel Oscar walking around on the pillow above my head and feel him settle into my neck. I cry myself to sleep surrounded by two animals I didn't know I needed as badly as I did until that moment.

I wake up feeling heat and pressure along my back and a gentle vibration against my stomach. My eyes are crusty and my throat hurts. I stretch as much as I can which, given the lack of space, isn't much. The movement wakes the animals and they stretch too and then climb off the bed. Felix stands at the side of the bed staring at me, which I guess is an indication that he would like me to get up and take care of both of them. I do my business in the bathroom and go downstairs. I let Felix out into the backyard, and mentally add calling a pooper scooper company to schedule weekly backyard pickups. I'll pick up the occasional poop on a walk, but I know myself well enough to know that there's no way I'm going to routinely patrol the backyard looking for poop. Plus, I learned a horrifyingly disgusting fact when I took Felix on a walk yesterday - Great Dane poops are HUGE!

I fill their food and water bowls and then make coffee. After I let Felix back in, I decide to make myself breakfast. I don't typically eat breakfast but along with every other thing in my life that is changing, I'm finding that my appetite is slowly coming back. I make Turkish eggs, which are essentially poached eggs over an herbed yogurt with a chili spiced butter. I don't mind a little heat, but the original recipe calls for more chili than I can handle so I typically tone it down with a little sweet paprika. I take my coffee and breakfast to the living room and sit down with my laptop.

I spend the next several hours being completely dazzled by this thriller. I have read and edited dozens upon dozens of psychological thrillers and this one had twists I never could have seen coming. I'm beyond excited for this author and for the readers who are going to get to read it once it's ready. I still have to go through it for a second edit, but that won't take very long and then I can send it to the publisher once the author looks at the edits I recommended. I send a quick email to the author and fangirl over the novel. I let them know it should be ready to send back to them in the next day or two.

I stand and stretch and decide that I need a break and Felix probably needs a walk. I change out of my pajamas, one of the perks of working from home, into a pair of loose denim overalls and a kelly green tight tee shirt. I slip on a pair of black flip flops and grab Felix's leash. I take him for a walk around the neighborhood and wander to a local dog park that I had never noticed before. I'm not really sure how dog parks work, so I observe for a couple of minutes. There are only a handful of dogs here, and none of them seem particularly interested in us. Felix just sits by my feet and seems to be observing with me. A beautiful Golden Retriever runs over and stops about ten feet from us, barks at Felix once and then runs in a circle. It repeats the process two more times. I look down at Felix who looks up at me. I shrug because what the hell do I know. I unhook his leash and hope I'm doing the right thing.

Felix walks over to the Golden but stops about three feet away and just looks at her.

"She's friendly," a male voice calls and I turn. There's a guy in khaki shorts and a white tee shirt approaching me. He's about five foot ten and really good looking. He's got shaggy brown hair, a clean-shaven face and glasses. He waves as he gets closer. "I'm Max and that's Daisy," he introduces.

"Ali, and that's Felix. I, ummm, just got him yesterday so I'm not really sure how this works. He's super sweet and the shelter said he is good with other dogs but I have no experience with how dog parks work."

He calls Daisy to his side and tells her to sit. "Well Daisy is a great dog for him to start with," he says. "Do you mind?"

"Umm no, you can," I wave my hand between the dogs, "do whatever."

He calls Felix over and Daisy sits as Felix sniffs her. Then he backs up, woofs, and turns in a circle. Max nods to Daisy and she races over to Felix, runs around him and then runs away. She stops, turns and looks at him, barks once and runs a little further. Felix catches on and runs after her. They chase each other around while Max and I watch.

"So you just got Felix yesterday?" Max asks.

"What? Oh, yeah. I adopted him and a cat he was bonded to. They are really sweet together." I know this is just a casual conversation but I suddenly feel super uncomfortable. With the exception of Henry, I haven't had a real conversation with a man since Will died. "Oh cool. He's a nice looking dog. It's too bad his family put him in a shelter."

I bristle at that statement and feel instantly defensive of Felix and Oscar's family. "Actually," I say a little snottily, "they died in a tragic accident and no one in either one of their families could take them in."

He looks properly chastised and I instantly feel bad. Great! More guilt.

"Oh damn! That sucks," he says. Then he brightens and smiles and says, "But hey! You got to have them so that's cool."

Oh my God! Did he really just imply that it's cool their family died tragically so I could benefit from their deaths? He did. He pretty much just said that. Suddenly I don't feel an ounce of guilt. I call Felix over to me and clip on his leash. "We need to go," I say in a rush. "Have a good day." I led Felix away when Max calls my name. I turn and look at him.

"Think I could get your number? Maybe we could get a drink or something?" Max asks.

I hold up my left hand and say "Sorry, no." I turn and Felix and I leave the dog park. I whisper under my breath to Will "Stop laughing. It's not even remotely funny."

When we get back Oscar meets us at the door meowing his displeasure at both of us having left him alone for longer than five minutes. I bend down and pet him and apologize, while Felix gives him licks on his face. This appears to placate Oscar and he saunters away, his tail twitching.

I wash my hands in the kitchen sink and then bake up a batch of the lemon basil tarts I made the other night. Then I pack them up and head over to MUD.

I pull the door open and am greeted by the scent of sugar and coffee. MUD is quiet, so I clearly have great timing. Valerie is behind the counter and calls hello to me when I walk in.

"Hey Valerie," I say as I approach the counter. "I brought you something," I hold up the box the tarts are in.

"Really? No one ever brings me anything. Usually they come here to get something."

I laugh and tell her about the tarts I made the other night. "I thought you might like to try one. I can give you the recipe if you want."

Valerie's eyes light up. "Oh gimme," she says, reaching out and making grabby hands. She takes the box and opens it. "Oh damn Ali, these are beautiful. The candied lemon circles are perfect." She picks one out and takes a bite and moans indecently. "Holy shit. These are amazing."

I smile at her. I knew she would like them. "Yay! I'm so glad you think so."

She shoves the rest of the tart in her mouth and mumbles something unintelligible. I wait while she chews and swallows for her to repeat herself. "I need the recipe. These might be one of the best desserts I have ever had. I want to make some for tomorrow and see how they do. Do you mind?"

I chuckle "No of course not. That's why I brought them. Hang on," I fish my phone out of my purse and text her the recipe.

"Awesome," she says. "Hang on a second, I'll be right back." She disappears into the back and returns about three minutes later carrying a chocolate brown box with MUD across the top in yellow. "Goat cheese tarts, raspberry lemon squares and lavender honey scones," she says handing me the box.

"Val seriously? You didn't have to do that," I say, taking the box of offered treats.

"I know, but I really love those lemon basil tarts and this is my way of saying thanks. I think they will be a huge hit tomorrow for sure!"

"Well thanks! I guess I know what I'm having for dinner tonight."

She laughs and says, "I'm very familiar with that kind of dinner. Seriously though, thanks again. Come in tomorrow if you have time and let me know if mine are even close to as good as yours."

"Umm I'm pretty sure they will be a million times better. I'll definitely come by so be sure to save me one," I say as I carry my box and head out the door.

"Hey Al," my mom says when I answer the phone the next morning. "Guess what?"

"Would you ask if I am twelve again if I say 'chicken butt'?" I ask.

She laughs and says, "No. I would ask if you were five."

"Fair enough. Umm, you went to the shelter?"

"I did," she confirms. "First of all, can I just say that Candi is...energetic."

"Mom, that is like saying grass is green."

She laughs again and says, "I have never met someone so excitable. And she was beyond thrilled when I told her that I was there to adopt Princess Diana. I told her who I was and she asked how you and Felix and Oscar were doing. She also asked how Linx and Wilson were doing. She's a lot, but she's also very sweet."

I agree, "Yes, she is. I mean, I definitely couldn't spend an extended amount of time with her but she is a sweet girl. So you adopted Princess Di?"

"I did. I took one look at her and knew you were right. It took about fifteen minutes to coax her to the front of her cage so I could pet her, but I was patient and talked to her softly the entire time and eventually she came forward enough so I could pet her. The second I started she climbed out of the cage and into my lap and started purring. I thought Candi was going to cry."

"Aww that's so great. How's she doing now that you have her home? Is she hiding?"

"Actually, no. I thought she would, and Candi told me to expect that, but she's been following me everywhere I go. She doesn't seem in distress or anything - she's not meowing or crying or whatever. She just seems to want to be wherever I am. She also ate, which I know the shelter was having trouble getting her to do."

"This makes me so happy," I say, and then I sigh. "Mom, would it sound crazy if I told you that I've been mostly happy the past couple of days and that that makes me feel unhappy?"

"Crazy? No. But tell me why it makes you unhappy to be happy."

I take a deep breath. "Everything feels like it's happening too fast. I've been in therapy for a little over two months and in those two months my emotions have changed so fast that I feel unstable. I mean, I went from a level of fury that seemed incomprehensible, to the deepest most profound grief possible. Then I started to do things because Dr. Whitman gave me assignments, and I enjoyed them, which made me feel guilty, so I cried more. But I also felt happy doing some of those things, so I did more things that made me happy, like dinner with the girls, the museum with you. I am still really sad, but I'm also happier this week than I have been in the last eight months. It just all feels like it's happening too fast. I didn't believe Dr. Whitman when she said part of the grieving process is the healing process because when she told me that everything was still so raw, and my grief was still too new. But clearly she was right and healing happens even if you don't notice it's happening, and that makes me feel unhappy."

"But why Al? I mean, we've talked about this before, but I'll say it again, Will and Tabby would *want* you to be happy. They would want you to laugh and enjoy life. So are you unhappy because you're happy, or are you unhappy because you think being happy is happening too quickly?"

I start to cry and then choke out "Yes."

"Honey, that was a two-part question. Yes isn't really an answer," she says gently.

I sniffle and say "It's happening too fast. And I yeah, I finally do believe they would want me to be happy, but this week I've been more happy than sad and that feels so fucking wrong."

"Beautiful girl, there is no timetable for what is acceptable for sadness or happiness. You are healing and moving forward in the way that is exactly right for you. Do you know how I know?"

"No," I pretty much whine.

"Because you're doing it. Dr. Whitman may have given you some assignments to get you started, but you took it upon yourself to do more things. Allison, look at all the things you did this week. You supported Julia through telling Linx about Tabby. You did that. And you did it because you wanted to be there for both of them. Even though it hurt you to do it, you did it anyway. Do you not even see how amazing that is? You had Henry and I over for dinner and talked about books and food. You laughed and joked and I never once saw a shadow of sadness pass over your face. We went to a museum, and yes, we had an emotional conversation in the car, but after that the whole day was about art and having a good time. You adopted two pets because you recognized you were lonely and wanted to fill that void. You are living your life, and baby girl it is beautiful to see. But more than that, it's the way things are supposed to be and I'm so proud of you."

"Okay I get what you are saying, but Mom, look at this week compared to last week. It's insane that things changed that quickly. Like, I don't even understand how it's possible to go from a crying disaster, to this person I am this week."

"Ali, I don't know the answer. I have never been where you are. It's not the same at all, but when your dad left me it took me about four months to crawl out of my hole and start living again. And I didn't have the benefit of therapy helping me do that. It just sort of happened." She takes a deep breath and continues, "I don't think there is a timeline for grief. I think it's different for everyone. But it's not like you woke up this week and declared 'Hey I'm not sad anymore'. You still have really sad moments, and that's to be expected. But it's also to be expected that you will have more and more really happy ones. You can't be tragically sad forever Al. I don't think the human mind works like that."

I take a minute to get my crying under control and then I mumble "That's what Dr. Whitman said. That I can't be sad forever."

"Well how about this. You can be sad right now. Take as much time as you need to cry and be sad. And then why don't you come over and we can go shopping. We can make a day of it. We can get some new clothes, get mani/pedis, shop and then have an early dinner. How does that sound?"

I sniff a couple of times and use the base of my palms to wipe my eyes. "Umm okay. Yeah, that sounds nice. Do you think Felix will be okay though?"

"He's housebroken right? He doesn't have accidents at night?"

"No he's totally fine at night. I guess it will be alright. I'm going to have to find out at some point I guess. Right?"

"Right," she agrees.

I sigh and say, "Alright. Can we leave in like an hour? I need to walk him and get ready, and I think I need a little more time to cry too."

"You take all the time you need Al. Call me when you are ready and I'll come pick you up. I love you sweet girl."

"I love you too," I say and hang up. Then I sink to the floor and sob at the unfairness of everything and at the guilt from letting go a little more each day. When I'm done, I get up and get ready to do more things that make me happy.

CHAPTER NINETEEN

I arrive at Dr. Whitman's office for my next appointment excited to tell her about my week. I'm wearing one of the new outfits I bought while shopping with my mom, and I have to admit it's nice to wear clothing that actually fit me properly. I have on a pair of low-rise beige cargo pants and a tight black silky tee shirt. I have on my trusty black flip flops and my hair is in a sloppy bun. Today Dr. Whitman is wearing a pair of black leggings with a short-sleeved navy smock dress with gray elephants and big pink flowers printed on it with black wedge sandals. I really need to know where she gets these dresses but don't ask. I feel like it might be a little creepy to tell her about my ongoing obsession with the dresses she wears.

I have a lot of things to tell her and ask her about so last night I made a list. I run through my week, the good and the bad, and manage to tell her everything without breaking down. The only thing I didn't bring up was how I was going to manage the anniversary and upcoming birthdays. I decided I wanted to try and spend a little more time thinking about those on my own before I ask for help. Dr. Whitman tells me how impressed she is with all that I have done, and even goes so far as to tell me she is proud of me, which was really nice to hear. We talk about some of the questions I have, and her answers are basically the same as my mom's, just more clinical.

"You have really done amazing work on your grief Allison. And you have come very far in your healing process as well. But there is still really hard work to be done, and I'm sorry to say that is going to start today."

I freeze in my seat. What else can there be? I mean, yes I have birthdays and the anniversaries and holidays I'll actually be aware of coming up, but what other hard things can there possibly be? I think of the one thing we haven't ever discussed, only because she has never asked, but even that I think I can manage. I decide to beat her to the punch and ask, "Do you want me to go to the cemetery?"

Dr. Whitman blinks at me, "What?" She looks surprised which I find surprising. I thought this was where she was going with this.
I shrug and say, "The cemetery. Is that my next assignment? I haven't been since the funeral, and you said there's really hard work to still do, and that's the only thing I can think of in my life that we haven't addressed."

"Actually, no. I had that planned for closer to the anniversary date. I'm actually surprised you brought it up, but that shows me how far you really have progressed. You heard me say we still had hard work to do, and you volunteered what is likely the hardest thing you can think of. Physically confronting the proof that they are gone."

I feel the tears sting my eyes and nod my head, "I know they are gone. I just haven't been ready to go to their graves. But if that's not it, then what other hard thing could there be?"

Dr. Whitman crosses her legs and gently says, "Tell me about Justin."

"What?"

"Justin. Tell me about him."

"Why? I don't understand what Justin has to do with my grieving process. Or my healing process," I say, truly confused.   "Yes, Justin is the reason this all happened, but he has nothing to do with my moving forward or dealing with my loss."

"I think he does, and I think it's important to talk about him. Does it make you angry that I asked?"

I shake my head, "Surprisingly, no. I'm just confused as to why he matters."

She nods, "Okay, so it doesn't make you angry that I asked, and the lack of anger surprises you. Tell me about that."

I shrug, "I honestly have no idea. It seems like I have no control over my emotions anymore. If you had asked me three weeks ago if talking about him would piss me off, my answer would have been yes. I hate him. I hate him with every fiber of my being. He took everything that matters from me. But...okay you know those flip books?" I ask her.

"Flip books? The ones that have a drawing on each page and you zip through it quickly and it forms an image moving?"

I nod, "Yes, those," I confirm. "My life feels like that. Each page is an emotion and the more work I do with you in therapy the faster the pages turn. Sometimes I feel like I'm healing too quickly, like we discussed when I got here. Three weeks ago you asking about Justin would have hurt too much to talk about and would have pissed me off. Now I just don't know why he matters beyond the obvious."

"That makes sense. So if you can talk about him, even if you don't understand why, tell me about him."

I sit back in my chair and fiddle with my thumb nail. It's a bright berry color which is a departure from my normal pale pink, but I like it because it's different. I sigh and ask "What do you want to know?"

"What do you know about him?"

I shrug, "He was an eighteen-year-old high school senior. He was on his way home from football practice and was texting his mother to let her know he was running late. He ran a red light and t-boned Will's car in between the driver's door and the passenger door. Tabby was in her car seat behind Will. He hit them both." I say this all matter of factly.

Dr. Whitman is about to say something, when I interrupt her, "Why can I do that?"

"Do what?"

"Tell you that, but do it without emotion. Like, talking to Julia about Tabby going to Heaven hurt more than I would have thought possible. But this, it feels almost clinical."

"What would happen if you saw Justin as a person?" she asks.

I blink a few times because that question throws me. "I don't understand. What do you mean?"

"Alright, a better question is, do you see him as a person?"

"Not as one who matters I guess."

"Okay, so he's not a person who matters. What about his family? Do they matter?"

I shake my head, "I actually thought about this a few weeks ago. When I first joined the grief group. There was a woman who posted that her family had died in a car crash with a drunk driver. He also died and I was jealous because she didn't have to live knowing the person who killed her family was still alive. Logically I know that Justin has a mother who loves him and would be devastated if he died, but I don't care. So I guess the answer is no, they don't matter."

"So if Justin isn't a person who matters, a person with value, and his family doesn't matter, then it makes sense that talking about him isn't emotional, just factual."

"It feels weird. Like I should have more emotions or feelings discussing him."

"I have a theory about that, but first I'm going to ask you a really difficult question and I want you to really think about it before you respond. Don't just give me the first answer that comes to your mind, because that will be an emotional answer. Can you do that?"

"Umm," I hedge, "maybe?"

She nods and chuckles, "Fair enough. Do you think Justin intended to hurt your family? Did he get drunk or high or drive recklessly with no thought to the people on the road with him?"

I bite my tongue because instinctively I want to say yes, but Dr. Whitman asked me to think about my answer and after so many weeks I trust her, so I do what she asked. After a minute I answer, "No. He wasn't drunk or high, and the police said he wasn't speeding either."

"Did he have any kind of police record?"

I shake my head, "Not that I know of. The police never said anything and neither did the D.A. when they discussed the case with me."

"Did it go to trial?"

"No, thankfully. He pled guilty to negligent homicide and received three and a half to seven years in prison. According to the D.A. that means he must serve three and a half but the max he will serve is seven. I was furious because that's nothing, but I wasn't asked and didn't get a say. I don't think it is nearly enough time, but I am glad that there was no trial. I'm in a much healthier place now than I was back then, and even now I wouldn't be able to handle a trial. When everything was so fresh I definitely wouldn't have been able to handle it. I was so angry, that it scares me to think about what I might have been capable of having to see him every day."

Dr. Whitman regards me and then asks, "Have you ever done anything you wish you could take back that hurt someone?" She does this often - asks a question that in her head is relevant to the conversation we are having, but to me just feels like a sudden and random topic change.

"I used the last of the milk that day."

"I'm sorry, what?"

"That morning, I gave Tabby cereal and used the last of the milk. I had planned on making meatloaf and mashed potatoes for dinner because it was Will's favorite, so I figured I would just stop and get more milk while we were out that day." I take a breath and take a tissue from the box on the table next to me. Tears stream down my face as I recount how I am to blame for my family dying. "But then on the way home from the park Tabby was crabby and I didn't feel like dealing with a cranky toddler in the grocery store so I took her home instead. I was going to ask Will to pick some up on his way home, but it completely slipped my mind. When he got home he offered to go out and I asked him to take Tabby with him so I could have thirty minutes to myself. They never came home." I'm sobbing in earnest now. "I was selfish and stupid and I put my needs above theirs multiple times that day and it cost me my family."

Dr. Whitman scoots to the edge of her chair and reaches forward and squeezes my hand, "Oh Allison, there's no way you could have known. It was a normal day in a normal family doing normal family things."

I shake my head vehemently, "But if..."

"'But if' is a dangerous game," she interrupts. "You could go back day after day after day playing that game."

"I know that but it's hard not to. If I had done one thing differently, I would still have my family."

"Were any of the choices or decisions you made that day cruel? Hateful? Malicious?"

I shake my head vehemently, tears flying off my cheeks at the force of it, "No, of course not. They were normal decisions I've made a hundred times." I slap my hand over my mouth and stare at Dr. Whitman who is nodding.

"Exactly. You made normal everyday decisions that you've made plenty of times before without anyone dying. There was absolutely no reason to think that day would have been any different."

I cry for a couple of minutes thinking about what she said. I work on getting my tears under control and once I seem to have a handle on things Dr. Whitman continues. "Now, have you ever done something that hurt someone that you wish you could take back?"

I think about this and inwardly cringe because I know Dr. Whitman well enough by now to know where this conversation is going to lead, and I know the answer will cause me to question everything. It's funny how quickly the brain can skip ahead from point A to point B to point C in the blink of an eye.

I take a deep breath and bite my lips between my teeth, nodding. Dr. Whitman patiently waits while I prepare emotionally for where this conversation is going to go. "When I was sixteen," I start, "I had a fight with my mother. It was over something stupid but when you are sixteen everything is a major catastrophe." I pause for a few seconds, and then continue, "I had had my license for about two months, and in my anger I didn't check the mirrors properly while I was backing out of the driveway. I was also changing the CD at the same time." I stop because I do not want to share what happened next.

Dr. Whitman nods and asks, "What happened next?"

My eyes slide to the side and I say "My neighbor Mrs. De Luca, actually my friend Sasha's mom, was out walking, and as I backed out of the driveway I hit her. She was okay, bruised and scared, but nothing was broken or anything."

"How did you react? How did you feel?"

"Oh my God I felt awful. I cried more than she did. I was afraid to drive for months afterward, and I brought her dinner I made myself every night for two weeks, until she finally asked me to stop. She told me she knew it wasn't on purpose and that she forgave me. She told me it was a tough lesson to learn, but that it would make me a much more careful driver. She wasn't wrong about that."

"Alright," she starts, "So, I know I just said the 'But if' game is dangerous, but in this case it's not a desperation to change the past, but more of an examination of what could have been. Do you understand the difference?"

I nod. "Okay," she continues, "so what if it had been an elderly neighbor? What do you think might have happened to them?"

"They probably would have broken a hip or fell and hit their head. They definitely would have been more hurt than just a bruise."

She nods in agreement and asks, "What if it had been a child running down the sidewalk ahead of a parent? Do you think they would have been okay?"

I swallow hard, and whisper, "No. They would have been badly hurt, maybe even killed."

"Allison, listen to me carefully because this isn't going..."

"I already know what you are going to say," I interrupt. I stand and pace. "You're going to say that I made a careless and stupid choice when I was sixteen. I didn't mean to hurt anyone, but I wasn't paying attention like I should have been, and I did," I bit out. "The difference between Justin and I is that I was fortunate enough to only hurt someone, but that it very easily could have been me that killed someone. Right?"

"Yes," she confirms, "although I would have used gentler words. Do you know the saying, 'There but for the grace of God go I'?"

I nod, "Yeah of course."

"I don't bring it up for religious reasons, but more because it is a common colloquialism. Tell me what you think it means."

I stop pacing and move to stand by the window. I stare out at the bright blue sky and say, "It means that one small change and I would have been someone's Justin." I turn and look at her, my arms crossed over my chest, "You think I shouldn't blame him? That he isn't responsible for killing my family?"

"Absolutely not. That isn't what I am saying at all." She nods her head in the direction of my chair and says, "Allison, come sit. Please."

I move back to my chair and sit on the edge. I haven't felt this way since my first appointment with Dr. Whitman. I'm not angry exactly, but I'm uncomfortable and restless and feel irritable.

"You are exactly right that one small change and you could have been someone else's Justin. And if the situation had been different you would have been just as guilty as he is. But what would you have been guilty of Allison?"

"Of killing someone."

She nods, "Yes, okay. But with intention? With purpose?"

"No, of course not. I was angry with my mom and not paying attention. I was playing with the CD player when I should have been watching out my back window. I didn't mean to hit my neighbor, and I wouldn't have meant it if it had been an elderly person or a child either. It would have been an accident." That word - that word that I hate so much - it's like a punch to the gut. Because it's true. I start to sob uncontrollably. Dr. Whitman waits for me patiently.

"You told me several sessions ago that you hate the word accident," she says, matter of factly.

I nod through my tears, "I did. I do," I affirm.

"But you just said it was an accident that you hit your neighbor and would have been an accident if you had hit a child or older person."

"Yes," I choke out. "I didn't mean to hit her."

"No, of course not. And you weren't drunk or high, selfishly disregarding the lives of others. You were not going a hundred miles per hour down the highway risking every person you passed. You were also sixteen, not thirty. Do you think that makes a difference?"

"I don't know. Maybe?"

"So why do you hate the word accident in relation to what happened to Will and Tabby? Do you think Justin purposely drove through the intersection? Do you think he made a conscious decision to kill your family?"

I dig my fingernails into my palm. This is exactly where I knew she was going to go, and I don't know how to make it stop. It's like being on a roller coaster and we are climbing the biggest hill, and I know that it's too late to get off and the drop off is going to make my stomach fall. "He was texting and driving. He wasn't paying attention."

"You were playing with the CD player and weren't paying attention," she counters.

"It's not the same thing," I shout.

"Why? Why is it different?" she challenges.

"Because they died!" I shout again. Then I cover my face with my hands and dissolve into tears.

"They did," Dr. Whitman says softly. "And I'm so very sorry for you for that. And I am in no way saying that you need to forgive Justin. But I do think that part of the reason you speak about him in a clinical manner is because if you spoke about him in an emotional one, if you saw him as a person who matters, then you would also need to consider how what happened is also affecting him. Think of how guilty you just told me you felt hitting your neighbor. I imagine Justin feels exponentially worse, don't you?"

"Why do I have to care how he feels? Why does it matter?"

"It's not that you have to care how he feels. But he matters in this because part of the grieving and healing process is dealing with how you feel about him. I think that part of you needs to hate him and hold him to a different standard than you would have held yourself to, because if you see him in the same light that you saw yourself, then there would be no reason Will and Tabby died. Because then it would just be a pointless accident caused by a poor decision by an otherwise good kid."

I shake my head and stand up. "Is our time up? I want to leave," I announce. I feel like a cornered animal and I'm desperate to leave. I don't want to hear this anymore and I'm not ready to process why or what it means.

She regards me and then nods, pushing up to stand. "Yes Allison, our time is up. But I have an assignment for you. I want you to write Justin a letter." She holds up her hand to stop me from interrupting, "Wait," she says. "You do not have to mail it. It does not have to be nice or forgiving. It can be mean and nasty if you want. The only thing it must be is honest. However that comes about. Alright?"

I glare at her, and for the first time since I started therapy with her, I think I hate Dr. Whitman. I hate her for making me question how I feel about someone I have vilified for months. I do not want to see him as a kid who made a poor choice. I want to be able to hate him without feeling guilty about it, or thinking about how he is dealing with living with the knowledge that he killed two people.

"Allison, okay?"

"Yes," I say harshly. "Fine. I'll write the damn letter."

She nods. I wonder if she is used to patients being angry at her when she pushes them past their comfort zones. I decide she probably is.

I take my card for my next appointment and silently stalk out the door, wondering if I lied to Dr. Whitman, and if this will be the first assignment that I flat out refuse to do.

CHAPTER TWENTY

I walk into my kitchen and slam my purse on the counter. Felix follows me and woofs at my display of frustration. I crouch down in front of him and give him pets, assuring him everything is okay. Not wanting to be left out, Oscar runs over and hops onto my thighs. I give my new friends some love and cuddles to help settle them, and in return they do the same for me.

I try to process how I'm feeling, but I'm too conflicted to deal with it myself. It's a giant jumble of emotions and I am having trouble making sense of them. I mentally run down a list of people I can talk to about this - my mom, obviously, Julia, Lola and the girls, and the grief forum. I haven't posted on there yet, but that might be the best place to start since so many of them actually understand my loss, versus my mom and friends who simply want to be there for me but don't fully understand what I'm going through.

I make a cup of tea and take my tea and laptop to the kitchen table. I log into the grief forum and click on the 'Post New Topic' icon. A text box opens, and I sit and stare at it for several minutes. I start to type several times and backspace to clear the text. I take a deep breath and tell myself it's time. I need advice and these are the best people to give it to me.

1124 Oizys writes: I have been a reader on this forum for several weeks now, and with the exception of one comment, I have never been able to bring myself to post my story. I'm not even sure how to do it or where to start. I just know I need to talk about something, and while my friends and family would try to understand, they can't really know what I'm feeling like you all can. This past November my husband and three-year-old daughter were killed in a car crash. I spent the first six months furious at the whole world. I drove away everyone in my life except my mother, and that wasn't for lack of trying. I buried my grief so deep under my anger that I never even cried. Not when I got the news, not at the funeral, not for six months. In those first six months I cut out any and everything that could potentially bring me any kind of joy. I never cried, but I never laughed or smiled either. I wrapped myself in my anger and just kept feeding it. My mother more or less forced me into therapy and that's when things started to change. My therapist is...amazing. She would end each therapy session with an assignment. I did them, but I never understood the point of them except the first one. For the first one she had me buy a ton of second-hand ceramic dishes and then take them outside and smash them against the fence. It shattered something in me and all of the grief I had been holding in exploded to the surface. I cried more in those first days after the fence assignment than I have ever cried in my life. She gave me rules to follow during coffee with friends, she had me start sleeping in my bed, cooking family favorite meals...little by little, week by week, she gave me new assignments and built on previous ones and before I realized what was happening I was living again. I go out with friends now, I do things with my mother, I laugh...I mean, I still cry...a LOT, but I'm living again. Today we talked about the car crash. My family was killed by a high school senior on his way home from football practice. He was texting his mother to let her know he was going to be late, and ran a red light and hit my husband's car. He wasn't speeding or drinking or doing drugs. But I have spent the last eight and a half months vilifying him and hating him with a passion. He took a plea deal and is in prison, but I don't think he got nearly enough time. Today we talked about him for the first time. While we were discussing him she asked me if I had ever done anything in my life that hurt someone that I wish I could take back. I told her when I was 16 I was backing out of the driveway after a fight with my mom, and was paying more attention to the CD player than the mirrors and I backed into a neighbor out for a walk. We talked about what would have happened if it had been an elderly person or a child running down the sidewalk, and she pointed out that I could so easily be where the kid who killed my family is now had things been just slightly different. It hurts to think about that. She pointed out that maybe I need to see him as a villain rather than a good kid who made a bad decision because I need a reason why my family isn't here anymore. I don't want to let myself think about that because if she's right then there's no one to blame for my family dying, and I NEED someone to blame. My assignment this week is to write him a letter. She specifically said I wouldn't have to mail it, and that she's not saying I need to forgive him. The only requirement is that I am honest. Except - I don't think I can be because it will change everything. I think I need help.

I sit with what I wrote for a long time and almost delete the whole thing half a dozen times, but I don't. I mean, it's probably the crappiest thing I have ever written in my entire life, but I don't have the mental bandwidth to worry about making sure it's a literary work of art. I need advice, or feedback or something. Okay that's a lie. I need people who know what I'm going through to tell me it's not a betrayal to allow today's therapy session to change how I see things, because I'm afraid that it might have and that makes me feel things I am not ready to explore.

I hit post, close my laptop, and curl up into a ball on the sofa and sob harder than I have ever cried before. Nothing in the past eight months has hurt as much as what I am feeling now. I thought I had experienced the worst of my grief so many times, but this outweighs everything I have ever felt by a mile. I cry so hard I have to run to the bathroom and vomit. I retch and vomit over and over until there is nothing left inside me. I feel hollow and empty, and not just in my stomach. It feels like there's an endless void inside of me. All the progress I have made in the past eight months seems to slip away, any happiness or joy I felt in recent weeks just gone, leaving me with a pit of despair and sorrow that feels bottomless.

I hear my phone ringing from the kitchen counter but I ignore it. I rinse my mouth and go back to the sofa. Felix comes over and nudges me with his soft wet nose and instead of allowing him to comfort me, I turn my back to him and pull the blankets over my head. He makes a whining noise and pushes his head into my back. I ignore him and burrow deeper under the blankets and cry myself to sleep.

I wake up to the sound of my mother calling my name. Not for the first time in my life I wish for the power of invisibility. I turn over on the sofa and flip the blanket off of me. I roll to sitting on the edge and realize I have a pounding headache, likely from crying so hard.

"Ali?" I hear again and I sigh. At least she's still in the foyer.

"Living room," I say back and rest my head in my hands, elbows on my thighs.

"I've been calling....Ali? What's wrong? Are you okay?" She rushes over and sits close, her hand on my back.

I shake my head, but I don't answer. I start to cry again and turn into my mom. She holds me close and rubs my back. "Ali, what's wrong? Did something happen?"

I nod but I don't respond. I am crying too hard to talk. I can't make it stop. It hurts so much, even more than the day at the fence.

"Okay my beautiful girl. Okay. It's okay," she croons, pulling me deeper into the sofa. I roll so my head is resting in her lap. She runs her fingers through my hair and waits for me to cry myself out. It takes an exceptionally long time. When I'm quiet for a couple of minutes my mom puts pressure on my shoulder and I sit up. I turn towards her on the sofa and tuck one leg under me.

"Can you tell me what happened now?" she asks, taking both of my hands in hers.

I shake my head no, but I start telling her anyway. I recount everything that Dr. Whitman and I talked about in therapy, intermittently stopping to get my crying under control. When I get to the part where I screamed at her my mother whispers "Oh Ali."

"Why did she even need to bring him up? I was doing so good. I was doing everything she told me to and more. Everything! I even got pets for fucks sake. And she ruined it. She ruined everything," I rail.

"Okay, I need some guidance here Al. Do you need me to just listen? Do you need me to just agree? Do you need me to tell you what I really think? I need you to tell me what exactly you need."
I groan and say "I don't know. I don't know what I need or want. I want to go back to this morning and not go to therapy today."

"Oh Ali. Okay listen," she takes a deep breath and reaches out to take both of my hands in hers, "I was worried about this. I figured at some point she would ask about Justin. If I'm being totally honest, I can't believe she waited this long."

I flop back against the arm of the sofa and stare at the ceiling. "Mom, do you understand, she ruined everything. I was getting to a good place. I really was. And now, now I feel...I don't know exactly, but it's bad."

"Everything isn't ruined Ali. Come on honey, did you really think she would never ask you about Justin? Really?"

"Yes!" I sort of shout. "I don't see why we need to discuss him. He killed them. There. We've discussed him. Why does it need to be more than that?"

"Because there's so much more to it baby girl," she tips her head towards one shoulder as she shrugs it and finishes, "and I think you are only just now realizing it."

I look at her in horror, "You don't blame him," I accuse. I sit up so fast that I feel lightheaded and jump off the sofa. "You don't!" I shout. "You think it was an accident." I sneer the word accident with as much sarcasm as I can infuse into that word.

My mother nods her head slowly, "I do Ali. I understand why you need to believe it was more, but baby girl, I don't. And Ali, it doesn't change anything. It doesn't take away from your loss. It doesn't undo the horribleness of it all. But I do think it was a terrible, horrible, tragic accident."

I pace the room like a caged animal, drawing the attention of Felix. He whines and paces with me, nudging my thigh with his nose each time I turn directions. I feel confused and hurt by my mother's admission. I needed her to say she blamed Justin just as much as I did. That she thought he was selfish, and thoughtless and that what happened was all his fault. I needed her to help me undo all these thoughts that Dr. Whitman set free in my head by telling me she was wrong. Fuck!

"When she asked me about if I had ever hurt someone and wished I could take it back, I totally knew where she was going to go with the conversation. And I knew when I told her about Mrs. De Luca that she would have even more ammunition to make her case that it was an accident." I'm seething now. I guess I figured out how to access my anger after all these months. I mean, it's not like I believed I would never get angry again, obviously. It's just, this is the first time in months that I have been truly angry, and it feels a little uncomfortable.

"Ali, I don't think she was looking for ammunition, like you said. That makes it sound like she is against you, and you have to know that just isn't the case. Dr. Whitman is there to help you."

"She's clearly not on my side," I interrupt, turning to face my mother, hands on my hips. Will used to call it my 'angry woman pose' which I suppose is a pretty accurate description since right now I am currently furious.

My mom gives me a look of disappointment and says, "Ali there are no sides here. She isn't 'not on your side'. Her job is to help you, and part of that is dealing with your feelings about Justin. He's a huge part of your loss, and in order to continue to heal and move forward you need to work through your feelings about him too."

I shake my head, stubbornly refusing to acknowledge out loud what I am really angry about.

"Ali, when you hit Sasha's mom, was it on purpose? Or was it just an accident?"

I glare at my mom, and instead of being gentle with me, she does something I never expected. She glares back at me. This goes on for several moments, until I sigh and flop back down on the sofa. "It was an accident," I say softly. "I would never have hurt her on purpose. I felt horrible for months. I was young and stupid and never ever meant to hit her."

My mom gentles her facial expression but still continues to look at me. "It's not the same thing," I say.

"How is it different?" she asks.

"Are you serious?" I demand. "Mom, he *killed* them! He didn't bump them and give them a couple of fucking bruises! He *killed* them!"

"I know that, Ali. And nothing and no one can take away how absolutely horrible that is. But baby girl, you must know somewhere deep inside that this was a tragic, tragic accident."

I crumple. There's no other word for it. I collapse into the sofa and crumple into a ball, inside and out. My mom reaches over and squeezes my hand. "Look at me Ali," she says softly.

I slide my eyes towards her and take a deep breath. "Mom, I need this," I cry. "I need him to be the bad guy. I need him to be at fault. I need it to be more than just a tragic accident. Don't you understand that?"

"I do Ali. I really, really do. But the reality is that it's not. And Ali, he may have legally been an adult, but you and I both know that an eighteen-year-old high school senior is basically still a child. He was a kid, on his way home from football practice texting his *mom*. He wasn't a kid with a gun in a school or a store. He wasn't coming home from a keg party drunk out of his mind. He wasn't driving ninety miles an hour through town. He did a really stupid thing, yes. Should he have been texting and driving? No, absolutely not. It was a stupid, stupid decision made by an otherwise really good kid. And baby girl, you felt like shit for weeks and Mrs. De Luca only had a few bumps and bruises. Can you imagine, Ali honey, think about it, can you please imagine if you had taken not just one, but two innocent lives that day. Can you imagine living the rest of your life with that knowledge?"   There are tears running down my mother's cheeks, and I know that while some of them are for me and what could have been, they are mostly for Justin and everything he must be feeling now.

I feel the tears slide down my own cheeks, but I'm unsure who exactly they are for at this point. "Logically, I know everything you are saying is true. I do. And I get it, if I had, God forbid, killed Mrs. De Luca and oh my God a child too, I don't think I would have ever been able to live with it. I can't even imagine," I stop and take a breath, and then another, in an attempt to control the tears and overwhelming emotions I am feeling. I suddenly hurt desperately for what Justin is living with and that feels like a huge betrayal to my family which just only adds to my sadness and confusion. "I can't even imagine what Justin is living with. But Mom, if I say this was an accident, then my family is dead for no reason! And if I let myself feel bad for him, then I'm betraying them." I break down sobbing, again. I'm so fucking sick and tired of crying all the fucking time. It's exhausting.

My mom pulls me to her and kisses the top of my head. "I think the problem is that you are equating being an accident with being blameless and that's not the case. Justin did something that caused the accident. He, and he alone, holds the blame for that. He caused the accident that took their lives, just like you caused the accident that knocked over Mrs. De Luca. That doesn't mean it wasn't an accident. An accident is something that happens without any malicious intent. Justin certainly didn't mean to kill Will and Tabby. And I honestly believe that when he was texting his mom to let her know he was running late he thought he was being a good kid, not doing something that would end in a horrific tragedy." She gentles her voice and continues, "Justin lost his life that day too Ali." She gives me a squeeze when she feels me stiffen at her words, "Wait," she says, softly but firmly. "I know you don't want to think about that, but it's true. Will and Tabitha aren't the only ones who lost their lives that day."

"I lost everything that day. Everything."

"But you didn't, Ali. You didn't lose your life."

I flinch as if she had slapped me. "I can't believe you just said that to me," I hiss as I shoot to my feet. "Get out," I demand, pointing at the door.

"Ali, listen..."

"No!" I interrupt her. "No! I will not listen. I will not listen to you tell me I didn't lose my life that day. How dare you?!" I am seething now.

"You lost your family. Not your life. You are still here, baby girl. You are living!" She stands and walks close, stopping just short of touching me. "We have talked about this dozens of times. You are grieving, and healing, and living. You suffered a horrible, terrible, devastating tragedy that is absolutely heartbreaking. No one is denying that or diminishing that. But Ali, you did not die that day. And you did not lose your life."

"It feels like I did," I cry. Tears are streaming down my cheeks and my breathing is erratic. It takes everything I have to calm myself because I know, rationally, that my mother is right. I am still here and I am still alive. My life is different, but I still have one. I am not dead. I am not in prison. I am learning to live a life that is different from the one I had planned, but I still have one.

She reaches out and takes my hand and leads me to the kitchen. She guides me to a chair and gently presses down on my shoulders until I sit. I watch quietly as she moves around the kitchen and makes two mugs of tea. She brings them to the table and sits down next to me, pushing a mug in front of me. She opens her mouth to say something, but I beat her to it.

"That day, I asked Will to take Tabby with him to the store to get milk so that I could have thirty minutes to myself," I start softly. "I could have gone by myself but I was tired and just wanted to sit on the sofa and be alone for a little while. The only reason they were on the road when Justin hit them was because I sent them both out."

"Baby..." my mother whispers.

"If Justin isn't guilty, if he isn't the monster I made him out to be, the murderer I have seen him as for the past almost nine months, then that means I am just as much to blame for being a selfish bitch for wanting to be alone."

My mother reaches over and takes both of my hands in hers and gives them a little shake. "Did you talk to Dr. Whitman about this?"

I nod but don't say anything.

"Did she tell you that sending Will and Tabby to the store so you could have alone time is something that thousands of mothers do daily because they need a break?"

I shrug my shoulders and admit, "Basically. She told me that I did a normal thing that normal families do every day without ending in tragedy."

"You know she's right, right?"

"I mean, yeah, logically." I groan and stand up. I'm restless again and I feel the need to move around. My mind is a huge tangle of emotions and uncomfortable thoughts. "Look, I know I sound like a lunatic. But don't you get that if I see it your way, if I admit that it was an accident, that it was no different than what I did with Mrs. De Luca except with a far more tragic outcome, then I will hurt for him too, and Mom, I can't. I can't betray Will and Tabitha like that."

"Why would it be a betrayal? Allison, Will was one of the most generous, kind people I have ever known. Do you truly believe he wouldn't hurt for Justin if the situation were reversed? Because the man I knew absolutely would. And Al, being able to say it was an accident, hurting for a child who lost his whole future and has to live with the horrific outcome of his decision, does not mean you have to stop blaming him. No one is saying you have to forgive him. Those things aren't contingent on one another. Justin is to blame, absolutely. But he is also a child who made a mistake and caused a tragic and terrible accident and I think you know that."

I nod because I know deep in my soul that she is right. And I know that Will would have seen it the same way. His heart would have broken for himself, but also for Justin. I think of Tabitha, imagine her at eighteen and in the same position as Justin, and I would hope that the me in that scenario would show her grace, something I haven't been able to do for Justin.

"I have to write him a letter," I tell her.

My mom draws her eyebrows together and says, "What? Why? Ali, coming to terms with it being an accident doesn't mean you have to immediately write him a letter and tell him that."

I shake my head and give a half smile, "Mom, seriously? No. It's an assignment from Dr. Whitman. She said I don't have to mail it, just write something honest."

"Oh! Well actually that might be helpful. A way to get out some of what you are thinking and feeling, especially now with this change in your perspective."

I sit back down in my chair and sip my tea. "It's really annoying," I muse.

"What is?"

I cross my arms on the table in front of me and put my chin to them. "That once again I'm easily swayed."

My mom bursts out laughing, "Baby girl if you think anything about this conversation was easy, then we have very different definitions of that word."

"Fair enough," I say with a chuckle. "But you know what I mean. I've said before that I feel like it's really easy for you and Dr. Whitman to talk me around to your way of thinking. Sometimes I feel like I have no real stance on anything. My emotions are kind of a freaking mess, and apparently my view on basically everything is negotiable."

My mom sighs and says, "I don't think you are being fair to yourself Al. I think it's more that everything is changing so fast and all of this is something you have never experienced before, and sometimes having someone offer a different perspective helps you see or accept things you hadn't considered."

I nod slowly as I think about what she said. I decide she isn't wrong and say, "You're right."

We look at one another and both burst out laughing.

CHAPTER TWENTY-ONE

Justin,

I'm pretty sure if I had to make a list of the things I was least likely to ever do, writing to you would probably be number one. I mean, I'm sure you never expected to get a letter from me either. And I guess I think if you did have to imagine what a letter from me would be like, you would have expected it to be full of anger and hate. And I guess if I had written this three months ago, or three weeks ago or hell even three hours ago, you probably would have been right. Honestly, I don't even know if I am going to mail this or not. It came as an assignment from my therapist, and her only requirement was that I be completely honest. So that is what I am going to try and do.

When I was originally given this assignment this morning, I had an entirely different idea of what I was going to say to you. But then tonight I was telling my mother some of what my therapist said today in advance of giving me this assignment and it led to a very emotional and difficult conversation about you and the crash.

Look, I'm sure it comes as no surprise that I have spent the past nine months demonizing you, blaming you, hating you. I needed for someone to be responsible for the fact that my family isn't here anymore. I refused to allow anyone to say the word accident when talking about the crash because I felt like it diminished what happened to my family. That somehow the word accident made it feel like there was no reason that they were gone.

When I was sixteen I had a fight with my mom about some stupid teenage nonsense. I left the house in a fit of anger and was backing out of our driveway, not paying attention, too busy being pissed off and worrying about finding the perfect "my mom sucks" song on the CD I had in so I could blare it at full volume, to check my mirrors. I backed into my friend's mother, who was out walking. I was beyond lucky that she suffered only minor bumps and bruises. As pointed out by my therapist, the outcome would have likely been drastically different had it been an elderly person or a small child running ahead of their parent. In a different life, I easily could be where you are now.

I've been thinking about Tabitha, not frozen in time as a three-year-old, but instead as a feisty, headstrong eighteen year old girl. I think about her coming home from school, running late from cheerleading or soccer or French club, or whatever extracurricular activity she would have been a part of, and sending me a quick text to let me know she was running late. I think about how, in the blink of an eye, she could take the life of two people and destroy her entire future. And then I think about her having to live with that for the rest of her life, and my heart bleeds for the imaginary eighteen-year-old Tabitha.

I don't think I will ever be able to forgive you, not in the traditional sense of the word. You took the most precious things in my life from me and I have to live with that loss every day. But, I do understand now that it was an accident. It's taken me months to get to this place, but I am finally here and believe it or not there is some measure of peace in that.

I spent some time tonight doing something I didn't think I would ever do. I googled you. By all accounts you were a good kid. An excellent student, a fantastic athlete, a leader among your peers. Well respected by your coaches, your teammates and your classmates. You clearly had a bright future ahead of you. I read how you were being scouted by big name colleges to play football and how full ride scholarships at competing universities were a given with your talent and your grades.

It's a strange thing to have spent months feeling one way, and then in a single day have that completely turned upside down. I never thought there would be a day where I would hurt for you. I know I hurt because of you, but I didn't expect that I could also hurt for you. Yet here I am - hurting for you. Not only for what you lost, because while it took me some time to get there, I do know you lost huge in this too. You lost a future you had planned. You lost a life you thought you were going to lead. And yes, you temporarily lost your freedom. But more, I hurt because with the things people in the papers said about the kind of person you are, no amount of punishment will ever compare to the guilt and self-hatred you must feel for taking two lives.

I wish I could tell you I forgive you. I wish I could show you the same grace my friend's mother showed me when I was sixteen. I wish I could show you the same grace I would want someone to show Tabitha if she were in the same situation you are in. But I didn't kill my friend's mother, or anyone she cared about. And Tabitha at eighteen in your same situation is a fiction that is impossible because she will never grow beyond three years old. For the first time in months I wish I were capable of being the bigger person, but no matter how much I want that, I am not there. I honestly do not think I will ever be there. But then again, I didn't think I would ever get here either, so maybe one day I'll surprise myself and get there too.

Mostly, I guess, I just want you to know that I don't hate you. I think that's where I am right now. I don't hate you. My heart breaks for you. I have to live with my loss for the rest of my life. But you might have to live with something worse. I don't know. And I don't know if it helps you to know that I don't hate you, even if I can't forgive you, but my therapist told me to be honest and that's about as honest as I can be.

Allison

CHAPTER TWENTY-TWO

I spent the week leading up to my next therapy appointment reading and rereading the letter I wrote to Justin. I must have decided to mail it and then changed my mind a hundred times. I know Justin can't write me back; I'm considered a victim of his crime and he isn't allowed contact with me even if I do mail my letter. I'm not even really worried about that part. I'm not even really sure what is keeping me from sending it. I didn't lie to him when I said I didn't hate him. It feels so crazy to say that, but I don't. I understand now that it was truly a tragic, terrible accident with the absolute worst possible outcome, with everyone involved paying different, but no less horrific prices. Will and Tabitha lost their lives. I lost my family. And Justin lost his future and has to live with knowing what his choice cost the three of us.

It feels strange to have pity for the person who killed Will and Tabitha. But it no longer feels like a betrayal.

My mother wasn't wrong when she said that Will would have hurt for him. Hell, he probably would have not only hurt for him, he would have forgiven him, and likely even visited him to tell him to his face. And he wouldn't have seen it as a betrayal either. For all intent and purposes, Justin is still a child, and Will would have struggled with allowing a child to bear such a heavy burden alone. His big, beautiful heart is one of the things I loved most about him, and while it took me a while to get there, I honestly think Will would have been disappointed in me if I didn't get to a place where I could accept that it was an accident.

The morning after my mom and I had our talk, and I wrote to Justin, I wake up and check the grief forum to see if I have any feedback on my post. There are several comments and I read each one carefully, grateful for the gentle words and thoughtful input. The one that hits me the hardest though is the reply from the woman whose story I read weeks ago; the one whose daughter drowned while she tended to her other child.

0005 QueenBee34 writes: Twelve years ago my two year old daughter drowned in our family swimming pool. I was outside spending the afternoon playing in the pool and the yard with my children. My son tripped and scraped his knee. I took my eyes off of my daughter just for the time it took to clean his scrape and put a bandaid on it. It's crazy, because I was always so worried about something happening to my kids if I ever had to run inside, that I always brought drinks, snacks, extra towels and a first aid kit outside with me. I didn't have to leave the yard to get a bandaid. I only had to take my attention away from one child in order to put a bandaid on the other. In those moments my daughter wandered down the steps of the pool and drowned. I was thirty feet away. Here is what I learned after twelve years of therapy - I am to blame for my daughter drowning, AND it was an accident. The two aren't mutually exclusive. It sounds to me like this is what you are struggling with. The boy who killed your family is, of course, to blame. But it was also an accident. An accident is something that happens - well - on accident. It is without intention. But in your post you said you couldn't look at it as an accident because you needed to be able to blame him - for there to be a reason this happened. Accident or not, what you want is a reason, and unfortunately there isn't one. This is something that a lot of us struggle with - the desperate need for there to be some divine reason our loved ones aren't with us any longer, and the harsh truth is that there will never, ever be an answer to that question. I'm also going to guess that you are equating being able to say this was a tragic accident with absolving him of blame. Like it somehow means you forgive him. Trust me when I tell you that is not the case. They are not the same thing. Obviously my perspective is quite different because I am the person responsible for my loss. I am to blame. It took me over a decade to be able to forgive myself, and I was only able to do that through the unwavering support of my friends, my family, my husband and my therapist. I had to be able to forgive myself because I had to be able to live with myself and the loss I caused. You do not owe this boy forgiveness. Look, no one in this group can tell you how to grieve or how to feel - all we can do is offer you support and share our own experiences and hope that what we share helps you work through your grief. So here is my two cents - you are entitled to feel however you want to feel. You can be angry, you can hate, you can laugh, you can cry, you can feel your loss in whatever way you want to. BUT - from someone who has not only been there, but been the victim and the villain of my own story I can say this - One of the biggest steps in healing was being able to accept that regardless of how it happened, my daughter's death was a tragic accident. I was at fault, yes. But it was an accident all the same. It wasn't on purpose and that is an important distinction. I hope some of what I have said here helps you. Please continue to reach out to this group for support, feedback, or even just to vent. We are here for you.

I close the laptop and just sit, thinking about everything she wrote. I think about what I wrote to Justin, the conversations I had with Dr. Whitman and my mother, and the internal conversations I have had with myself. I fought so hard against accepting that this was an accident, because QueenBee is right, what I really wanted was a reason, and I will never get one. It's why I struggled so much with needing Justin to be a monster. If he was the monster I portrayed him as then in the mental gymnastics I performed in my head he was also the reason. When I finally accepted that it was an accident, Justin stopped being a monster, and became a kid who made a terrible, stupid choice that cost more than just me and my family dearly. But there also stopped being a reason. And it is going to take me a long time to accept and work through that.

The night before my next therapy session I invite Julia, Lola, Audrey and Sasha over for dinner. I make sure to tell them this is a rules free dinner, something Julia asks me numerous times if I am sure I am ready for. I answer her honestly each time, that no I am not sure, but that it is something I need to do regardless.

I've been experiencing so many rapid changes lately, not just in how I am living this new life, but also in so many of my thoughts and emotions. I've found I can be happy and have moments of true joy. I've been able to identify my feelings of loneliness and restlessness when I'm in my house by myself and set about doing something to change that. I've found support for my questions about the future through reading posts from those who have been there on the grief forum. And I have worked through some pretty significant feelings surrounding Justin and the accident. I miss my family and the life and future we had planned, but I know now that I need to continue to make changes and move forward because my mother was right; I need to live not only for myself, but for Will and Tabby too.

The girls all arrive within minutes of one another and we make small talk and laugh as Julia gets everyone set up with drinks and I finish up dinner. Once dinner is ready we move to the table. I went with a simple dinner of steak fajitas and cilantro lime rice and set the table with sour cream, cilantro lime crema, salsa and guacamole.

I look at my friends, take a deep breath, raise my margarita and say, "I want to propose a toast." I look each of them in the eye and continue, "When Will and Tabby died, I believed my entire world died with them. I couldn't allow myself to feel their loss because it was too big and too overwhelming. Instead, I wrapped myself in as much anger as possible because it kept me from feeling anything, and at the time I thought I needed that. I let that anger protect me, but I also used it to alienate everyone. I said hateful, horrible, wretched things to every single one of you. Things I can't take back, and you guys will never know how incredibly sorry I am for that. I don't know how you guys found it in yourselves to not only forgive me, but none of you ever even asked for an apology. Instead, you showed up after months of me basically telling you to fuck off, and did it with smiles and hugs and acceptance. You followed rules that had to be difficult, and never made it feel like you were following rules. You are the best friends anyone could ever ask for and I just want you all to know how much I love and value you. I'm so sorry I forgot that, but I'm so grateful that you all gave me a second chance when I probably didn't deserve one."

"We love you," Julia says, swiping at the tears on her cheeks. "You don't owe us anything. We are here for you no matter what."

Sasha is nodding and agrees, "We do Al. And Al, none of us judged how you dealt with your loss. How could we?"

"I know, but still. I was really horrible to you guys and you all just took me back like I didn't act like a screaming bitch for months on end."

"Yeah, because that's what friends do," Audrey puts in. "You needed time and you needed to deal with your loss the way you needed to deal with it. And I think I speak for all of us when I say not one of us took what you said personally. You lost huge Ali. And honestly, if taking some of that anger out on us gave you even a little bit of what you needed then great. We will happily be your kicking posts, because we love you."

Lola wipes her tears and adds, "Seriously Ali. By the grace of God none of us know what you were and are going through. We can be there for you, but we don't know what that kind of loss feels like. I never looked at you and thought you were a screaming bitch. I looked at you and thought you might be the strongest person I have ever known to keep going day after day."

Audrey raises her glass and says, "Here here!"

The others follow with cheers of their own. I take in my friends, one by one, and this time the tears that fall are ones of gratitude and love.

Dinner conversation is light. Audrey shares the latest gossip from work which involved an executive's wife tracking his phone to a seedy motel and finding him tied spread eagle to a bed with a ball gag in his mouth and an apparatus inserted into his nether region. Apparently she posed as management to get his coworker to crack open the door, barreled through and then proceeded to take numerous photos which she forwarded in an email to his entire company. According to Audrey this has caused quite the uproar at work, as one would expect. We toasted the unknown wife and her very impressive revenge.

Sasha and Lola both finished a book I had recommended and had vastly differing opinions on it which led to a slightly heated conversation. I obviously side with Lola since I loved the book, hence the recommendation. Julia jumps in having read something else by the same author and, having hated his writing style, sides with Sasha on principle.

"Have you guys read any of the dinoporn books?" Audrey asks with mock innocence, effectively ending the book debate.

It's unfortunate that I chose that moment to take a sip of my margarita, because I end up choking on it.

"What?!" Julia asks in what can only be described as a shriek. "Oh God please please please tell me you are not fucking with us. Please tell me there is actually such a thing."

Audrey laughs and nods, "Yup it's a real thing. Hang on," she says as she scrolls quickly through her phone. Once she finds the book she is looking for, Audrey proceeds to read to us excerpts from this absolute trainwreck of a book. While the writing borders on middle school quality, the story has us in stitches, laughing so hard we are crying.

Lola jumps up from her seat and runs to the bathroom shouting, "Oh my God, I'm going to pee. I'm going to pee," which only makes us laugh harder.

Lola returns and announces, "Made it. Whew!" and collapses back into her chair, which starts a whole new round of giggles.

We chat for a while longer and then the girls help me clean up from dinner. We move to the family room with coffee and individual pints of Ben and Jerry ice cream that Lola brought over for dessert.

"So this has been a really nice evening and at the risk of ruining that, I have some information and a question for you," Lola says.

I brace, because this sounds like it might be difficult and emotional, and I honestly don't know how much more I can take.

"Okay," I say, hesitantly.

Lola leans forward and rests her elbows on her knees. "Okay so technically this is a pretty big breach, and I could get in a lot of trouble at work, so this needs to remain between us. Elizabeth Cooper is going to call you tomorrow and you absolutely cannot let on that you already know. Seriously, Ali, I could lose my job."

I hear her but I also don't. I'm stuck on the name Elizabeth Cooper. I know that name. She was the transplant coordinator who talked to me about donating Will and Tabby's organs the day they died. Lola also works as a transplant coordinator, but obviously, because of our relationship, she was not the one who spoke with me about it that day.

Julia takes my hand and gives it a squeeze. "Ali?"

"Yeah, umm, shit. Okay," I say.

"Ali this isn't something bad," Lola reassures me. "I wouldn't bring it up if it was bad. It's just big, and I think having us here with you when you hear about it is better than being alone when Elizabeth calls you. Like I said, I could get in trouble, but I know you, and I don't think this is information you should get alone."

I nod and say, "Elizabeth Cooper is the transplant coordinator."

Lola confirms this, "Yes. She's the other coordinator in the area. She got a phone call yesterday and I just happened to be in the office with her when she got it. It is the only reason I know about this. Anyway, the mother of the child who received Tabitha's heart called…"

I gasp and my hand flies to my mouth. The tears are instantaneous, and my heart is beating so hard it feels like it might break through my chest. "Oh my God," I moan.

Julia moves in closer on my left, and Sasha moves and pushes in on my right. They each take a hand and anchor me as I prepare for whatever Lola is about to tell me.

"Her son is four. He was born with a congenital heart defect that required a transplant and he received Tabby's heart. His mother almost lost him several times while they waited for a transplant. She reached out because they would like to meet…"

"Yes!" I say without thinking. "Yes. Absolutely."

"Okay well, hold on. They want to meet to thank you, but also because they have a thank you gift for you."

"When?" I want to meet them now. This instant. I want to see the flush on the cheeks of the child whose blood is pumping because of my baby girl.

"Alright that's the thing. The law says she has to wait until the one-year mark. That is roughly three months away. We aren't allowed to facilitate a mutually agreed upon meeting until that time. However, when Elizabeth informed her of this, she was distraught. She insisted that if they had to wait the time out for the full year that she wanted to know if the thank you gift can be given to you prior to that. I don't know what it is, but she said it was really important to her and her family for you to have it. Elizabeth agreed to have the gift overnighted to her and promised to call you when it arrived. It came in just before we closed today, so she is going to call you first thing in the morning and ask if you would like to pick it up."

My disappointment feels palpable. I don't want to wait three more months. Not when I know now that meeting them is an option. It never occurred to me that

that was even a possibility. I start to wonder about the others out there living their best lives thanks to my husband and child. I wonder if there are more people out there who would be willing to meet with me so that I can see the proof that they live on in others.

"I know waiting sucks, but we have that rule for a reason," Lola says, seeing my obvious disappointment. "And Elizabeth did ask her what the gift was, because it can't be anything that identifies them or contains their name. I didn't ask what it was though. I wanted to, but I also knew I was going to tell you about the conversation and if I knew what the gift was I wouldn't be able to keep it a secret, and I didn't want to ruin it."

"I wonder what it could be," I say, curious.

"Whatever it is," Julia reassures me, "I'm sure it is thoughtful and something that will mean a lot to you."

"Do you think there are others who would want to meet? Is this something that happens often?"

Lola leans back and crosses her legs. "It happens pretty often. Usually it's the family that received the donation reaching out. It's really hit or miss if the donating family agrees to meet. For some it is too hard. They donated their loved ones' organs because ultimately, it's a beautiful and selfless gift, but not all of those families want to be confronted with the visible reminder that someone else is alive simply because their loved one is not."

I completely understand this. It's not something I struggled with, although that still surprises me from time to time. But I do get why it would be hard to be face to face with a physical reminder that someone else is alive because the person you love died.

"When it gets past the one year mark," Lola continues, "Elizabeth can help by reaching out to some of the families if you decide you would like to request to meet them."

"Why do they make you wait a year," I ask.

Lola looks a little sad as she answers. "Not all transplants are successful. Sometimes the organ is damaged in a way that isn't obvious during harvest. Sometimes the host body rejects it. Sometimes despite the transplant the patient dies anyway. We wait a full year because generally speaking if a patient survives until the one year mark we consider them to be 'out of the woods' medically. It would be devastating for the donating family to meet a recipient two weeks post op, only to have that patient end up rejecting the donated organ and dying anyway. Our goal is to ensure that if a meeting does take place, that the outcome has already been established as a good one."

I nod because that makes sense. I imagine how much harder it would be to meet the person who received Will's lungs only to find out shortly after that that person died anyway. It would be like losing a piece of Will all over again. Not to mention grieving for the family that lost their loved one too.

"Are you okay Ali?" Audrey asks.

"I am. I mean, obviously I want to meet this mother and her child now that I know it's a possibility, but I also understand the thought process behind waiting. I'm just grateful it's even a possibility. I have been dreading the year anniversary, trying to imagine how I am going to get through that day. I belong to this online grief group and one of the things I read was about this family that lost their child to cancer. Every year on the anniversary of her death, her parents dress up as superheroes and spend the day at the hospital in the same children's cancer ward that their daughter died in. I think it's such a beautiful way to honor her memory. Several other members commented on that post talking about the ways they spend the anniversary of their loved one passing and each one of them is so inspiring. But my family died in a car accident. There isn't much that I can do to honor them that day. Knowing that I could potentially meet people who are alive because of them around that time might make that day a little less hard."

"Oh my gosh, that is so beautiful," Sasha says, squeezing my hand. "What a terrific way to honor their daughter."

"Right?"

"Oh yeah, definitely," Julia puts in.

"We can help you plan something," Lola says. "I know of one family that does something I think you might be interested in. It's an older lady with two grown sons. The dad died about five years ago and they donated pretty much everything. I think they ended up with about eighteen people who are alive or leading better lives because of his gift. As the first-year mark approached, they asked us to reach out to the recipients and invite them to a big party. Of the eighteen people, twelve of them, along with their families, attended. It was a huge to-do, and now they do it every year. They rent a space and have it catered, have a DJ, a cash bar, the whole nine yards. The wife explained it to me like this - she and her sons can choose to spend that day grieving their loss and being sad, or they can choose to celebrate the fact that he lived on in all these other people. She said being with them on that day makes her feel closer to her husband because she can see the proof of his life outside of his death. Elizabeth and I have gone to each party, and it's truly one of the most beautiful things I have ever seen. The first year there were a lot of tears from pretty much everyone, but as the years go by it's more like one big family getting together for a fun, and sometimes rowdy, reunion. It is by far one of my favorite days of the year. Actually, at the last party the wife told me that what was the worst day of her life, is now the best day of the year for her."

I wipe at the tears that are sliding down my cheeks and nod my head vehemently. "I want that. I want to do that. I so completely love that idea. Can you and Elizabeth help me with that?"

Lola nods, "Absolutely. But I'm going to wait to bring it up with Elizabeth until after tomorrow. It will seem fishy if I bring it up before she calls you. She knows we are friends so my asking for help in reaching out to Will and Tabby's recipients two days after she gets a call from one of them will be a dead giveaway that I broke protocol and told you about the phone call."

"Oh yeah, no definitely wait until after. That's totally fine. And when she calls me tomorrow I will act surprised and not let on that I know anything. Thank you for the heads up though. I'm not sure how I would have handled it if she just randomly called me to tell me this. Sometimes I surprise myself, but I think this would have been a little too hard to hear without support, even if it is good news."

"We are here for you Ali, for the good and the bad. Always," says Julia.

"Always," the others repeat.

"Always," I say.

CHAPTER TWENTY-THREE

I carry the box Elizabeth handed to me this morning into Dr. Whitman's office. I purposely picked it up just before my session with her so that I could open it here. I figure whatever it is will cause some pretty big emotions and I've long since stopped trying to manage the big shit by myself. I also have a copy of the letter I wrote to Justin in my purse. There is another copy of this letter in an envelope in a big blue post box outside the post office.

"What's this?" Dr. Whitman asks, nodding to my box, as I enter. I take in her outfit and today she really does not disappoint. She is wearing a short sleeved dress in traffic cone orange with psychedelic rainbow cats. It is an absolute abomination and I have to stifle a giggle as I take the whole thing in.

"It's a gift from the mother of the child who received Tabby's heart." I tell her the whole story, including Lola and her heads up. I know she can't share anything I say to her and I think Lola will understand why I wouldn't want to tell half-truths or lie to my therapist. "I picked it up before I got here. I thought it would be good to open it with you in anticipation of a big emotional breakdown," I say with a chuckle.

"Alright. Well, do you want to start with this or with the letter you were supposed to write to Justin?"

I reach into my purse and pull out the letter, unfolding it and smoothing it out on my lap. "I wrote it. I also mailed a copy this morning, although I wasn't sure if I was going to. I kind of went back and forth all week on whether or not I would. I decided this morning to just go ahead and send it. He can't write me back, which helps, and I think Will would have wanted me to send it."

We spent some time discussing my conversation with my mom, the feedback I received from the grief forum and how finally being able to accept that this was an accident feels. I read her the letter - I've read it so many times I pretty much have it memorized, but the act of reading it out loud had a different impact than reading it in my head.

"How do you feel?" Dr. Whitman asks when I am finished.

I sit back deeper into my chair and sigh. "I feel…" I pause and then finish, "like Will would be really fucking proud of me."

Dr. Whitman chuckles and agrees, "I bet he would be. I know I am. I imagine that it was really difficult for you to accept the fact that this was an accident."

"It was. But that lady from the grief forum wasn't wrong when she said that I needed Justin to be the bad guy because then there was a reason. I guess in my mind if Justin was evil - some monster who purposely killed my family then by that deduction, Justin was also the reason."

"And now?"

"I guess now I understand that it was just a terrible thing that happened. It happened to me and my family and the people who love Will and Tabby, but it also happened to Justin and the people who love him."

"Allison, that is huge. You know that right? Being able to see that, to realize that this was a tragic accident that also happened to Justin is a major step."

"I expected it to feel horrible. Like I was betraying them. Instead I feel proud of myself, because I know it is what Will would have wanted me to do. Honestly if the situation were reversed and I had been the one who died, Will would have personally gone to the prison and told Justin to his face that he forgave him. I'm not that big a person. I don't know that I will ever be that big a person."

Dr. Whitman chuckled and affirmed, "And you never have to be. We talked a lot about how grief is a journey and part of that journey is healing. Think of it this way - loss, especially one as big as the one you experienced - leaves a wound. A huge gaping wound. And when you don't tend to it, like you weren't in the beginning, that wound festers. It gets infected and spreads. It takes over. But when you treat that wound, when you get it the help it needs to heal, it starts to close. But it will never, ever go away. It takes time, longer for some than for others, but over time it becomes a scar. Your scar will differ from someone else's scar, even if they experienced the exact same type of loss. So maybe part of your scar will be that you can never forgive Justin. And that's okay."

"I like that analogy. It helps me be able to visualize the changes I've made the past several months. Like each assignment you have given me to start living my life again helped to stitch closed a section of that wound. Do you think…well, do you think Justin has a wound too?"

She shrugs one shoulder and says, "I don't know. I don't know what kind of person he is. In my experience good people who cause great harm or pain to someone else are wounded too, just in a different way. You said you googled him and that by all accounts he was a pretty terrific kid. So what do you think?"

"I think if even a fraction of what I read about him is true, then he is hurting in a way I can never understand. Obviously, I'm not saying it's less than how much I hurt. I think I understand now that his pain, his loss, it's different from mine. And maybe in some ways it's worse. I'm the one who lost, but he is the one who took and that is a really big thing to have to live with. So yes, I guess I think he probably does have a wound. And while I didn't have that imagery when I made the decision to send my letter, I think I did understand on some level that hearing that I realized it was an accident and that I didn't hate him might help him even heal a tiny bit. I've seen him for so many months as a monster, but in the past couple of days I have been able to see him as a kid, and that might be the thing that changed my entire perspective."

Dr. Whitman smiles at me, a big, bright, smile that I feel deep into the center of me.

"So," she tips her head to the box, "should we see what that is?"

I nod emphatically. "I'm nervous though. I'm assuming that whatever it is is going to cause some pretty big feelings, and quite honestly, I'm pretty freaking sick of big feelings."

Dr. Whitman laughs, "I'm sorry to tell you that big feelings are likely going to stick around for a while. You still have a lot of 'firsts' to get through and each one of them is going to cause some 'big feelings'".

"Oh! Speaking of firsts. I have something to tell you after we find out what this is."

"That sounds like it might be part of a big feeling," she replies.

"So big," I confirm.

Dr. Whitman walks over to her desk and comes back with a pair of scissors that she hands to me. I use them to slit open the tape on the box and fold the flaps back. Inside, under some tissue paper, is a white stuffed bear in white dress with angel wings. I pull it out of the box and hold it gently in front of me.

"Oh my," Dr. Whitman breathes.

I look up at her, confused. "What?"

"Allison, squeeze its belly."

I do as she says and the sound of a heart beating fills the space between us.

Tears instantly fill my eyes as I ask "Is that? Oh God, is that Tabby's heart?"

I look up and through my tears I can see that Dr. Whitman has tears of her own. She nods and says, "I believe it is."

I press the belly a second time and there is the beat again, strong and sure. I press it again and again and again as the tears stream down my face.

Dr. Whitman gets up and comes over to crouch in front of me. She reaches into the box and pulls out a card, handing it to me.

"Can you?" I ask.

She nods and says, "Of course."

Dr. Whitman opens the card and reads, *"Thank you seems so inadequate for the gift you have given my family, especially because in order for us to have this gift you had to lose the most precious thing in your life. Please know that I will treasure your child as much as I treasure my own child. I truly believe that their life lives on within my son. I will make sure my son knows the priceless gift he was given in ways he can understand as he grows. I will replace this bear as many times as you need throughout my son's life, as I am sure you will wear the sound out, as I know I would if our situations were reversed. With more love and gratitude than I have the words for, K's Mom."*

Dr. Whitman places the card back in the box and then excuses herself. I hardly notice her leaving the room as I hug the bear to my chest and sob into its fuzz.

It takes her about five minutes to return, in which time I have listened to Tabby's heartbeat dozens of times and managed to somewhat collect myself.

"I'm sorry," Dr. Whitman says as she returns to her chair.

"For what?" I ask, genuinely confused.

"I have been a therapist for decades, and I have never once cried in front of a patient. I have cried for patients after they have left, but I have never been so unprofessional to do so in their presence and I am very sorry."

I laugh as I say, "Seriously Dr. Whitman? I probably owe you like six Costco sized packs of tissues I have cried so much in your office. Besides, you're human. You're allowed to have honest emotions. One of the things that I like most about you is that you aren't some stuffy, buttoned-up doctor. You laugh, smile, and evidently if the feelings are big enough, you cry. Please do not feel like you need to apologize for that."

She nods and says, "Well thank you for that. I appreciate it." She clears her throat and continues, "So, that's a pretty spectacular gift. And the card was pretty special too. How are you feeling?"

I stroke my hand down the softness of the bear's leg and swallow hard. "I never dreamed I would hear that sound again. It's very overwhelming, in a wonderful way. I'm so grateful to K's mom for realizing how much this would mean to me. And honestly, having her say that she would treasure my child the way she treasures her own was possibly the most beautiful thing anyone has ever said to me. I mean, she has one of the last living parts of my daughter and the fact that she says she believes that two children live within her son's body means the world to me. It means she will never forget that Tabby was not just an organ, but a child that was loved and cherished."

"It's a very special way for someone to look at an organ donation," she agrees.

"Speaking of organ donation," I say, "I have a plan for the first anniversary of Will and Tabby's death."

"Wow! Okay, that's big. What kind of plan?"

I tell Dr. Whitman all about the day I saw the superhero post and the different comments others posted about how they spend the anniversary of their loved ones' deaths.

"Well those are absolutely beautiful tributes to the lives that were lost. I think it's really special that they choose to do something that gives back or celebrates their lives, rather than spend that day being depressed."

"Right?" I agree. "So I was really struggling with that because I love the idea of being proactive and having a plan for that day, especially a plan that honors Will and Tabby, but none of those situations really apply to us or their lives."

"Okay," Dr. Whitman nods in agreement.

"Okay, so like I said when I got here, my friend Lola is one of the regional transplant coordinators. When she told me the family of the child who received Tabby's heart wanted to meet, she explained how they require all donor and recipient families to wait a full year. She gave me a bunch of reasons, but the bottom line is that it's mostly to make sure the transplant takes, and the person doesn't die or reject the organ."

"That makes sense."

I nod and continue, "I told Lola and my other girlfriends the same thing I told you about the post I read. I told them how the possibility of meeting that family gave me something to look forward to during a time period that would otherwise be absolutely horrible. She told me this amazing story about a family who donated their dad's organs and how on the anniversary of his death they have a huge get together with a dozen of his recipients and their families. She told me that she and the other transplant coordinator could help me at the year mark reach out and plan something similar if I wanted. I love this idea. I love the idea of being surrounded by all the lives that are possible or better because of Will and Tabby. I mean, I know that this year that day is going to be horrible, and that this celebration can't take place on the actual day because I have to wait out the year, but at least it will give me something to look forward to during that time period."

"Ali, that is a really lovely way to celebrate their lives. And I am especially proud of you for proactively looking for a way to do something joyous rather than spending that time being profoundly sad. And yes, you are correct. This year, that day will be difficult. Although, for some people it's the second year that is harder. The second anniversaries, birthdays and big holidays."

This surprises me. "Why would the second year be harder?"

"People tend to brace for all the firsts. They anticipate how hard they will be and mentally prepare as much as possible leading up to those days. The second year, they don't. I imagine that is because with the first year they ensure they have the proper support and are so prepared for it to be horrific, that it's bad, but not as bad as they had anticipated in their heads. They assume the second year will be the same, but they don't tend to brace as hard, or make sure they have the same support and when those days hit they hit harder than expected."

"Well that's good to know. It sucks to know it too though. Does it ever get, I don't know, easier, I guess?"

Dr. Whitman nods, "I have found, through decades of helping people learn to live again, that the third year is generally the 'magic' year. It's the year that there are moments of sadness, but mostly joy. There are a lot more 'remember when' stories that elicit laughter instead of tears. It also tends to be the year the dead stop being perfect."

I raise one eyebrow and ask, "Perfect?"

"Yes. Obviously, it's different for everyone, but in general, for the first two years the dead are perfect. Think about Will. Tell me five things you remember about him."

"He was exceedling kind. He had this amazing, infectious laugh. He made the best eggs benedict. He loved cookies and candy and anything sweet. And he was the best kisser on the planet." I rattle them off easily without even having to think about them.

"Perfect," she states.

I blink and ask, "What?"

"I didn't ask you to tell me five things that were good about Will. I asked you to tell me five things you remembered. Note that you didn't say he left the toilet seat up, or he clipped his toenails in bed, or he couldn't find the kitchen sink with a map and always left his dirty dishes on the counter next to said sink. I didn't hear you say he left dirty clothes on the floor or beard clippings in the bathroom sink. Everything you said was perfect. In fact, I bet if I had asked you for ten things, you would have given me ten perfect things."

"Shit," I laugh. "You're right."

"Now tell me five things about Will."

"He was exceedingly kind," I repeat. "He never put his dirty clothes in the laundry basket. He snored so badly that sometimes I would go sleep with Tabby. He was the best kisser on the planet. And he really did make the best eggs benedict."

"Better," Dr. Whitman says. "But that is what I mean. I bet if his snoring was so bad that you had to leave your bed to sleep with your daughter, that it was a huge source of annoyance for you and likely would have made the top five immediately if he were still alive. This isn't a bad thing Ali. I'm not judging you at all. It's a fact of death that the dead, temporarily, are perfect. Sometime around year two but more by year three, they stop being perfect and all the wonderfully hilarious 'bad' stories start to come out. That's the year things start to hurt less. When people can joke about their loved ones and not feel like they are dishonoring them."

"That makes sense when you explain it like that. It kind of sounds almost like a honeymoon period where everything the person you love does is adorable. And then when it wears off you discover that their little idiosyncrasies are actually annoying as hell."

Dr. Whitman laughs and says, "Exactly."

She checks her watch and says, "So our time is pretty much up. Today was a big day full of big feelings. You impress me each week with your willingness to do the hard work, and to take on your own hard work to bring in to discuss each week. I think we are going to skip an assignment this week. I figure you'll do your own thing anyway whether I give you one or not."

I chuckle and agree, "Probably."

I take my next appointment card, hug the bear containing my daughter's heartbeat to my chest, and smile as I walk out into the sunshine.

EPILOGUE: SIX YEARS LATER

"I can't believe this is our last appointment," I say as I take my chair in Dr. Whitman's office. Today she is wearing a teal and pink A-line dress with darker teal and pale pink stripes with fluffy white bunnies on it. I've long since moved from weekly, to bimonthly to monthly appointments with her and have seen dozens and dozens of her crazy animal print dresses but this is by far the absolute worst and I'm thrilled she chose it for my last session.

"It's time Ali. You don't need me anymore. You haven't in a really long time. That doesn't mean you can't ever come back if something happens and you find you need help processing it. It just means you no longer need monthly sessions anymore."

"Is it weird that I'm going to grieve leaving my grief therapist?"

She chuckles and says, "Not at all. Ironic though isn't it?"

"So ironic."

"Is everything all set for tonight?"

I rest my hands on my belly and answer, "Yes. Finn took Jasper with him to meet up with my mom and Henry, Julia, Ethan and Linx, and Lola and her brood at the venue to make sure everything is all set up for tonight. I'm so excited to see everyone."

"Jasper must be getting so big. Is he excited about becoming a big brother?" she asks, indicating my belly with her head.

"He is! He's three so I figure the excitement will wear off by day two of a new baby crying, but for now he tells everyone he meets that he's getting a new baby brother. He's going to be sorely disappointed if this baby turns out to be a girl," I say, laughing.

"I imagine it won't take him long to get over it if that is the case though."

"No, probably not. He's such an easy, happy boy. Which means," I say, rubbing the spot where my child is incessantly kicking me, "this one will be a hellion."

Dr. Whitman nods, "You aren't going to get lucky three times in a row, so I suggest you get used to the idea of a hellion."

I laugh, "God Tabby was such an easy baby, and Jasper was even easier than she was. I'm a little terrified this one is going to be more than Finn and I can handle together."

"How is Finn?"

"He's great. He basically planned this year's donor reunion himself because he was worried about me being stressed out while I'm pregnant."

"Aren't you due pretty much any second?" Dr. Whitman asks.

"Five more weeks. But I feel as big as a house."

"You look wonderful and nowhere near as big as a house."

I laugh and say, "I thought therapists weren't supposed to lie?"

"It is frowned upon," she chuckles. "So tell me how you are handling things this year. I don't think the celebration has ever fallen on the actual day Will and Tabby died, has it?"

I shake my head and say, "No this will be the first time it's on the actual day. I think if it had been two or three years ago, it would have been really hard, but I'm doing okay today, all things considered."

"Meaning?"

I sigh and say, "It's different this year. Jasper is the age that Tabby was when she died. He is starting to do things, learn things, that she never got the chance to learn or do, and that's hard. I mean, obviously I'm excited to see my son grow and change, but there's also a sadness there too because Tabby should have done those things first and she never will."

"We talked about this when you were pregnant with Jasper, remember? Having a child after the loss of a child is no less joyous, but it can be very hard in some ways because there will be a hundred different 'firsts' for you to celebrate, but also to mourn. And Ali it is okay to feel that way. When Jasper learns to tie his shoes you will celebrate with him, but that doesn't mean you won't feel some sadness that Tabby never got the chance. It will be the same with this baby, although it will likely be less."

"I know. And honestly, Finn is so great about helping me process my feelings when those things happen. Obviously since they are roughly the same age there haven't been many, but I know they will start coming more often."

"And after six years of therapy, I promise you that you have the tools to handle each one of them," Dr. Whitman reassures me.

I nod and say, "I know." And I do know. I will never stop being grateful to my mother for forcing me to come that first day, and I will never stop being grateful to Dr. Whitman for helping me learn how to live again after losing my family. Without her I don't think I would be living the life I am today. I would never have moved forward enough to allow Finn into my life, which means I wouldn't have Jasper and a new baby on the way. I owe her everything and then some.

"So does the new baby have a name yet? Last time we met there was a hot debate going on at home over names."

I chuckle because she is not wrong. "God, who knew picking a name for a child could be so hard. When we named Jasper it was so easy. We both agreed on his name by like, the second month of my pregnancy. We didn't pick a girl's name for him because I just couldn't, and we agreed that if he was a girl we would cross that bridge when it arrived. For this baby we decided to pick one of each and the name debate was not pretty. Ultimately we ended up taking your advice and put a piece of paper on the fridge and each of us would just add names we liked and cross off names we hated. I'm happy to say we *finally* agreed on Leo for a boy and Nora for a girl. Middle names are still up for debate, but I think we are leaning towards James and Annabelle."

"I love those. And I'm glad my advice helped. Naming a child can be contentious," she says with a laugh.

"It doesn't help when your husband suggests names like Herman and Gurtrude."

"Oh God," Dr. Whitman says, sounding appropriately horrified.

"Exactly."

"Have you been to the cemetery today?"

I nod and say, "Yes, I went just before coming here."

"And how was that?"

I sigh and say, "Hard. Easy. Confusing."

"Break that down, Allison."

"It will always be hard to go see Tabitha. I miss my daughter every single day and that will never change. I don't break down daily, I don't cry all the time, but that doesn't mean I don't miss her desperately. Someone in the grief forum described it best when they said you don't get through that kind of pain, you just get used to it. And it's true. It's not as sharp or as crippling as it was in the beginning, more like an ache I'm accustomed to living with, but it's there every day all the same. Going to the cemetery just brings that pain into sharper focus while I'm there. Going to see Will is easier, which is sometimes confusing and makes me feel guilty."

"I thought you had let the guilt go a long time ago Ali."

"I did, which makes me feel guilty," I say with a wry laugh. "Look I know I am not the same person I was when Will died. I worked through the knowledge that losing him changed me in such a fundamental way, that it's almost like I'm an entirely new person, a long time ago. And I no longer miss him like I did in the beginning or like I miss Tabby. I miss him in a 'the world is a poorer place without him in it' kind of way, but not in a 'God I want my husband back' kind of way. It took me a long time to accept that if Will suddenly came back, and he and Finn were standing side by side, that the me that I am now would choose Finn. There was a lot of guilt I had to work through over that, as you very well know. But this is where my life is now, and that is partly because the me that I am now is who I am *because* Will died."

Dr. Whitman asks, "Okay, so what is it you feel guilty about?"

I shrug and reply, "I don't know. I mean, I buried them together, which is a decision I have never regretted. Knowing that Tabby is wrapped in her father's arms gives me a sense of peace because she isn't alone. But when I go to the cemetery and I cry for Tabby, it is out of longing. When I cry for Will it is out of a general sense of sadness that the world is missing out on such a great guy. I know it's going to sound so incredibly stupid, but I'm worried his feelings are hurt that he doesn't get the same level of grief from me."

"Okay first of all, that doesn't sound stupid. It didn't sound stupid years ago when we discussed this, and it still doesn't sound stupid now. Second of all, I will tell you what I told you back then, it is not a competition between how sad you are over Tabby and how sad you are over Will. They are two entirely different people and while everything was a smushed jumble of grief at first, as you started to heal grief for each of them was naturally going to be different. It is completely normal that you would grieve your child in a significantly different way than you would your spouse. You know this. So what is really going on?"

I start to cry and tell her the truth, "I don't want to leave you. I'm not ready."

"Oh, Allison, you are. You are so ready. We have spent this past year preparing you for today. Do you honestly think, if I thought for one second that you weren't in a place where you no longer needed grief therapy, that I would stop our sessions?"

"No," I admit.

"No," She confirms. "It's natural that you are sad that our time together is coming to an end. I'm sad too. I will miss our sessions, because believe it or not, I have learned just as much from you as you have from me. But it's time and that is a wonderful thing."

I swipe under my eyes and say, "I'm a mess. Pregnancy hormones do not help. And I know you are right. I know it's time. I think maybe today is just a really big day. It's the anniversary of their deaths, it's my last day of therapy, and it's our donor reunion - couple that with the fact that I am thirty-five weeks pregnant and eighty-seven thousand pounds - well it's all just a little bit overwhelming."

Dr. Whitman nods in agreement but says, "I'm not so sure you are anywhere close to eighty-seven thousand pounds."

"Alright but everything else is true."

"Yes, everything else is true. It's also not more than you can handle. You went to the cemetery and had your moments with Tabby and Will. You are having your moment with me now, and then in a few hours you will get to walk into a celebration full of people you love and have an amazing, incredibly special bond with. Speaking of, how is Kyle?"

"Oh my gosh, he is getting so big! He just had his tenth birthday. Finn and I took Jasper and flew out to celebrate with them. And I don't think I told you but Brooke, the girl who got one of Will's kidneys, is getting married, and we got her wedding invitation in the mail a couple weeks ago. I love every single one of these people, and I love how they have embraced me and Finn and Jasper as part of their extended family. When I'm with them, individually or as a group, I feel closer to Tabby and to Will. And I'm so grateful that they allow me and my family to be a part of their lives."

"I would think that the gratitude goes both ways. I'm quite sure if you asked them, they would say they were grateful that you allow them to be a part of your family and your life."

I laugh because she is so right. "Yes, when we all get together it is a bit of a 'mutual admiration club'. There are always lots of 'thank yous' and tears, but so much fun and laughter too."

"That sounds wonderful. It's a very special connection you have with each of those families."

"I wish you would come to the celebration. I mean, I'm technically not your patient anymore after today, so you could come without violating any professional boundaries."

Dr. Whitman chuckles and shakes her head. "No, Ali. I appreciate the invitation, but it's not appropriate and you know that."

I nod in agreement, "I know. I know."

We spend the rest of the session making small talk. Finally, Dr. Whitman looks at her watch and says, "It's time Allison."

I feel the tears as they start to form. I am going to miss this woman so much more than I could have ever imagined the first time I walked in her door.

I push up to standing, bracing the small of my back with one hand. I move towards Dr. Whitman and embrace her in a fierce hug, working hard to keep the tears from becoming full-fledged sobbing.

"Thank you. For everything. You changed my life. You helped me live again during a time I never imagined that would be possible. I could not have done it without you and for the rest of my life I will be grateful. There aren't enough words to tell you what you mean to me. I love you and I am going to miss you so much."

Dr. Whitman hugs me back just as fiercely and I hear her sniffle and know she is experiencing her own emotional struggle. "I am so proud of you Allison. So proud. You take care of yourself and the beautiful family you are building." She lightly grips my forearms and leans back so she can look me in the eyes and says, "It's unprofessional, but after six years it would be a lie if I didn't tell you that I love you too Ali."

She gives me one more tight hug and then lets me go. I walk to the door and turn and give her a big, teary smile. Then I open the door, and without a card with my next appointment written on it, I walk out.

ABOUT THE AUTHOR

Broken is Dawn Michele's debut novel. She is an avid reader and a lifelong lover of books. It has been her dream for decades to be a published author, and she has plans for numerous novels beyond this one. Her second novel is currently underway. Dawn is a mother of three grown children, the youngest of which is still in college. She lives in Pennsylvania with her fiancé.